AUNT BESSIE QUESTIONS
AN ISLE OF MAN COZY MYSTERY

DIANA XARISSA

ISBN: 1984034200
ISBN-13: 978-1984034205

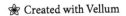 Created with Vellum

For everyone still looking for their happily ever after.

AUTHOR'S NOTE

It's hard for me to believe it, but this is book seventeen in the Isle of Man Cozy Mystery series. When I first wrote about Bessie in my romance, *Island Inheritance,* I had no plans to ever write about her again. There was something about her, though, that made me want to tell more of her story. This series came out of that desire. As she'd recently passed away in the romance, this first book in this series was set about fifteen years before the romance novel. (The first mystery was set in 1998, therefore.)

While the books in the series can be read in any order, I always encourage readers to start at the beginning and work their way through the books in (alphabetical) order. My characters do change and develop as the series progresses.

As with all of my books, this book is a work of fiction and all of the characters are fictional creations. Any resemblance they share with any real person, living or dead, is entirely coincidental. The Isle of Man is a real place, and I encourage everyone to learn more about this unique and historic country. I often mention the various historical sites on the island in my books, and they are all real as well. The events in the books that take place within those sites are, however, fictional. All of the businesses in the story all also fictional and any resemblance that they bear to any real businesses is also coincidental.

Because of the setting of the books, I use British and Manx spellings and terms. There is a glossary at the back of the book which explains some of them for readers in other parts of the world. As I've been living in the US for several years now, I suspect an increasing number of Americanisms are sneaking into my books. I apologize for those and will try to correct them if they are pointed out to me.

Hearing from readers is one of the best things about being a writer. There are various ways to get in touch with me, and they are all listed on the "About the Author" page at the back of the book. I have a monthly newsletter all about new releases. You can sign up for it on my website. I'd love to include you!

CHAPTER 1

"Thank you so much for coming along," Helen Baxter told Bessie. "I just know I'm going to forget everything that the vicar says tonight."

Elizabeth Cubbon, "Bessie" to nearly everyone, smiled at her friend. "I'm happy to come along," she assured her, "and I'll do my best to remember all of the instructions for tomorrow."

Helen nodded. "I'm sure Pete will remember them as well. He's not nervous at all. But then, he's done this once before."

"I should think that would make him more nervous."

"He told me that he's much more sure this time. I hope he wasn't just saying that. Do you think he was just telling me that because he knows I'm nervous?"

Bessie took the woman's hands and held them tightly. When Helen looked into her eyes, she replied. "Pete loves you, and he wants to spend the rest of his life with you. But even so, he's not the type to say something just because he thinks you want to hear it. If he said it, he means it."

Helen nodded. "I'm making myself and all of my friends crazy," she said apologetically.

"You aren't making me crazy, at least not yet. Just try to relax. Tomorrow is meant to be the happiest day of your life, after all."

"I don't think it will be," Helen replied. "I'm hoping the honeymoon will be happier. I really just want to get tomorrow over with."

Bessie nodded. "I can certainly understand that, but it is a special day, and I'm sure it's going to be wonderful."

"Elizabeth did her best, anyway. I know she'd have been able to do a lot more if we could have afforded it."

"Money can't buy happiness," Bessie reminded her.

"I'm not sure Elizabeth would agree with that," Helen chuckled.

Elizabeth Quayle, the daughter of one of Bessie's dear friends, had taken on the role of wedding planner for Helen and her fiancé, Peter Corkill. Having grown up a spoiled only daughter of wealthy parents, Elizabeth had needed to be convinced that weddings didn't have to be lavish or costly. Still, from what Bessie knew, the girl had worked hard to arrange a very special day for her clients.

"Elizabeth is just grateful that you were willing to let her plan your day," Bessie said. "Now she has one reference for her new wedding and event planning business."

"Once she gets one of her wealthy friends to let her plan their wedding, she won't need to bother with me anymore."

"Having met a lot of her friends, I can't imagine any of them having weddings in their near futures."

"Really? Are they all too busy making money and travelling?"

"Among other things," Bessie told her.

"Do I look okay?" Helen asked, smoothing her blonde hair back and licking her lips.

"You look lovely."

"This is the last time I'll see Pete before I walk down the aisle tomorrow. I want him to remember me looking beautiful."

"I'm sure he always thinks you look beautiful."

Helen shrugged. "Okay, I want everyone else to think I look beautiful."

"Everyone? Who else is going to be there tonight?"

"No one, just you and John Rockwell, since you're going to be our witnesses. I suppose I mean random people walking past the church or something," Helen said with a sigh. "I don't even know what I'm saying. I'm so nervous that I feel as if I'm going to be sick."

"Do we have time for some tea?"

Helen glanced at the clock on Bessie's wall. "Not really. We should probably be going. I don't want to be late."

Bessie got up and collected her handbag from the table. "I'm ready when you are," she told her friend.

"I'm as ready as I'm going to be," Helen replied. "I should have come over earlier and had tea with you, I suppose. I was just pacing around my flat, worrying myself into a tizzy."

"You would have been more than welcome. You're welcome here after we're done at the church, as well, if you want to come back."

"We'll see. I think I'll probably want to get home and get some rest. I don't think I'll sleep, but I can try."

"You know you can still change your mind about staying here tonight, if you'd like," Bessie offered.

"I know, but I think I'll sleep better at home, and if I can't sleep, at least I won't be keeping anyone else awake while I pace around my flat, muttering to myself."

"Elizabeth said she offered you a room at Thie yn Traie, but you didn't want to stay there, either."

"They have staff," Helen said. "I can't even begin to imagine what it would be like staying there. I'm not comfortable with the idea of having people doing things for me like that."

Bessie understood what Helen meant. Thie yn Traie was a huge mansion not far from Bessie's cottage on the beach. A home that large needed staff, but Bessie was sure she would feel similarly to Helen if she ever tried staying there. She found it strange enough when she went for lunch or tea with her friend Mary, Elizabeth's mother. Maids, cooks, and butlers seemed to be everywhere in the home.

Helen and Bessie headed out to Helen's car. Bessie locked up her cottage behind them and then climbed into the passenger seat. She'd never learned to drive, relying on friends or, more often, a car service that provided taxis to her on a regular basis. The original owner of the company had been a dear friend who had given Bessie a preferential rate. When he sold the company to a Douglas-based firm, Bessie had continued using them, as she liked nearly all of the drivers.

"I don't expect this to take long," Helen said as she drove. "The vicar just wants to walk us through what to expect tomorrow. Apparently, he usually does it a week or more before the wedding, but as we made our arrangements on rather short notice, this was the best he could do."

"I don't have anywhere else to be tonight," Bessie replied cheerfully. "If it takes a while, that's fine with me."

"Thank you," Helen said, "and before I forget, thank you for being a witness for us tomorrow. I'm not sure if I thanked you before or not."

"You did. You've thanked me at least ten times," Bessie chuckled, "and you know I'm honoured to have been asked, truly I am. I'm so very happy for you and for Pete."

"Thank you. It's strange getting married when you are older. I don't have a circle of female friends, and my parents aren't around anymore, either."

"You aren't that old," Bessie said firmly.

"I felt old when I was wedding gown shopping," Helen replied. "I'm going to be forty this year. All of the other brides in the shops seemed to be about nineteen, with glowing skins and gorgeous figures. I felt like a frumpy old maid."

Bessie laughed. "You're beautiful and slender, and I'm sure no one thought you were an old maid. Of course, I fit that description better than anyone."

Bessie had never married, and now, aged somewhere between sixty and a hundred, she felt she was highly unlikely to ever do so. She'd stopped counting her birthdays once she was old enough for a free bus pass, and had no intention of paying them any more notice until she received her first telegram from the Queen.

"You don't seem at all like an old maid to me," Helen told her. "I can't imagine anyone would think that of you."

"I don't really mind if they do. It's true, after all."

"I'm sure someone told me that you were a widow," Helen said after a moment. She pulled the car into the church car park, and once she was safely in a parking space, looked over at Bessie. "I can't remember where I heard that, though."

"I'm not a widow, although my cottage is called 'Treoghe Bwaane,' which is 'Widow's Cottage' in Manx." Bessie replied. "I did have a romance or two in my younger days, but I never married. The one man that I would have wed, given the opportunity, passed away before we were able to marry. I bought Treoghe Bwaane right after his death. The cottage already had its name when I bought it, but it seemed incredibly suitable to my devastated eighteen-year-old self."

"If you don't mind, I think I'd like to hear the whole story," Helen said. She glanced at her watch. "Maybe on the way back to your cottage?"

"I don't mind at all. It was a long time ago."

"There's Pete," Helen said, nodding towards a car that was just turning into the car park.

The pair got out of Helen's car and stood next to it while Pete parked. He joined them a moment later. Pete's dark brown hair looked as if it had just been cut, and its sprinkling of grey gave him a distinguished air. His usual frown seemed to turn itself into a grin as he looked at Helen.

"You look gorgeous," he whispered to Helen before kissing her cheek. Bessie got a hug.

"Are you excited about tomorrow?" Bessie asked him.

"Excited? I'm not sure that's the word I would use," Pete said with a shrug. "I'm really looking forward to it all being over. I can't wait to get away for a while and just spend some time with my bride."

"Your plans sound wonderful," Bessie replied.

"New York, Los Angeles, and Las Vegas," Helen said. "It's all so exciting. I never dreamt I'd take a trip to the US, and now I'm actually going for more than a fortnight."

"I'm sure you'll have a lovely time," Bessie told her.

"I'm sure I'm going to gain twenty pounds," Helen replied, "but once I get through tomorrow, I don't care. As long as my wedding gown fits tomorrow, nothing else matters."

"I don't care if you walk down the aisle in jeans and a T-shirt," Pete told her. "Just make sure you turn up."

"I'll be here," Helen promised.

Bessie blinked back a tear. She was incredibly happy for the couple, who had actually met during a murder investigation over a year ago. Another car turned into the car park before anyone else could speak.

"That will be John," Pete said. "He rang to warn me that he'd be bringing his kids with him."

"They just arrived a few days ago," Bessie said. "I wonder how everyone is adjusting to their being here."

A moment later John Rockwell joined them, his children following behind him. John was tall, with dark hair and gorgeous green eyes. Both of his children had the same stunning eyes. He greeted Bessie and Helen with hugs and then shook hands with Pete.

"I hope you don't mind my bringing along the kids. I didn't want to leave them home alone, not on their second night on the island," he said.

"It's not a problem at all," Helen assured him. "I just hope they aren't too bored."

"They brought their handheld electronic games," John told her. "They'll be happy for hours."

Bessie thought that the looks on both children's faces suggested otherwise, but she didn't voice her opinion. Instead she greeted the new arrivals. "Thomas, I believe you've grown over a foot taller since the last time I saw you," she told John's fifteen-year-old son.

"Yeah, Mum reckons she's been feeding me too much," he replied, grinning at her.

"And Amy, my goodness, I'm not sure I would have recognised you if I'd passed you on the street. You're a good deal more grown up now, aren't you?" Bessie continued.

Amy looked at Bessie and shrugged. "Maybe," she muttered, looking down at the ground.

Bessie knew the girl was thirteen and that thirteen was a difficult age. "Welcome to the island, both of you," she told them.

"Thanks," Thomas replied. "We're both happy to be here, really. It's better than being at home with Mum and Harvey, anyway."

John's former wife, Sue, had never stopped loving Harvey, even though they'd been broken up for some time before she'd started seeing John. Sue and John had been married, with their first child on the way, before Sue told John that she was still in love with her former boyfriend. The couple had tried to make their marriage work for many years in spite of that fact, but in the end, when Sue and Harvey crossed paths again, the marriage had failed. Now Sue and Harvey were honeymooning in a developing country where Harvey's medical training would be useful, and the children were staying with John for several months.

"Mum's not bad," Amy said softly.

"Not on her own," Thomas agreed, "but when Harvey's around, she goes all stupid and tries to make sure he's included in everything. I don't like Harvey."

Amy looked at him for a minute and then shook her head. Bessie was sure she could see a tear in the girl's eye.

"Have you met Pete and Helen?" Bessie asked them.

"They know Inspector Corkill," John said, using Pete's title. "I don't think they've met Helen. Thomas and Amy, this is Helen Baxter, but after tomorrow she'll be Helen Corkill."

"Actually, I'm keeping my maiden name," Helen corrected him. "It makes things easier, and also, well, in memory of my father. He was a very special man."

"That's cool," Amy said. "Mum is going to change her name and then we won't have the same surname anymore."

"It's a tradition that seems to be dying out," Bessie said, "and I don't think that's a bad thing. Women shouldn't have to change their names just because they get married."

"When I get married, I think my husband should change his name," Amy said. "Then we can both be Rockwells. It's an awesome name."

"It is, isn't it?" Bessie said with a smile.

"You can take my name if you want," Helen told Pete.

"Too much trouble," Pete told her. "It's easiest if we both just keep our own names."

"What time were you meant to be here?" John asked, glancing over at the church.

"Seven," Helen replied. She looked at her watch. "Which means we're late."

"Only by a few minutes," Pete said. "I'm sure the vicar won't mind."

"Let's go and find out," Bessie suggested.

Everyone turned and began to walk towards the church. At the front, Pete climbed up half a dozen steps and pulled on the door. It stayed firmly shut. He shrugged and then tried the other door. It didn't open, either.

"The vicar didn't say to use the side door," Helen said.

The little group trooped around the church to the door at the side. There was only a single step here. Pete pulled, but that door, too, refused to open.

"Maybe we're meant to meet him at the vicarage," Pete suggested.

"We aren't, because he said we'd go over where everyone is meant to stand tomorrow and the seating and everything," Helen said.

"Maybe he's forgotten we're coming," Bessie said.

"That's more likely," Helen said. "Elizabeth said she had a hard time getting him to agree to the meeting."

Bessie could hear the panic in her friend's voice. As she turned towards Helen, Bessie smiled as Pete obviously heard the same thing.

"It's okay," he told Helen, taking her hand. "It will all work out in the end."

"Let's try the vicarage," John said. "It's only a few steps away. Maybe the vicar's housekeeper will be able to help, if he's not in."

The quickest way to get to the vicarage from the church was through the old cemetery at the back of the church. John set off down the narrow path with Bessie right behind him. Helen and Pete followed with Thomas and Amy lagging behind. They already had their electronic toys out and were only half-watching where they were going as they walked.

When John stopped suddenly, Bessie walked right into him. "I am sorry," she exclaimed, taking a step backwards. A look at John's face made her heart skip a beat. "What is it?" she asked quietly.

John nodded towards a cluster of graves some distance from the path. "Something doesn't look right," he whispered. "Take the kids back around to the front of the church, please."

Bessie glanced over and then shivered. There appeared to be a foot sticking out from in between the gravestones. "Thomas, Amy, let's go around the other way," she said, wincing as she realised that her voice was far too loud.

Thomas looked up from his game and stared at her for a minute. "What's going on?" he asked.

"I'd like you and your sister to go with Bessie," John said firmly. "Wait by the cars, please."

"Why?" Thomas demanded.

"Later," John said.

Thomas put his game into his pocket and then looked around. "Is that a foot?" he asked, pointing.

"A foot? Where?" Amy asked.

"Please go with Bessie," John repeated himself.

"But if it is a foot, you'll need the crime scene technicians, and we'll be here for hours," Amy said. "Let us stay and watch, at least."

John shook his head. "I don't know what we're dealing with yet, but you're both too young to be allowed to stay. Please go with Bessie."

"Only if you promise to tell us all about it," Amy retorted, "and I want to see the photos."

John sighed. "Just go, please."

Amy narrowed her eyes at him and then shrugged. "I suppose we don't have a choice."

"No, you don't. Bessie, can you ring Doona and see if she can come and get the kids, please. They don't need to stay here," John said.

"I assume you want me to stay," Bessie said.

"For the time being, yes. It may turn out to be nothing but a Guy

Fawkes effigy or something, but, well, at this stage, yes, please stay," John replied.

Bessie turned and followed Thomas and Amy back towards the church. A few minutes later, they found a bench near the car park and settled onto it.

"I wish Dad would have let us stay," Thomas grumbled.

"Tell me about it," Amy replied. "I want to be a crime scene technician. I could have learned a lot."

"Well, I want to be a police inspector, so I could have learned a lot too," Thomas said.

"What does your mother think of your plans for the future?" Bessie asked them.

Thomas looked at Amy, and then they both shook their heads. "She thinks we should both be taking our inspiration from Harvey," Thomas replied after a moment. "She wants us both to go to medical school and become arrogant oncologists like him."

"I understand that he saved your grandmother's life," Bessie said.

Amy rolled her eyes. "To hear Mum tell it, he saves billions of lives every minute of every day. If it wasn't for Harvey, there would hardly be anyone left in the UK; everyone would have died from cancer by now. He's only just the tiniest step away from being some sort of god or magician or something."

"I'm sure she's just very proud of what he does. Becoming a doctor requires a lot of hard work and dedication, and I understand that he's one of the best in his field," Bessie replied.

"Yeah, we know," Thomas said. "Mum tells us that every single day."

Bessie thought about arguing further, but she needed to ring Doona and get the children away from what was probably about to become a crime scene.

"Doona, it's Bessie. I'm at the Laxey Church with Thomas and Amy, and John was hoping you might be able to pop over and collect them. There's a bit of a problem here."

"What sort of problem?" Doona asked.

"I'm not sure yet, but, well, let's just say John's probably going to be working for the next several hours."

"Oh, dear, that doesn't sound good. I'll just change and be on my way."

"Doona will be here in a few minutes," Bessie told the children after she'd dropped her phone back in her bag.

"Do you think she and Dad are a couple?" Amy asked.

"I know they're good friends," Bessie replied. "As they're both single, they may become more than just friends one day, but as far as I know, they're just friends now."

"She's really nice, but I'm not sure I want Dad getting married again," Amy said.

"You're being selfish," Thomas told her. "We're both going to be off to uni in a few years, and Dad will be all alone. It would be good for him to find someone special."

"I suppose so," Amy sighed. "I still don't understand why he and Mum couldn't just stay together."

"Adult relationships are complicated," Bessie said. "Even though I'm an adult, I rarely understand why people do the things they do in their relationships."

"Dad told us that you've never been married," Amy said.

"No, I haven't. I was deeply in love once, but the man I loved passed away before we could marry. Now, looking back, I wonder if our relationship would have worked, but at the time I was sure we were perfect for one another."

"That's very sad," Amy said. "You never found someone else to love?"

"There was another man, but he wanted me to move to Australia and I wasn't prepared to leave the island for him," Bessie replied.

"Aren't you lonely?" Amy asked.

Bessie smiled at her. "When Matthew first died, I felt incredibly alone, but not lonely, if you see the difference. That was a great many years ago, and I've lived a full life since then. I have many friends, including your father, and I've acted as something of an honourary auntie to many generations of Laxey children. I enjoy living on my own, and no, I'm not lonely."

"Do you think..." Amy stopped as a car turned into the car park.

"There's Doona," Bessie said. "Wait here a minute, won't you?"

She stood up and crossed to the car that had just parked. Bessie's closest friend, Doona, climbed out a moment later.

"What's going on?" Doona asked, glancing from Bessie to the children and back again.

"We were walking between the church and the vicarage, and John spotted something in the graveyard," Bessie said softly. "It looked very much like a leg sticking out from between the tombstones."

Doona sighed. "And if it had been anything other than a dead body, John would have let you know by now that everything is fine."

"Yes, I suspect so," Bessie sighed.

"I hope the kids don't mind staying at my house tonight," Doona said. "I'd be surprised if John gets finished here before the wee small hours of the morning."

"Can you manage?"

"Oh, yes. John and I talked about it a lot before the kids arrived. I stocked up on extra food and drinks, and John gave me overnight bags for each of them, just in case. He wanted to be prepared in case work got in the way, as it usually does."

"It does indeed."

Doona crossed over to Thomas and Amy while Bessie followed. Doona Moore was forty-something and seemed an unlikely friend for a woman of Bessie's age. They'd met three years earlier in a Manx language class and had bonded over their struggles to learn anything other than the basics. Doona had just ended her second marriage and spent many nights crying on Bessie's shoulder about the man she still loved, who had cheated on her. Bessie gave her tea, sympathy, and tough love, and Doona was still hugely grateful to her friend for helping her through the difficult time.

Over the past year or so, Doona had been able to repay the kindness by supporting Bessie through a number of murder investigations.

It had been Bessie's turn to provide support when Doona's second husband ended up as a murder victim, though. Bessie suspected that Doona and John had feelings for one another, but they were taking things slowly, which Bessie felt was a good thing. That John was relying on Doona to help with his children made Bessie happy, though.

"We'll head off, then," Doona said brightly. "I have microwave popcorn and a dozen new movies that your father probably won't want you to watch. Let's go."

The children both stood up. "What movies?" Thomas asked.

"American police comedies," Doona replied, "and some scary thriller-type detective dramas. Movies that your dad would say aren't realistic."

Amy laughed. "He's always complaining about the police procedures when we try to watch that sort of thing with him."

"Yeah, I've told him I won't watch anything on telly with him anymore if there are police in the show. It's rather limited what we can watch, but it saves him complaining," Doona laughed.

Bessie gave each of the children a hug and then squeezed Doona tightly. "I'm sure I don't have to tell you how grateful John will be to know that the children are being looked after," she said as Thomas and Amy climbed into the back of Doona's car.

"Are you staying here, or would you like a ride home?" Doona asked as she pushed the door shut behind Thomas.

"John wants me to stay," Bessie told her. "I suppose I'm a witness or something."

"And being that we're in Laxey, you probably know whoever it is," Doona added. "You know everyone in Laxey."

"Not quite everyone, but nearly," Bessie replied. "Anyway, you go and enjoy your movie night with the children. I'll let John know that they've gone."

"Thanks. They're really good kids, and I like spending time with them. I just wasn't expecting to have to start looking after them the day after they arrived. I'm sure John was hoping to get to spend some time with them before a big case came up."

"Maybe this will be something simple in the end," Bessie said hopefully. "Maybe whoever it is died of natural causes."

"We can hope," Doona said. She opened her door and slid behind the steering wheel. Bessie took a few steps backwards and then waved as Doona drove out of the car park.

Bessie walked back over to the bench and sat down. A moment later Helen walked out from behind the church and joined her. She'd obviously been crying, and Bessie quickly dug around in her handbag for a tissue.

"I don't normally cry," Helen said after she'd wiped her eyes. "I'm a nurse. I've seen lots of really sad things, and I've never once broken down. I've seen dead people before, too, lots of them."

"I'm sorry," Bessie said, rubbing the woman's back.

"I don't even know why I'm crying," Helen said, "or rather, I think I do know, and it's so awful that it makes me cry more."

"I'm not sure I understand you."

"No, I don't suppose I'm making sense. John had me take a look at the body, just to see if there was anything anyone could do. But he's well and truly dead. And I'm afraid I'm only crying because now that the vicar is dead, I don't know if Pete and I can get married tomorrow or not."

CHAPTER 2

*B*essie put her arm around Helen. "You've had quite an upset," she said soothingly. "You were already under a great deal of stress, anyway. Just have a good cry, and then we'll see what we can come up with to sort things."

Helen sobbed for a minute or two on Bessie's shoulder and then drew a long, shaky breath. "I'm okay," she said. "I'm sorry as well. I'm not usually so emotional."

"As I said, you're under a lot of stress. Don't be so hard on yourself. It's okay to be emotional sometimes."

"Yes, but please don't tell Pete that I was crying. I gather his first wife used to cry at just about everything. That was one of the things that caused difficulties in their relationship. I'd rather he continue to think of me as stronger than that."

"It won't do him any harm to find out that you're human," Bessie said stoutly. "Seeing a dead body is upsetting under any circumstances."

"John didn't want to ask me to look, but, well, I insisted, just in case I could do something. As it happens, John was right, though. I shouldn't have looked. I'll probably have nightmares for weeks about what I saw."

Before Bessie could reply, a police car, lights flashing and sirens blaring, pulled into the car park. Bessie smiled as she recognised the man who climbed out of it.

"I don't think you needed the sirens," she told Hugh Watterson, a young constable who was also her friend.

"John said to hurry," Hugh replied. "The crime scene team is behind me, and I need to get the scene ready for them."

"How are you?" Bessie asked as the man rushed past them.

"I'm fine and so is Grace," he called over his shoulder. "The morning sickness is finally getting better, but she still has one or two days a week where she's ill. She's taking it in her stride, though."

Hugh disappeared behind the church before Bessie could reply.

"Grace is pregnant?" Helen asked. "I hadn't heard."

"She is. They're very excited," Bessie confirmed.

"And now I'm sad again," Helen sighed.

"Do you want to talk about it?"

"I'm nearly forty, and the chances of my getting pregnant are pretty slim, at least without help. I always thought I'd have children, that's all. I mean, I always thought I'd find the perfect man, get married, and then have a few kids, all before I got anywhere near forty. Instead, it took me all of this time to find a good man who I actually think I might be able to spend the rest of my life with, and now it's probably too late for me to have kids."

"What does Pete think about children?"

"He doesn't mind either way, or so he says. He and his first wife were planning on having some, but then things didn't work out. After they split, he told me he thought he'd never find anyone else, so he stopped thinking about having children one day. Now, if they arrive, he'll be happy, but if they don't, he won't be disappointed. Or at least that's what he's telling me."

"There are all sorts of ways to become a parent without having your own children," Bessie pointed out.

"Oh, I know. I read happy adoption stories all the time. I read about the various medical treatments that can help, too, but I don't

16

know. I suppose we'll get married and then see what happens. It's too soon to start thinking about medical intervention or adoption."

"All I can do is wish you luck. If you ever need someone to talk to about everything, you know where I am."

"Thank you. I may take you up on that. I feel as if all of my friends have babies, and they simply don't understand."

A police van pulled up next to Hugh's car. "Do you know where we're going, Aunt Bessie?" one of the crime scene technicians asked as he walked away from the van.

"Behind the church, in the graveyard," Bessie told him.

"That's a bit creepy," the man replied. "At least we'll have daylight for a while longer. If it were January, we'd have to work in the dark."

Bessie and Helen sat and watched as the three technicians unloaded various pieces of equipment and then headed off along the path behind the church.

"You said it was the vicar who was dead?" Bessie asked after a moment.

"Yes, and I don't know what that means for tomorrow," Helen replied. "It's awfully short notice to get someone else to marry us, if the police will even let us use the church."

"At least it happened in Laxey, so it's John's jurisdiction and not Pete's," Bessie pointed out. "Were you able to tell what had happened to the man? Did it look like a heart attack?"

"Only inasmuch as there was a giant knife stuck in his heart," Helen replied, her voice quavering slightly.

"Oh, no," Bessie exclaimed.

"I'm probably not meant to be telling people that," Helen said, frowning.

"I won't repeat it," Bessie promised, "but who on earth would want to kill a vicar?"

"I've no idea, but then I barely knew the man. I met with him once or twice to discuss the wedding, but I'm not sure I would have recognised him on the street if I'd seen him in Douglas or elsewhere."

"I only met him a few times myself," Bessie said thoughtfully. "He'd only been on the island for a short time."

"He did mention that he'd only been appointed recently, but I wasn't really paying that much attention. Elizabeth did most of the talking."

"I wonder if we should ring her. Maybe she could start looking around for another vicar."

"We probably need to wait until John or Pete says it's okay," Helen replied. "I'm sure they don't want people knowing about the murder until they're ready to release the information."

"Yes, but you're meant to be getting married tomorrow afternoon. Someone needs to start ringing around soon."

"Let's talk about something else, or I might just start crying again," Helen said. The pair chatted about nothing much for a few minutes before John appeared around the side of the building.

"Sorry to keep you both waiting," he said. "The crime scene technicians are hard at work now, and Hugh is helping Pete. I'd like to take statements from you both."

"I don't think I've anything useful to say," Bessie told him. "I barely knew the man, and all I saw at the scene was a shoe."

"Nevertheless, I need a statement from you, and I should talk to each of you separately. We're just, ah, there he is." John nodded towards the man who was just climbing out of his car.

Bessie smiled at James Clucas, the church's caretaker. She'd known the man for many years. He'd been looking after the church, the church hall, and the grounds for a great many years.

"Mr. Clucas, sorry to disturb you at home," John said to the new arrival.

"I'm used to being called out to deal with things," the man replied good-naturedly. "What's the problem tonight, then?"

"I'm afraid my friends and I discovered a body in the graveyard tonight," John said solemnly.

"That's the place for them," James replied. "I mean, there are a good many bodies in there."

"Yes, but this one didn't belong there, at least not yet," John said.

The man frowned. "I'm sorry. I don't think I understand what you're saying."

"We found the body of a murdered man in the graveyard," John explained slowly. "Our crime scene technicians are working there now."

James stared at John for a minute and then began to shake his head. "Murdered? In the graveyard? But that doesn't make sense."

Bessie stood up and took the man's arm. "Sit down," she urged him. James was well over six feet tall and nearly as broad. Having seen the colour drain from his face while John was talking, Bessie was worried that he might lose consciousness. He could get quite badly hurt if he fell to the ground.

James dropped heavily onto the bench, still staring at John. "I'm sorry, Inspector, sir, but I still don't understand."

"I know it's a lot to take in," John replied. "I was hoping you might be willing to let some of our team into the church to take a look around and also that we might be able to use the church hall to talk to witnesses."

"I don't mind you going through the church, as long as you're properly respectful, but I'll need to get permission from the vicar. Give me a minute, and I'll ring Reverend Doyle. You're probably best talking to him directly, and then he can tell me what he wants me to do," James replied.

John held up a hand as James pulled out his phone. "I'm sorry to be the one to tell you, but it's Reverend Doyle who is dead."

Even more colour left the man's face. "But, no, I don't, I mean..." He stopped and looked at Bessie. "It's Reverend Doyle?" he asked her.

"I haven't see the body," Bessie said softly, "but Inspector Rockwell knows Reverend Doyle well enough to know whether it's him or not."

"I don't understand," James said.

"That's why we're here," John replied. "We're going to do our best to work out exactly what happened to Reverend Doyle. If you could open the church and the hall for us, it would help."

"Of course," James said, sounding dazed, "but I should ask someone. Let me think for a minute."

"Why don't you have the inspector ring the bishop's office," Bessie suggested. "I'm sure someone there will be able to grant you permission to let the police in."

"That's a good idea," John said, shooting Bessie a grateful look. "I'll do that. Give me a minute." He walked a short distance away and pulled out his phone. James stared straight ahead, his eyes on the ground, while they waited. Bessie opened her mouth a dozen times to try to start a conversation, but she simply couldn't work out what to say. Before she'd managed to come up with anything, John was back.

"Mr. Clucas, the bishop's office would like a word with you," he said, handing James the phone.

Bessie could only hear James's side of the conversation, and that seemed to consist of nothing but monosyllables. They were accompanied by a great deal of nodding that was lost on the person on the other end of the line. When James handed the mobile back to John, he stood up.

"I'm to let you into the church and the hall," he told John, "and the vicarage, which you hadn't mentioned before."

"We'll leave the vicarage for last," John said. "For now, let's just make sure that the door is locked. Going through it will take some time."

"Ms. Hamilton might be home," James said. "She usually is in the evening."

"Who is Ms. Hamilton?" John asked.

"Reverend Doyle's housekeeper. She lives in. She moved across with him when he came here from Dorking," James explained.

"It's a very small vicarage to have live-in staff," Bessie exclaimed.

"It is, aye. Ms. Hamilton was always complaining about how small the house was and how cramped they were, but Reverend Doyle said he was too used to have her living in. He didn't want her getting a flat somewhere and just coming in to do the cooking and cleaning."

Bessie nodded. "I'm sure it was convenient for him, even if it was uncomfortable for her," she said tartly.

"Anyway, she's probably at home," James said. "You'll have to tell her about Reverend Doyle, won't you? She'll be devastated. They were very close."

"How close?" John asked.

"According to Reverend Doyle, Ms. Hamilton started working for him twenty or so years ago when he was given his first parish. She kept moving around with him as he moved from place to place."

"And neither of them ever married?" John asked.

"Not as far as I know," James replied. "You'd have to ask her, though, to be sure."

"Oh, I will," John said, "but we sent a man to check the vicarage and no one answered the door. Maybe we'd better go and have a look around, if you think Ms. Hamilton should be there."

"Oh, goodness, I hope nothing has happened to Ms. Hamilton too," James exclaimed. "Losing Reverend Doyle is bad enough."

He and John took a few steps away before Bessie spoke. "John, just one minute, please," she said.

"What is it?" John asked.

"Helen and Pete are meant to be getting married here tomorrow. Obviously, they need to find someone else to perform the ceremony. Is it okay if Helen starts ringing people?" Bessie asked.

"I believe Pete is already working on that," John told her. "He rang Elizabeth Quayle a short time ago and spoke to her about it. That's one of the reasons why I'm so anxious to get into the church. We need to go through it, and hopefully clear it so that the wedding can take place as planned."

"Assuming they find another priest to marry them," Bessie said, glancing over at Helen, who was staring at the front of the church.

"They'll find someone," John assured her. "Pete told Elizabeth that he's prepared to pay whatever it takes, but he's not going to bed tomorrow night without his legal wife by his side."

Bessie smiled. "I didn't realise he felt so strongly about it."

"He's absolutely crazy about Helen," John said softly. "It will all work out. Pete will make sure of it."

John and James walked away, heading towards the vicarage, as Bessie sat back down beside Helen.

"Pete rang Elizabeth and told her to find someone else to perform the ceremony tomorrow," she told the woman.

Helen blew out a long breath. "That makes me feel a bit better," she said. "Now we just have to worry about whether we can use the church or not."

"If you can't, there will be options," Bessie told her. "You can always get married at Thie yn Traie or on the beach below it. You can even get married on the beach behind my cottage, if you'd like. I can't promise you won't have dozens of guests from the holiday cottages standing around watching the whole thing, but with all of the police that will be there, I'm sure they'll keep to a respectable distance."

Helen laughed. "Okay, I feel better now," she said. "Maybe Pete and I will still be able to get married tomorrow. That doesn't mean I'm not worried about the honeymoon, though."

"What about the honeymoon?"

"I'm just afraid that Pete won't want to go because of the murder investigation," Helen explained. "I know how he is about his work. He takes it very seriously, and I don't blame him for that."

"But this is John's case, not Pete's," Bessie said. "Anyway, I know how much Pete is looking forward to your trip. He's not going to let a murder investigation get in the way of it."

"I hope you're right," Helen replied. "I'm incredibly excited about the trip, which feels all wrong, sitting here with a dead body on the other side of the church."

"You can't stop living your life because someone you barely knew died," Bessie told her.

"But who would want to kill a vicar?" Helen asked.

"I really should have told you two not to talk," John said.

Bessie jumped. "I didn't see you there," she told the man.

"I came around from the other end of the car park," he explained.

"Was Ms. Hamilton at home?" Bessie asked.

"No. The vicarage was empty," John told her. "I've left a constable at the door in case she comes home before we start searching the building."

"You don't think she killed the vicar and then left the island, do you?" Helen asked.

"At this point, I don't think anything," John replied. "We've a great deal of evidence to gather and examine, and many people to speak to about what's happened."

"It's odd that she's not home," Bessie said. "James seemed to think that she should be there."

"It's far too early to start speculating," John said firmly. "For right now, I'd like to get statements from both of you. Then you can both head home and try to relax. Helen has a big day tomorrow."

"Assuming we find someone else to officiate and somewhere to have the ceremony," Helen said.

"I have a team going through the church right now," John said. "Thus far they haven't found anything that suggests that we'll need to restrict access to the building. We won't be letting people use the side door, but that shouldn't be a problem."

Bessie got to her feet, and Helen followed suit. "James has the church hall opened up for us," John told them as they walked. "I don't expect this to take long."

The church hall was basically one large room. Bessie sighed as she looked around the space. Only a few months ago, she'd been taking Manx language classes there. Those were hard work, but she much preferred them to being questioned about murder.

"Bessie, if you could wait here for a few minutes, I'll start with Helen," John said.

There were a few folding chairs set up near the door. Bessie sat down on the first one and stretched out her legs in front of her. She nearly always had a paperback book in her handbag, but she hadn't bothered with one tonight. The trip to the church with Helen was only meant to be a short one.

John continued across the room to the back wall. A long table had been set up, with two chairs on either side of it. John slid into a seat and motioned for Helen to sit on the opposite side of the table. While Bessie watched, he pulled out a notebook and his mobile. Bessie assumed, from what she could see, that he was sending a text message. A moment later, the door swung open and Hugh walked into the room. He gave Bessie a smile and then joined John and Helen at the table in the back.

Bessie could hear the low rumble of their voices as the trio talked, but she couldn't make out any words. After a while, she quit trying and amused herself by running through the multiplication tables backwards. She hadn't quite finished them all when John and Helen walked over to her.

"Helen, if you want to go home, I can make sure Bessie gets back to Treoghe Bwaane," John offered.

"I'll wait for her if she won't be too long," Helen replied. "I'm not sure I want to be alone right now."

"We'll be as quick as we can," John promised. He led Bessie over to the table and held out a chair for her. "Let me send a text, and then we'll get my questions out of the way," he told Bessie before pulling out his mobile again.

Bessie smiled at Hugh. "How are things with the house?" she asked.

"Getting there, but slowly," Hugh replied.

He and Grace were buying a large house in a new development on Laxey Beach. The row of houses stretched along the beach some distance beyond Thie yn Traie, and Bessie was looking forward to having her friends as neighbours, even at a distance.

"Grace is worried that we'll never be able to afford furniture for the whole house," Hugh added, "especially since she doesn't want to bring all of my old furniture with us. She's right that a lot of it is pretty beat up, but most of it came from my relatives when they were getting rid of it to get new things. Constables don't make a lot of money, and neither do teachers," Hugh sighed.

"It won't hurt you one bit to have to use secondhand furniture for a while," Bessie said. "If you put aside a little bit of money each month towards a furniture fund, you'll be able to buy new things eventually."

Hugh shrugged. "I suspect that once the baby gets here, all of our money will go towards making him or her happy. I'm pretty sure Grace won't care about furniture, as long as Baby Watterson has every single thing he or she could possibly want or need."

Bessie nodded. "That sounds like Grace," she said. "You'll have to start saving now and try to get a few things bought before the baby comes."

"Except the first thing Grace wants to do is furnish the nursery," Hugh replied.

"You need to have a baby shower," Bessie told him.

"A baby shower?"

"It's an American tradition," Bessie explained. "All of the expectant mother's friends get together and buy presents for the baby. You can even tell them exactly what you want."

"That sounds, well, weird," Hugh said.

"That's just because it isn't usually done on this side of the pond," Bessie replied. "We don't have bridal showers, either, but that doesn't mean they aren't a good idea. Actually, I don't much like bridal showers. Most brides these days have everything they could possibly need or want, but baby showers are different. A baby shower is exactly what you and Grace need. Several of us could go in together and get one or two of the big expensive items like the cot and the pram."

"That would be a huge help," Hugh said, "but I'm not sure Grace will agree. She doesn't like to feel as if we're being treated like a charity case. Besides, you all just paid for our glorious honeymoon. I'd feel funny asking people to buy us presents again."

"But if it was a surprise, then Grace couldn't complain," Bessie said. "I've never been to a baby shower, but my sister used to tell me all about them in her letters from America. She went to plenty when her children got old enough to have children. She had ten, you know."

"Your sister had ten children?"

"She did, and I can't even remember how many grandchildren. Anyway, I know exactly what's meant to happen at a baby shower. I think I'll get Elizabeth to help with the planning. Don't say a word to Grace. We'll make it a surprise."

"I wish you hadn't told me about it," Hugh said miserably. "I'm not sure I can keep anything secret from Grace."

Bessie looked disappointed. "If you can't keep it a secret, maybe I won't bother," she said. "That doesn't mean I won't be buying you two a few things for the baby, but maybe a shower isn't such a good idea."

Hugh shrugged. "As I said, it seems odd to me."

Bessie nodded. If Hugh didn't think it was going to happen, he couldn't tell Grace about the shower. Now Bessie just needed to talk to Elizabeth and start making plans.

"Sorry about that," John said as he put his phone away. "I just wanted to let Pete know that Helen's upset. I really appreciate his help, but he should be with her now, not worrying about my case."

"She worried that they won't be able to get married tomorrow," Bessie said.

"I'm sure it will all work out," John told her. "I might need a gallon of hot coffee in order to stay awake for the ceremony, but otherwise, it should be fine."

"I forgot to tell you that Doona took the children home," Bessie said.

"She texted me once they got back to her house," John replied with a smile. "They were all in their pyjamas, stretched out across the couches, eating popcorn and watching some movie I probably wouldn't normally let them watch."

"It's a good thing she was home," Hugh said.

"Yes, I must remember not to take her for granted," John replied, frowning. "Let's get your statement and then you can get home too," he said to Bessie.

"I don't know what I can tell you," Bessie replied, suspecting that she knew where John was going to want her to start.

"Just run me through your day, starting with the time you got up this morning," John said, exactly as Bessie expected.

"I woke up at six, just like I nearly always do," Bessie began. She told John and Hugh all about her rather ordinary day, right up until Helen appeared at her door a few minutes before she was due.

"How did Helen seem when she arrived?" John asked.

Bessie stared at him. "You can't possibly think that she had anything to do with Reverend Doyle's death," she gasped.

"Not at all. I'm just making sure I'm being thorough," John assured her. "If I didn't know Helen or you I would ask, so I'm asking. The chief constable will be taking a very close interest in this case, especially as two inspectors just happened to find the body. We have to make sure that we do everything by the book."

Bessie nodded. "Helen seemed frazzled and incredibly worried about the wedding tomorrow. She was looking forward to getting tonight's meeting over with, so that she'd have a clear idea of what was going to be happening tomorrow afternoon."

"Okay, let's continue. Take me through your conversation with Helen before you left for the church," John said.

Bessie repeated what she could remember of that conversation. John didn't stop her again until she was recounting his own arrival in the car park.

"Before I arrived, did either Helen or Pete seem anxious or worried about anything?" he asked.

"You mean besides the wedding?" Bessie asked. "I'm pretty sure they were both worried about the wedding, but nothing else. No, wait, I'm also pretty sure that Pete was worried about Helen. He kept trying to calm her down and reassure her."

"Neither of them behaved in an atypical manner?" was John's next question.

"Not that I noticed, although it's hard to say what's typical for either of them on the day before their wedding," Bessie replied.

John sighed. "I know, and that's the problem. They were both edgy and anxious, but I didn't have any reason to suspect that they were worried about anything other than tomorrow."

"There's no way either of them killed Reverend Doyle," Bessie said steadily.

"What if he told them he wouldn't marry them?" John asked.

Bessie took a long deep breath before she replied. "I know you're just doing your job," she said eventually, "but you know them both as well as I do. There's no way either of them would kill anyone under any circumstances."

"You know full well that isn't true," John said quietly. "I believe anyone can kill, given the right provocation."

"You may be right, but Helen and Pete would both need very strong motives before they would consider such a thing. I won't believe it."

John nodded. "I'll leave that for now, then. Finish telling me about your day, including what you and Helen were discussing while you were waiting, please."

Bessie obliged, telling John everything that she could remember. "I hope that's everything," she said at the end, "because I'm exhausted."

"I just need you to tell me everything you know about Reverend Doyle," John said.

"As I know next to nothing, that won't take long," Bessie replied. "He'd only been on the island for not much over a month. I could talk for hours about the man he replaced, but he left the island in May."

"Where did he go?" John asked.

"Nice," Bessie replied.

"In France? I suppose it won't be hard to find out if he's still there."

"I'm sure he is. Several of the older ladies in the congregation have kept in touch with him. I get regular updates. He's actually thinking about coming back for a visit some time in the autumn, but not before then," Bessie said.

"So when he left, Reverend Doyle was appointed? Any idea how that works?" John wondered.

"None at all. I'm not as active in the church these days as I used to be," Bessie said. "Even when I was more involved, I was never privy to how the bishop made his appointments. You'll have to talk to him about that."

"I have an appointment with him tomorrow morning," John replied. "But you must have picked up some skeet about Reverend Doyle over the past month, surely?"

Bessie grinned at the man's use of the Manx word. "A few of my friends have complained about the way he conducts his services," Bessie said, "but there are always complaints when someone new comes into a parish. He simply didn't do things the way the former vicar had. People would have come around eventually."

"And you don't know anything about his personal life?"

"No, not a thing. Actually, now that you mention it, I'm surprised that I haven't heard more. I didn't even know he had a housekeeper, let alone a live-in one. I'm surprised that didn't have people talking.

Maybe Ms. Hamilton is considerably older than Reverend Doyle was, though."

"Do you know how old Reverend Doyle was?"

Bessie shrugged. "As I said, I only met him once or twice. I would guess he was around fifty, but that's just a guess. I think he dyed his hair, which made me think he was older than he wanted everyone to think he was."

"Isn't that unusual for a vicar?" Hugh asked.

"You'd have to ask the bishop about that too," Bessie replied.

"I'm going to walk you and Helen back to her car," John said, getting to his feet. "If I can tear her away from Pete, that is."

Bessie looked over and smiled. She hadn't heard the door open or seen Pete come in, but he was holding Helen tightly, and she was crying quietly on his shoulder. Pete was patting her back and whispering in her ear.

Bessie followed John across the room towards the couple. They were still a few steps away when the door suddenly swung open.

"What the bloody hell is going on around here?" a voice shouted from the doorway. "And where is William?"

Bessie looked over at John and shrugged.

"Ah, sorry about the interruption," James Clucas said from behind the woman. "But Ms. Hamilton has just returned home and the constable at the vicarage told her she couldn't go inside.

"And now I'd like some answers as to why," the woman said loudly.

Bessie raised an eyebrow. Ms. Hamilton was a thirty-something blonde in a tight skirt and four-inch heels. She was not at all what Bessie had been expecting. There was no way any of her friends knew that Reverend Doyle was sharing the vicarage with this woman. The complaints to the bishop would have been fast and furious.

"Come on, then," Ms. Hamilton demanded. "Tell me what's going on."

CHAPTER 3

"Ms. Hamilton, I'm sorry about the temporary inconvenience," John said. "Please come and sit down."

"I don't want to sit down," the woman snapped. "It's late and I want to go to bed. Where is William? I'm sure he isn't any happier about all of this than I am. Whatever has happened, you've no cause to keep me out of my home. I can't believe that William told you that you could take over the vicarage like this."

"As I understand it, the vicarage is the property of the church," John replied calmly. "We have permission from the bishop to search it, along with the church, and the church hall."

"Search?" The woman turned pale. "What are you searching for? And where is William?"

"Ms. Hamilton, please take a seat. I'll be with you in just a minute, and I'll explain everything," John replied.

The woman looked around the room and then stared at Bessie for a moment. "Who are all these people?" she asked.

"They were just leaving," John told her.

"You know where to find me," Bessie said in a low voice. She continued on her way to the door. Helen stood up as Bessie went past and fell into step behind her. James followed them to the door and then held it open so that they could walk out.

"What I wouldn't give to be a fly on the wall in there right now," Helen whispered as she and Bessie walked towards the car park.

"I'll just go back to the church in case I'm needed," James said, mostly to himself.

Bessie gave him an encouraging smile. "I'm sure the police are working as quickly as they can."

"Yes, I'm sure," James replied.

A loud scream startled all three of them.

"John must have told her about Reverend Doyle," Helen said sadly.

"I must say she wasn't what I expected," Bessie told her.

"It's not like her to be all dressed up like that," James said. "She usually wears clothes that look as if they're too big for her. I've never seen her wearing makeup before, either. She's younger than I thought she was, or maybe she just looks younger when she's all made up."

"I wonder where she was tonight," Bessie said thoughtfully.

"She looked as if she was at a party," Helen said. "I wonder if she's married or has a boyfriend on the island."

"I don't think she's married, not with the way she was living with Reverend Doyle and all," James said.

"It's a very small house for two people," Bessie remarked.

"It is, aye." James took a step closer to them and then lowered his voice to a whisper. "And from what I could see, they were only using the one bedroom."

Bessie gasped. "I know young men and women live together all the time these days, but I would have expected something different from a member of the clergy," she said sadly.

James shrugged. "I may be wrong, but there are only two bedrooms in the vicarage. They had a problem with the plumbing the other day, and when I was there, I noticed that the second bedroom was full of boxes, so full of boxes that you couldn't actually get into the room. Reverend Doyle said something to me about having trouble finding room for all of his things. I didn't like to ask any questions."

"I can understand that, but John needs to ask some now," Bessie said. "You need to make sure that you tell him everything that you know."

"I already talked to one of the young constables," James replied. "I didn't think to mention my thoughts on the sleeping arrangements in the vicarage, though. The police are searching it. Surely, they'll notice that the second bedroom isn't being used."

"They probably will, unless Reverend Doyle rearranged things once he'd realised what you'd seen," Bessie answered. "Whatever, you should still tell John what you saw."

"Okay, well, I've promised to lock everything up when the police are finished, so I'll talk to him then," James promised.

"Did you see anything else odd in the vicarage?" Bessie asked.

James shrugged. "As I said, there were boxes filling up the second bedroom. That was about the only room I saw, aside from the sitting room and the loo. The sitting room was tidy and neat, and the loo was just a loo."

"There's only one, so they must have been sharing that too, right?" Helen wondered.

"Yes, it's a small house, really," James told her. "The last vicar's housekeeper didn't live in. The church paid for her to have a flat nearby."

"I hope the police finish soon," Bessie told the man.

"I do as well. We have a wedding here tomorrow afternoon. There will be flowers arriving in the morning and lots to do," James replied.

"We know," Helen said. "I'm the bride."

"Oh, dear," James exclaimed. "I didn't realise, but I'm not sure what's going to happen, really. I don't know who can perform the ceremony. You may have to ring the bishop."

"That's already been done," Bessie assured him. "We'll see you tomorrow."

"You shouldn't," James said. "If everything goes right with the wedding, you shouldn't even know I'm here. But I will be, of course, just in case."

Bessie gave the man a hug and then she and Helen continued on their way to the car. They'd only gone a few steps when the door behind them swung open with a loud bang.

Ms. Hamilton stormed out of the church hall with John right behind her. "Ms. Hamilton, wait," he called.

She spun around. "I have nothing further to say to you," she shouted at him. "First of all, I don't believe you. William is fine. I don't know who or what you found in the churchyard, but it won't be William. Second of all, even if something did happen to William, you've no right to search my home. Now I'm going back to my house, and you and your men are going get out and leave me in peace."

John shook his head. "I'm terribly sorry, but I've met Reverend Doyle a couple of times since he's been on the island. The body was definitely his."

"Show me, then," Ms. Hamilton challenged him.

"The crime scene technicians are still working on the scene," John replied. "Once they've finished, and the body can be removed, we can make arrangements for you to see him."

"Fine, that's fine. So for now I can go home and get some sleep," she said.

"I'm afraid you can't stay at the vicarage right now," John told her. "I'll have one of my constables escort you inside so that you can collect an overnight bag. Then I'll have someone take you to a hotel."

"And you're going to pay for that?" Ms. Hamilton demanded.

John frowned. "I'm sure we can arrange something," he replied.

The woman stared at him for a minute, and Bessie could almost see the moment when she decided to change tactics. Ms. Hamilton tossed her hair and then walked slowly towards John.

"I'm sorry," she said breathily. "I'm really sorry. I'm just so tremendously overwhelmed by all of this. I rarely go out in the evening, and I certainly wasn't expecting to come home to this." She stopped and dug in her small evening bag for a tissue.

"I'm sure this is all terribly upsetting," John replied. "I'm sorry that I had to share such bad news with you, but I'm sure you can understand how important it is that we start our investigation immediately."

"Of course," the woman said, taking another step closer to John.

"I'm sure you can understand how devastated I am, though. I can't imagine going to stay in a cold and empty hotel room tonight. William and I were very close. I want to stay in what was our home so that I can feel close to him, at least for one more night." She wiped her eyes again.

Bessie watched closely, trying to see if the tissue was actually getting wet. She knew she was probably being unfair to the woman, but she'd taken an immediate dislike to Ms. Hamilton the moment she'd seen her.

"I'm sorry, I truly am," John replied, "but I can't let you stay in the vicarage tonight."

"And tomorrow the bishop will throw me out," Ms. Hamilton sighed. "The use of the vicarage went along with the appointment at the church. It was William's home. I only got to share it with him. With William gone, I'll be homeless. I probably already am."

"I'm sure the bishop won't throw you out into the street," James objected.

"I wish I had your confidence," the woman said sadly.

"Let's get you sorted for tonight," John suggested. "We can worry about the rest tomorrow."

Ms. Hamilton put her hand on John's arm. "You said I could collect an overnight bag, right? I'll just need a few minutes to gather up all of the things I need."

"Yes, of course. I'll have a constable escort you," John said. "Please limit yourself to what you actually need for tonight. Once we've been through the house, you'll be able to get the rest of your belongings."

She looked as if she wanted to argue, but after a moment she simply sighed and nodded.

"Let's go and get what you need," John said. "I'll escort you myself."

"I'd be awfully grateful to you if you'd do that for me," the woman simpered. "I'm sorry I didn't answer all of your questions earlier. Maybe you can ask me them again while I'm packing."

"Let's deal with one thing at a time," John replied.

As he and Ms. Hamilton walked past Bessie on their way to the vicarage, Bessie was struck by how tired John looked. It wasn't until they were out of sight that Helen spoke.

"I suppose we should go," she said. "I'm meant to be getting married tomorrow."

"And you will be," Bessie said firmly.

"I'd feel better about it if I thought Pete was going to get a decent amount of sleep tonight," Helen replied. "He's going to end up being too tired to enjoy our honeymoon."

"I doubt that," Bessie said.

The pair walked back through the car park to Helen's car. They were both silent on their way back to Bessie's cottage. Bessie was lost in thought, wondering what Reverend Doyle had done that had led to his murder, and curious as to his relationship with Ms. Hamilton. She could only imagine that Helen was thinking about the wedding.

When Helen pulled into the parking area for Bessie's cottage, there was a shiny red sports car parked there.

"It's Elizabeth," Helen said. "What is she doing here at this hour?"

"Whatever it is, I hope it won't take long," Bessie muttered as she climbed out of the car. She hadn't even shut the car door before she heard Elizabeth's door slam. Elizabeth was a very pretty blonde with an enviable figure and a penchant for short skirts and high heels. Tonight, though, she was wearing what almost looked like pyjamas.

"Helen, you poor thing," Elizabeth said as she rushed across the parking area to pull Helen into a hug. "I can't imagine how you must be feeling, but don't worry. I have everything under control."

"That's good to hear," Helen replied.

"Reverend Smith from Onchan is going to perform the ceremony tomorrow. He's going to be at the church at one o'clock. He'd like a few minutes with you and with Peter, separately or together, which-ever you'd prefer," Elizabeth told her.

"Oh, separately," Helen said quickly. "I don't want Pete to see me before the wedding. We don't need any more bad luck, not now."

Elizabeth chuckled. "I think you've already had more than your fair share," she said.

"That's for sure," Bessie exclaimed.

"But what if the church isn't available?" Helen asked. "We don't have that many guests coming, but we have too many to simply ring everyone to tell them about the change in venue."

"I spoke to the chief constable, and he's assured me that the church will be ready for you as planned," Elizabeth replied. "He and Daddy are good friends," she added.

"My goodness, Pete's not going to like that," Helen muttered.

"My job as your wedding planner is to make sure that your wedding happens," Elizabeth said. "If that includes me calling in a few favours from friends of mine, then that's what I'll do."

"John isn't going to be happy if he's told he has to clear the church before he's finished with it," Bessie said softly.

"That's why I came up with a backup plan," Elizabeth said proudly.

"Go on, then," Helen said in a worried tone.

"If we can't use the church, we can still use their car park," Elizabeth told her.

"I don't want to get married in the car park," Helen objected.

"No, no, I don't mean that at all," Elizabeth laughed. "I mean everyone can still turn up at Laxey Church and park their cars there. I have two buses and the church in Lonan on call. The church should be plenty big enough for your ceremony, and the two buses can take people back and forth from Laxey every five minutes or so."

"That's a great idea," Bessie said.

"And Reverend Smith will be waiting for me to ring him in the morning to tell him which church we're using. He doesn't mind either way," Elizabeth added.

"So I can still get married, no matter what," Helen said with a small sigh.

"Yes, you can," Elizabeth told her. "For now you need your beauty sleep. Come on, I'm going to follow you home and give you a facial before you go to bed."

"It's far too late at night for a facial," Helen argued.

"It will only take five minutes, and it will relax you," Elizabeth told her. "After the evening you've had, I think you need it."

Helen looked as if she wanted to argue further, but after a moment she sighed and turned to Bessie. "Thank you for everything," she said. "I suppose I'll see you tomorrow, then."

"I'll be at the church by one, just in case you need anything," Bessie told her. "Elizabeth can let me know which church I'm meant to be at."

"Elizabeth can do better than that," the girl replied. "I'll come and collect you around half twelve, if that works for you."

Bessie nodded. She's been planning to take a taxi, but she hadn't booked one yet. Getting a ride from Elizabeth would be much easier.

Bessie hugged both women and then let herself into her cottage. She waved from the doorway and then shut and locked the door behind herself. The message light on her answering machine was blinking frantically. Bessie was going to ignore it but then decided to clear the messages before she went to bed. Otherwise there was a real risk that the machine would be full before she got up the next morning.

Nearly all of the messages were from friends who had heard about the body at the church and wanted to get the full story from Bessie. After erasing every message, Bessie only rang one person back.

"Doona? I'm finally home, but I can't even guess when John might get away," she told her friend when she answered.

"He texted me about half an hour ago to say that the kids should just stay here tonight," Doona told her. "I don't know if he'll get any sleep at all before the wedding."

"I hope he'll manage a few hours," Bessie replied. "He's meant to be a witness, and he can't do that if he falls asleep during the ceremony."

Doona laughed. "That would be unfortunate, and poor Pete and Helen have had quite enough bad luck, I think."

"I agree."

"One of the reasons John is planning to work late is so that he can clear the church, and they can actually have the wedding, of course."

"Elizabeth has a plan in place in case they can't use the church. She's also talked to the chief constable and he's assured her that the church will be ready."

"Oh, dear, maybe that's why John sounded so unhappy," Doona sighed. "I didn't realise the chief constable was involved."

"I don't think Elizabeth understood the possible consequences of her ringing him."

"No, I don't suppose she did. But John would be doing everything he could anyway, as he wants everything to be perfect for Helen and Pete."

"We all do. Elizabeth was here when Helen brought me home. She's going to give Helen a facial when they get back to Helen's flat."

"I hope she stays with Helen tonight. Helen would be upset and anxious anyway on the night before her wedding. I can't imagine how she must be feeling under the circumstances."

"I should have insisted that she stay here tonight," Bessie said.

"Except she would have had to go home to pack an overnight bag anyway," Doona pointed out. "I'm sure Elizabeth will take good care of her."

"I certainly hope so," Bessie sighed. "I also hope John can solve the murder quickly. I don't suppose he said anything about having a suspect in custody already?"

"I wish," Doona replied. "It's far too early for that, I imagine."

"But you missed all the excitement," Bessie told her. "Reverend Doyle's housekeeper arrived just before I left."

"Really? I suppose I knew he had a housekeeper, but I don't know anything about her. Was she devastated?"

"I don't know. She wasn't at all what I was expecting."

"Oh? Do tell," Doona replied.

Bessie told Doona everything she could remember about Ms. Hamilton. Doona didn't say a word until Bessie had finished.

"She's only thirty-something?" was Doona's first question. "I'm sure Reverend Doyle was in his fifties, wasn't he?"

"Maybe late forties," Bessie replied, "but he dyed his hair, so he may have been older than he looked."

"Maybe she's older than she looked."

"Maybe, but whatever age she is, I can't believe they were living together and, we think, sharing a bed."

"That is shocking. I really hope that James is wrong about that. I don't mind people living together, I suppose, but it feels wrong for the vicar to be doing it."

"Yes, well, we'll have to see what John finds out. Maybe there's a logical explanation for it all."

The pair talked for a few minutes more before Bessie began yawning after every sentence. "I think I need to go and get some sleep," she laughed.

"We both should. We have a wedding to go to tomorrow, and I'm responsible for two children as well. I need as much sleep as I can get."

"Do you need any help with the children?"

"No, not at all. They're both really good kids, or at least they have been so far. We're going to walk over to John's in the morning so they can get ready for the wedding there. Then they'll come to the church with me, unless John would rather do things differently. I suspect he'll be working tomorrow, except for during the wedding, so I'll probably have the kids all day."

"If you need some suggestions for things to do with them, just ask. I'm sure they'd love to see the island's heritage sites, but if that doesn't appeal, I can ring a few friends and find out what children their age like to do during the summer months."

"Thanks, Bessie. I may take you up on that. I'm hoping that John can solve the case quickly, though, and then he can worry about entertaining Thomas and Amy."

Bessie put the phone down and made her way up the stairs to her bedroom. It took a few minutes for her mind to settle, but once she was asleep, she slept soundly. Her first thought when she woke up the next morning was of Helen. "I hope the poor woman is okay," she said to her reflection as she combed her short grey hair. "It's meant to be the happiest day of her life, after all." Her mirror image didn't bother to reply.

Toast with honey and a cup of tea didn't really satisfy Bessie this morning. She found a box of stale cereal in the cupboard, but that didn't appeal, either. What she really wanted was pancakes or waffles smothered in maple syrup, preferably with bacon. That was the breakfast of her childhood in America and something she often craved when she'd had an upset. It felt far too indulgent for most mornings, though, including this one.

A light rain was falling as Bessie headed out for her morning walk. It seemed to stop and start as she went, but she simply ignored it on her steady march towards Thie yn Traie. She felt like continuing, but she wanted to be available if Helen or Elizabeth needed anything, so she turned back for home once she'd reached the steps to the mansion.

"Ah, good morning," a loud voice called across the beach as Bessie walked.

Bessie forced herself to smile at the new arrival. Maggie Shimmin was a nice woman, really, and Bessie liked her and her husband, Thomas. The couple owned the holiday cottages that ran between Bessie's cottage and Thie yn Traie, and Bessie knew that they worked hard to make sure that their guests were good neighbours. It was just that Maggie tended to complain a lot and gossip even more. Bessie wasn't really in the mood for Maggie this morning.

"My goodness, what a miserable morning," the fifty-something woman greeted Bessie.

"It's a bit damp," Bessie agreed.

"Which makes our guests grumpy," Maggie said, "which means I have to come over and listen to them complain."

"I believe it's meant to improve later."

"I hope so. But how are you, Bessie?"

"I'm fine. How are you?"

Maggie rolled her eyes. "You know how it is. I've done something awful to my back, but I've no time to have it looked at during the summer, do I? Thomas is trying to do most of the heavy lifting and whatnot, but sometimes things need to be done, and I'm the only one available. He's doing all of the shopping now, because we have to buy so much for the cottages, but that means I have to deal more with the guests, which isn't my favourite thing to do. But you know me; I never complain."

Bessie hid a smile. "Of course not."

"But today's Helen Baxter's wedding day, isn't it?" Maggie asked before Bessie could start walking away. "She's marrying that inspector from Douglas, the one who's always frowning, isn't she?"

"Yes, Pete and Helen are getting married this afternoon. I must say Pete smiles a great deal more these days, though."

Maggie waved the thought away with a hand. "Yes, but they were getting married at the Laxey Church, weren't they? What are they going to do now?"

"As far as I know, they are still getting married at the Laxey Church," Bessie told her.

"Hmph, it's okay for some, I suppose."

"What is that supposed to mean?"

"When we had our little incident in our cottage, the police wouldn't let us back inside for days. Somehow, though, they've managed to make the church available in less than twenty-four hours. Doesn't seem quite right to me."

"In this case, the body wasn't found in the church," Bessie told her. "The area where the body was found will be surrounded by police tape for some time, I would imagine."

"But it's the church's vicar who's been killed," Maggie argued. "That must mean that the church is integral to the investigation."

"Maybe, but that's a decision for the police to make, not us."

"I'm just saying that if I were having a wedding there today, I don't think the police would be in such a hurry to accommodate me."

"Well, Helen and Pete have made alternate arrangements in case the police aren't done with the church," Bessie told her. "They aren't asking for any special treatment, either."

"But who would want to kill Reverend Doyle?" Maggie asked. "He's only been here for a few weeks. It must have been someone from across."

"I'm sure the police are doing everything they can to answer that very question."

"I hear he had a young woman living with him," Maggie said in a low voice. She glanced up and down the empty beach, as if worried about being overheard. "My source told me that she turned up at the vicarage last night dressed for a party."

"It's my understanding that the vicar had a live-in housekeeper."

"Ha! From what I've heard, that woman was not a housekeeper. The question is, why didn't any of us know about her?"

"That's a very good question," Bessie said. In a small village like Laxey, it seemed almost impossible that no one had noticed and commented on the woman's presence. Bessie knew that Maggie's circle of friends thrived on gossip and that many of her older friends were involved in the local church. Ms. Hamilton should have been the most talked-about person in the village.

"I knew he had a housekeeper," Maggie said, "but I never actually saw her. When I visited the vicarage, he made a comment or two about her, but she wasn't actually at home when I was there. And everyone I've spoken to says that same, that the vicar mentioned her occasionally, but no one actually saw her. I suspect we all would have started to wonder about her soon, though."

"No doubt," Bessie replied dryly. Everyone would have been prepared to give the new vicar time to settle in before they'd have started speculating on his household arrangements.

"I didn't like Reverend Doyle very much anyway," Maggie said. "He didn't seem very dedicated to his calling, at least in my opinion."

Bessie wondered what Maggie had wanted the man to do. Presumably he'd refused her request, which was why she was questioning his dedication. "I'd barely spoken to him," she told Maggie.

"There was just something odd about him. I didn't trust him."

By the end of the day, Maggie would be telling everyone that she'd suspected all along that the man would end up murdered, Bessie thought. She only wished that she spoken to Maggie about him before he'd died. No doubt she would have heard a very different opinion. "It's still tragic, what happened to him," Bessie said.

"Oh, yes, tragic," Maggie echoed. "Do you know exactly what happened? I mean, I'm told it's a murder investigation, but I don't know more than that. Was it very obviously murder? When you saw the body, could you tell right away?"

"I didn't see the body," Bessie replied. At least not most of it, she added to herself. "John Rockwell noticed that something wasn't right in between the gravestones, but he sent everyone away before he went to investigate."

"And he hasn't told you anything more?"

"I haven't even really spoken to him since the body was discovered. He took my statement last night, but he didn't tell me anything at all. He just asked me questions."

"You should ring him up and ask him what's going on," Maggie said.

"I couldn't possibly."

"Oh, but surely we all have a right to know what's happening. I mean, a vicar was murdered in his own churchyard. Surely the good people of Laxey need to know why. We could all be in danger, after all."

"No doubt Dan Ross at the local paper will take a similar position with the chief constable. I don't know how much luck he'll have, but I suggest you get your news from there."

Maggie frowned. "You will let me know if you hear anything, won't you? The guests will all be asking, you understand. Some of them are already edgy because of the unfortunate incident in the last cottage. Another murder might drive some of them away."

"John will be doing everything he can to work out what happened. In the meantime, you should hope that your guests are too busy enjoying their holidays to pay attention to the local news."

"At least this time the beach itself won't be swarming with police," Maggie said.

"Have you worked out what you're going to do with that cottage?" Bessie asked.

Maggie shrugged. "I think we should start trying to rent it out again, but the rental agency that we use in Douglas doesn't agree. According to them, at least half of the guests who book with us ask specifically not to be booked into that cottage. They reckon that if people were booked in there and then found out later what had happened there, they'd complain bitterly."

"I hope it isn't hurting your business too much."

"Oh, we raised the rates on all of the other cottages to cover for it," Maggie told her, "but we'll have to raise them ever higher if we're going to start tearing that cottage down to rebuild it."

"I hope you can find a solution. But now I really must go," Bessie said. "I have a million things to do before the wedding."

Maggie nodded. "And I've guests to see to," she said, turning and walking quickly away.

Back at home, Bessie checked her answering machine. No new messages. She paced around the kitchen for a few minutes and then looked at the clock. It was too early to start ringing people. She was standing in the middle of the kitchen and trying to decide what to do next when the phone rang.

CHAPTER 4

"*H*ello?"

"It's Helen," the voice on the other replied. "I didn't wake you, did I?"

"Oh, goodness, no. I get up at six every morning."

"I thought you'd be an early riser," Helen said. "I was hoping to lie in today, but, well, I can't sleep."

"Do you want to come here, or should I come there?" Bessie asked.

"Oh, I didn't, I mean, I don't know," Helen replied. "I'm just wide awake, and I don't know what to do with myself."

"What were you planning to do today?"

"Well, I thought I might get married," Helen laughed, "but I know what you mean. I was going to have a very lazy morning at home, take a long, hot bath, and then I'm meant to be at Thie yn Traie for eleven. Elizabeth is going to do my hair and makeup, and she said something about a light lunch before we have to be at the church for one."

"Well, you're more than welcome here at any time. I'll be home all morning. Then you'll only be a short distance away from Thie yn Traie."

"Maybe I will come up," Helen said. "I'm making myself crazy here, having all sorts of second thoughts about everything."

"You're more than welcome."

"I'll see you in a short while, then."

Bessie put the phone down and then spent a few minutes tidying the cottage. Once she'd finished that chore, she refilled the kettle and switched it on. Tea was going to be necessary.

"I'm sorry about this," Helen said when Bessie opened the door to her a short time later. "I'm far too old to be this frazzled about anything."

"Nonsense," Bessie replied. "It's your wedding day. I can't even imagine how stressed you must feel."

"I just want it to be over, really," the woman confessed. "I want to be Pete's wife, but I'm really not looking forward to today."

"I'm looking forward to it. I like seeing my friends happy."

Helen nodded. "I know, and I'm sure I'll have a wonderful day. I just feel as if there's so much that could go wrong, you know?"

"I do know, but as long as you end up as Pete's wife at the end of the day, nothing else matters."

Helen nodded. "I'm going to keep reminding myself of that all day," she told Bessie. "Anyway, our celebrant was brutally murdered the night before the wedding. Anything else that goes wrong will probably seem quite minor."

"Have you talked to Pete yet today?"

"No. I don't want to talk to him or see him before the ceremony unless I have to for some reason. I know it's an old-fashioned tradition, but it's one I'm hoping to keep. I know it might not be possible in the middle of a murder investigation, but the case is John's, not Pete's."

"So we aren't even sure if you'll be able to use the church or not yet," Bessie said.

"Elizabeth said she would ring the chief constable this morning if we hadn't heard anything."

"Which we'd prefer she not do, right?"

"Well, yes, I mean, I'd rather he not be involved, if at all possible. He's meant to be coming to the wedding, of course."

"Let me ring Doona," Bessie said. "She may have heard something from John by now."

"Good morning." Doona sounded tired.

"Helen is here, keeping me company before she's due to start getting ready. We were just wondering if anyone had heard anything about the availability of the church," Bessie said.

"I'll text John and get back to you," Doona replied.

Bessie made tea for her guest and piled a plate high with biscuits. Neither woman was in the mood for them, though. They sipped their tea in silence, waiting for Bessie's phone to ring. Even though she was expecting it, Bessie still jumped at the sound when it finally rang.

"Good morning, Bessie," John's voice came down the line. "How are you this morning?"

"I'm fine, thank you. But how are you?"

"Tired, of course, but I've had a few hours of sleep, at least. Doona said that Helen was there."

"She is, yes."

"You can assure her that Pete went home hours before I did," John told her, "and that we cleared the church before he left the site. It's a good thing it's a very small church."

Bessie held her hand over the receiver and repeated what John had told her. Helen seemed to visibly relax at the words.

"Is there anything else I need to know right now?" Bessie asked John.

"I don't think so. I fully intend to be at the church to perform my duties as a witness, even if I have to miss out on the reception afterwards. Doona is looking after the children today. I'm not sure how I'll ever repay her."

Bessie thought of a dozen different replies and discarded them all. "Let's hope you can work out what happened fairly quickly," she said eventually.

"It's looking more complicated than I'd like," John sighed, "but it always is, isn't it?"

"Yes, rather, so we'll see you at the church around half one, then," Bessie concluded.

"You will. As I said, I may not make it to the reception, but that isn't the place to talk about murder, anyway. I may want to talk to you later today, though."

"You know you're welcome here anytime."

Bessie put the phone down and looked over at Helen. "It sounds as if everything is okay."

"Does John think he'll actually make it to the wedding?"

"He'll be there, but he might have to miss the reception."

Helen nodded. "I thought as much. I'm just grateful that he'll be at the ceremony. Pete would be very disappointed if John had to miss that. He'd understand, of course, better than anyone, but he'd be disappointed."

With nothing else to do, and the rain having stopped, the pair took a long walk on the beach to fill their time.

"I feel so much better now, thank you," Helen said as they went. "Nothing like fresh sea air to calm the soul."

When they reached Thie yn Traie, Bessie spotted Elizabeth walking down the steep stairs behind the mansion.

"Good morning," she called as she bounced down the last few steps. "I've been ringing your flat all morning," she told Helen.

"I was too restless to be at home alone, so I came to bother poor Aunt Bessie," Helen replied.

"You should have come to Thie yn Traie," Elizabeth said. "You could have had a facial and a massage and bottles and bottles of champagne."

"I don't think I'll want champagne until after the ceremony," Helen replied. "I don't really like people fussing over me, either. I just didn't want to be alone."

"I should have stayed with you last night," Elizabeth said.

"But I told you to go home," Helen reminded her. "I wanted to be alone last night, but then this morning I didn't. I'm just a mess; that's all."

Elizabeth chuckled. "Maybe being a wedding planner isn't going to be such a great idea. I'm not sure I want to deal with brides all the time."

"I'm sorry," Helen said quickly.

"Not at all," Elizabeth replied. "I was mostly teasing, and anyway, you've been wonderful to work with. Last-minute jitters are totally understandable, especially after what happened last night. Anyway, I've learned a ton working with you. I'm really excited about my new business. Now I just have to find clients."

"I'm not sure you'll want to tell people you were involved in my wedding," Helen said. "People tend to be skittish about murder."

"I've been involved in murders before," Elizabeth told her. "At least it didn't happen during the ceremony."

Bessie shuddered. What a horrible thought that was. "I talked to John this morning, and they're done with the church," she said.

"Excellent. So I can cancel the buses and the church in Lonan and let Reverend Smith know where to be. Everything will be just perfect from here, I'm sure," Elizabeth said confidently.

Bessie wasn't sure that perfect was the right word, but things did seem to run fairly smoothly for the rest of the day. She ended up joining Elizabeth and Helen at Thie yn Traie for their "light lunch," which turned out to be enough food for a dozen hungry men, and included several bottles of champagne. Bessie limited herself to a single glass, and Helen didn't have more than a sip. Bessie was surprised when Elizabeth also limited herself to only one glass.

"I'm working," she said, winking at Bessie as she sipped her drink slowly.

They arrived at the church just before one o'clock. Bessie greeted James with a hug.

"I hope you managed to get some sleep," she told him.

"I got a few hours," he replied. "I'll have an early night tonight, and I'll be back to normal tomorrow."

"You aren't coming to the reception?" Helen asked.

"Oh, well, I mean, it was very kind of you to invite me, but I didn't really think that you'd meant to include me," he stammered.

"Of course we did," Helen said. "We invited Reverend Doyle as well. I must remember to invite Reverend Smith."

"That's very kind of you," James said. "I may just come out and join you for a short while."

Helen nodded, and then they followed James into the church.

"It looks wonderful," Helen sighed.

There seemed to be flowers everywhere. The old church really did look even more beautiful than normal.

"Ah, this must be the bride," a tall, slender man said, getting up from a seat near the front. "I'm Reverend Smith. I'd really appreciate a few minutes of your time."

Helen nodded and followed the man further into the church.

"I'd better watch out for the groom," James said. "She won't want him to wander in and see her before the service."

He headed for the door, leaving Bessie and Elizabeth in the church's foyer.

"I hope nothing else goes wrong," Elizabeth said. "I've really come to like both Helen and Pete over the past few weeks. I want their day to be perfect."

"I'll settle for almost perfect," Bessie told her.

"But what's happening with the murder investigation?"

"I've no idea. I only talked to John long enough to confirm that the church would be available for today. I was hoping he might tell me that he'd already made an arrest, but he didn't."

"Who kills a vicar? I mean, he's a man of God and all that. Although I did hear that he was living with a woman, and they weren't married. Surely that isn't very vicar-like behaviour?"

"John's investigating, and that's all I know," Bessie said.

Elizabeth nodded. "I was hoping I might see the housekeeper when we were here today. She seems like the most likely suspect to me."

Bessie didn't bother to reply. Helen walked back over to them a minute later, and then it was time to help her get changed. Elizabeth had done Helen's hair and makeup at Thie yn Traie, but because of the last-minute meeting with the vicar, Helen hadn't put on her wedding gown yet. Now James let them into the church hall, which gave them plenty of space for what needed doing.

"You look gorgeous," Bessie told Helen as she studied the woman. Helen had chosen a fairly simple white gown that still managed to look bridal. Undoubtedly, the crown of flowers and veil were part of that. Elizabeth made a few final adjustments to Helen's hair and then touched up her lipstick.

"You're perfect," she announced. "I'll get the photographer." After what felt like a hundred photos later, it was two o'clock.

"Is Pete even here?" Helen asked, looking worried.

"He arrived at ten past one and waited outside for his turn with the vicar," Bessie told her. "John was with him and texted me in case you asked."

"Oh, thank goodness," Helen breathed. "I just suddenly started to wonder what would happen if he didn't show up, and, well, let's just say my mind raced away with me."

"So now it's up to you how late you want to be," Bessie told her.

"Oh, I don't want to be late at all. If everything is ready, let's go and get this over with."

Bessie shook her head. "I'm not sure that's the right attitude," she said softly.

"No, and I don't really mean it, but I am incredibly anxious to see Pete."

Elizabeth went first, holding doors as she went. Bessie followed Helen into the back of the church. She was holding Helen's arm, which was shaking badly, when Pete turned around and looked back at them. Helen went still for a moment and then looked at Bessie.

"It's all good," she said softly before she marched down the aisle with a huge smile on her face.

Bessie wiped away more than one tear as the pair exchanged their vows. John looked exhausted, but he managed to stay awake for the ceremony. Doona looked tired as well, sitting next to Thomas and Amy, who behaved impeccably. The substitute vicar did a good job, at least in Bessie's opinion.

"It's never easy performing a marriage ceremony when you don't know the couple involved. I have to say that I was delighted today to find, after just spending a few minutes with both Pete and Helen, that I could stand here and feel confident that they will make their marriage work. I've been doing this for a long time, and I've rarely seen a couple so very much in love," he told the congregation.

Bessie was pretty sure that nearly everyone in the church was wiping his or her eyes after that remark. After the ceremony, and after Bessie and John had signed the register as witnesses, Helen beamed at them.

"We did it," she exclaimed. "Now we get to have fun."

"Congratulations," Bessie said to Pete.

"Thank you. I'm a very lucky man," he said, gazing at Helen with a huge smile on his face.

"You are, at that," John agreed. "I hope you'll excuse me now. I need to get back to work. I'm hoping to stop in at the reception later, but I can't promise anything."

"We'd love to see you, but we understand," Helen told him. "Thank you for making time to be here for the ceremony."

"I wouldn't have missed it for anything," John replied.

He gave the bride a hug and then shook Pete's hand. Bessie got a hug, too, before John slipped away.

"I love the food at the café in Lonan," Bessie told Helen. "I never would have thought to have a wedding reception there, though."

"It was Elizabeth's idea, and she got them to give us a really good price. This is the first time they've done a wedding. We just have to hope they know what they're doing."

"I know Dan and Carol, the owners," Bessie replied. "I'm sure they wouldn't have agreed to do it if they weren't positive that they could deliver."

Outside the church, everyone was making their way back to their cars. A limousine was waiting for the happy couple.

"Oh, Bessie, ride with us," Helen suggested.

"I promised Doona I would ride with her," Bessie said, not entirely truthfully. Pete and Helen didn't want to spend the first few minutes of their married life together with Bessie in the car with them, she was sure of that. "You go and enjoy a bit of luxury."

Helen giggled and grabbed Pete's hand, pulling him towards the long black car. The uniformed driver was standing by the door at the back, and he quickly pulled it open as they approached. Bessie waved and then hurried away to find Doona.

"Of course you can ride with us," Doona assured her a moment later. "We're all starving. Breakfast didn't exactly go to plan, and then we were running late and didn't get much lunch. I hope they have something out already when we get there."

"I never did find out what they're planning for food," Bessie said, "but I'm sure it will be delicious."

She climbed into the passenger seat of Doona's car while Thomas and Amy got into the back. Doona slowly pulled the car into the long queue that was leaving the church. They all made their way together from Laxey to Lonan, quickly filling the small car park at the café.

Bessie found herself pulled into a hug almost as soon as she walked into the building.

"I brought the cake, and Elizabeth insisted that I stay for the party," Andy Caine told her with a grin. "I hope it tastes as good as it looks. Though I'm saying it myself, I think it came out rather nice."

Bessie glanced over at the cake that was sitting on a large table in the corner. "It's stunning," she exclaimed. "Maybe you should forget about opening a restaurant and just open a bakery."

"We'll see. I have to finish culinary school first, although I have had three other wedding cake orders in the past week. Elizabeth Quayle is sending a lot of business my way."

"That's good to hear," Bessie grinned.

"It's filling up my summer break nicely, anyway," he shrugged.

"Bessie, there you are," Dan Jenkins, the café's owner, said in a loud voice. He came over and gave her a hug. "You must promise to be totally honest with me about everything after this is over," he said. "We're hoping to start doing more of this sort of thing, but I need honest and critical feedback if we're going to do it right."

"I'm sure everything will be lovely," Bessie told him.

"I certainly hope so," he replied.

"How's Carol?" Bessie asked.

"She's fine. She's at home, having a quiet weekend."

Bessie wondered what that meant. She knew the young couple was hoping to start a family; that was why Carol was no longer working at the café. Maybe they'd be making a happy announcement soon, she speculated.

The afternoon passed quickly. Bessie spent time chatting to many of her friends from around the island. Doona seemed to be coping with the children well, and the food on the extensive buffet was even better than Bessie had expected. After everyone had eaten and the cake had been cut, Dan and his staff pushed chairs and tables out of the way to make a small dance floor.

Wine and champagne flowed, and everyone seemed to have a wonderful time. Bessie was happy to spend a few minutes with Hugh and Grace.

"I wasn't sure you'd be able to be here," Bessie told Hugh.

"John is rotating us all through short shifts today so we can all spend some time here and still keep the case moving," he explained. "I can't drink anything, but I wasn't really planning on doing so anyway. As Grace can't, I don't think I should drink, either."

"Which I've told him is silly," Grace said. "I don't even miss alcohol. I was never much of a drinker. But I've told Hugh he can still have a glass of wine or whatever once in a while. Seeing other people drink doesn't bother me."

"I think it's sweet that he's not drinking because you're pregnant," Bessie told her. "But how are you feeling?"

"Better, I think," Grace laughed. "I'm having less morning sickness, anyway. I'm told the second trimester is the best, so I'm trying to enjoy it while I can. Now that school is out, I'm getting lots more rest, which is helpful. I seem to be tired all of the time, but the doctor assures me that it's all perfectly normal."

"You're growing a baby," Hugh said. "It must be incredibly hard work."

"Hugh said things are moving forward with the house as well," Bessie said.

"Yes, they seem to be going quite slowly, but they are moving," Grace agreed. "We should be in before the baby arrives, anyway."

"I'm so happy for you both," Bessie said, "and for Pete and Helen too. They look incredibly happy together."

"I've never seen Inspector Corkill smile so much," Hugh told her. "In fact, before he met Helen, I don't think I'd ever seen him smile at all. He didn't smile like that when he was married to his first wife."

"It was such a shame; the vicar dying right before the wedding," Grace said in a low voice.

"Yes, it was," Bessie agreed.

"I almost expected the inspector to cancel his honeymoon so he could stay and help with the investigation," Hugh confided. "I'm sure he thought about it."

"They have such wonderful plans," Bessie said. "It would be incredibly sad if they had to cancel."

Pete and Helen made their way around the room, hugging everyone and thanking them for coming.

"I had a wonderful time. Thank you for including me," Bessie told them both. "I hope you have an amazing time in the US."

"I'm sure we will," Helen replied.

"Thank you for everything," Pete said to Bessie. "I know you found Elizabeth for us, and she was brilliant, and you found Andy to do that amazing cake. We couldn't have done all of this without you."

"You'd have managed, but I was more than happy to help," Bessie replied. "I'm so very happy for both of you."

A short while later Doona found Bessie. "The kids have been behaving wonderfully, but they're both bored to bits. I'm going to take them home now."

"I'll come as well if you don't mind giving me a ride," Bessie said. "I think I've spoken to everyone I know at least once, and I'm getting tired. It's been a stressful twenty-four hours."

At Bessie's cottage, Doona insisted on coming inside to make sure everything was okay. "I hate when you fuss," Bessie told her.

"I know, but I'm going to do it anyway," Doona replied.

While Doona was peeking under beds and into wardrobes, Bessie told Thomas and Amy to have a walk on the beach.

"Splash in the sea if you want to," she added. "I'm sure you need a bit of fun after that long afternoon."

When Doona came down, she frowned at Bessie. "I was only gone for two minutes, and you've already lost John's children?"

"I told them to go and run on the beach for a bit. They need to let off some steam."

"Yes, you're probably right," Doona sighed. "I don't know a lot about looking after children, really."

"I'm sure you're doing a great job. Just try to remember what you were like when you were fourteen."

"I'm not sure I want to remember," Doona laughed. "I thought I was going to marry some movie star or other, and I wanted to be a supermodel. I was sure I was going to keep growing taller, but it turns out I never did. I've been five feet six since I was in my early teens."

"And thus a bit too short to be a supermodel."

"Yes, well, that wasn't the only reason I never managed to become a supermodel, but that's beside the point. I should go and see how the kids are getting on."

"I'll come along," Bessie said. "I could do with a walk on the beach."

As both women were still dressed for the wedding, they slipped off their shoes and tights before they left the cottage.

"I should have changed," Bessie remarked after a few minutes. "It's too warm out here for this dress."

"The kids should have changed," Doona said, nodding towards Amy and Thomas, who were happily splashing along the water's edge in their fancy clothes.

"I didn't even think about that," Bessie admitted. "I hope they don't ruin their good clothes."

"I hope everything is washable," Doona said. "At least the kids are."

The beach was crowded in the early evening sunshine. Bessie and Doona made their way through the groups of families on blankets and in folding chairs, collecting Thomas and Amy along the way. When they reached Thie yn Traie, the crowds began to thin. Only a few holidaymakers had bothered to walk beyond the beach immediately behind their own holiday cottages. A short while later Bessie and her friends had the beach to themselves.

"I feel as if I could walk forever," Doona said as Thomas and Amy chased one another around rocks.

"I know what you mean. After days like today, it's so good to get out and get some exercise. I wish I had their energy," Bessie added, nodding at the children.

As if on cue, the children stopped racing around and came over to join Bessie and Doona.

"That was weirdly fun," Amy said. "I haven't run around that way in a long time."

"Yeah, it was fun being a little kid again for a while," Thomas said.

Bessie laughed. "If you ever watch parents chasing their children around on the beach, you'll see that most of the parents seem to having as much, if not more, fun than the children. I think we're all in too much of a hurry to grow up and behave responsibly, and we forget to have fun and simply enjoy life."

"Yeah, I miss being a little kid," Amy said with a sigh. "All of my friends are worried about getting boyfriends, and I'd much rather still be playing with my toys."

"Stay as young as you can for as long as you can," Bessie told her. "You've many years ahead to find boyfriends and all of that."

The foursome walked a bit further before turning back towards Treoghe Bwaane.

"I hope you weren't too bored at the wedding," Bessie said.

"It was okay," Thomas shrugged. "The food was good, anyway."

"I just wish Dad had been there," Amy said softly. "I hope he solves the case quickly so we can spend some time with him while we're here."

"Like we spend so much time with Mum back home," Thomas said.

Amy giggled. "But we don't mind not seeing that much of Mum. She's too in love with Harvey to be any fun anyway. Dad's fun to spend time with."

"There is that," Thomas agreed.

"Well, I hope you enjoy your time on the island. I know you didn't like it all that much when you were living here," Bessie said.

"It wasn't that bad," Amy told her. "Mum hated it, and I think she tried hard to convince us that we hated it too. I made a few good friends when we were here, though. I'm hoping I'll get to see them during this visit."

"I made a few friends as well," Thomas added. "We're meant to try to get together, but we haven't made any firm plans because, well, because of the murder and all that."

"When we get back to my house, why don't you both see if you can make some plans for tomorrow? I have the day off, so I can drive you all over the island if you want," Doona suggested. "I'm pretty sure your dad is going to be busy tomorrow."

"Yeah, he told me after the wedding that things were more complicated than he'd expected with the murder. I don't think he'll be around much for a few days," Thomas sighed.

"As I said, I have tomorrow off," Doona said. "I can take you sightseeing, or you can make arrangements with your friends, or we can go to the park in Ramsey and play mini-golf and go paddle boating, whatever you want to do."

By the time Doona finished speaking, they were back at Bessie's cottage.

"We can talk about it on the drive home," Thomas said, "and thank you, Doona. We really appreciate you trying to make our visit fun."

"I'm happy to do it," Doona told him. "Your dad is a great guy, and he just happens to have some pretty terrific kids."

Amy gave Doona a hug, and then the trio got into Doona's car and drove away.

At least that seems to be going well so far, Bessie thought as she let herself into her cottage. No doubt there would be some bumps in the road, but for now the children seemed to be dealing well with their father's unavoidable absence. They seemed to like Doona and appreciate her efforts as well. Bessie hoped that the case would be solved before they began to get tired of one another.

She made herself a cup of tea and curled up with a good book. She was just a few pages away from finding out who'd killed the French maid and stolen the silver sloth when someone knocked on her door.

"I'm sorry to come by so late," John said as Bessie let him in.

"It's fine. I was just finishing a book," Bessie told him.

"I hope it's a good one."

"It isn't, really," Bessie sighed. "I could tell on page six who the killer was going to be, and nothing changed my mind in the next two hundred pages. If the killer turns out to be anyone other than the man I suspect, I'll be very angry, as the entire book points to him on every single page."

"Maybe it's all an elaborate bluff," John suggested.

Bessie shrugged. "He's the only character with any motive, the only character with the means to have successfully used the rather odd murder weapon, and one of only two characters who had the opportunity to be with the victim at the right time. Unless the author has deliberately misled us through the whole book, he has to be the killer."

John sighed. "Maybe that's why I don't read murder mysteries."

"But you aren't here to talk about fictional murders and missing sloths," Bessie said.

"Missing sloths?"

"The dead woman had a large solid silver sloth for some reason that isn't clear. It went missing when she was killed," Bessie explained.

"Okay," John said with a shrug. 'I'm not even going to ask. As fascinated as I am by the whole thing, we really need to talk about our real-life murder."

CHAPTER 5

*B*essie shivered. "I was really hoping that you were going to be able to solve this one quickly," she said.

"I always want to solve cases quickly, and much of the time we do. This isn't one of those times, however. I have a lot to discuss with you. I'd like to start by asking you to tell me everything you can about Reverend Doyle."

"I already did that. I don't know much at all about the man. He seemed nice enough when I saw him, and he conducted his services well." Bessie sighed. "I have heard some complaints that he went too quickly, but, well, I'm not one to complain about that."

"But he seemed to know his job?"

Bessie stared at John for a minute. "Seemed to know his job? What an odd question."

John sat back in his chair and didn't reply. After a minute, Bessie got to her feet. "Let me put the kettle on," she said. "While I do that, I'll think about your question."

"I'd rather you didn't," John told her. "Just tell me your initial thoughts on the matter. If you think too much about the question, you'll start to see things that aren't there."

"In that case, yes, he seemed to know his job. I mean, I only saw him at a couple of Sunday services, but they didn't feel significantly different from when the previous vicar was here. Everyone does things slightly differently, of course, and as I said, he was noticeably faster at getting through the service, but I never doubted that he was a proper vicar, if that's what you mean."

"Perhaps your opinion would have changed if he'd conducted Helen and Pete's wedding."

"Perhaps. I never spoke to him about the wedding. Helen, Pete, or Elizabeth might be able to address that, though."

"They have, although I will be following up with Elizabeth early tomorrow."

"Are you suggesting that Reverend Doyle wasn't a proper vicar?"

"Do you know anything about how his appointment was made?" John asked, ignoring Bessie's question.

"Not really. I was on a selection committee for a new vicar maybe thirty years ago, but I'm sure things have changed since then. The bishop at the time liked to have a handful of parishioners on the committee, but I'm not sure if the current bishop feels the same way. I'm less involved in the local church now than I was all those years ago."

"I have an appointment with the bishop tomorrow. I'm sure he'll have plenty to tell me."

"How could someone who wasn't properly qualified get appointed? It doesn't make sense. Surely the bishop's office would have checked the man's credentials?"

"More questions for the bishop," John replied. "Although in this case, it seems the Reverend William Doyle was perfectly well qualified for the job. It appears that the man who arrived on the island to take up the post, however, was not the Reverend William Doyle."

Bessie put the teacups she'd just taken out of the cupboard down on the counter and turned around to look at John. "He wasn't Reverend Doyle?" she repeated, feeling confused.

"No, he was not. And Dan Ross managed to get that information almost before we did. It's going to be all over tomorrow's paper, which is why I'm so eager to talk to Elizabeth early. I'd like to get her opinion of the man before she finds out he wasn't who he claimed to be."

"That explains Ms. Hamilton a bit better, then," Bessie said after a moment. "I did wonder at a vicar behaving like that."

"Yes, we've established that Ms. Hamilton was the man's girlfriend, although she did do a bit of cooking and cleaning around the vicarage, I've been told."

"So who was he really? And what was he doing on the island?"

"His real name was Walter Gray, spelled with an 'a', not an 'e', by the way," John replied. "As for what he was doing on the island, well, we're still working on that one."

"Surely, Ms. Hamilton knows the answer to that."

"If she does, she isn't willing to share it, at least not yet."

Bessie knew that John wouldn't tell her anything that the woman had said while she was being questioned by the police. She sighed. "She must have given you some sort of explanation."

"On the contrary, she's insisting that she only ever knew the man as Reverend William Doyle. She's even given an interview to Dan Ross about how betrayed she feels."

"My goodness, that's going to be a difficult lie for her to keep up, isn't it?"

"Most likely, yes. We know where Walter Gray was six months ago, and we know when he arrived on the island as Reverend Doyle. Once we fill in the missing six months, we'll find out when Ms. Hamilton arrived on the scene."

Bessie went back to making tea and then filled a plate full of biscuits for John. She sat back down opposite him once everything had been served. "How did you work out who he was so quickly?" she asked.

"When we searched the vicarage, we found several pieces of identification for Walter Gray, and very little in William Doyle's name. Because of the confusion, we ran the man's fingerprints."

"And you found them? He was a criminal, besides?"

"Assuming someone else's identity is a criminal act," John pointed out, "but, yes, he was already in the system. That's why we're quite certain of where he was six months ago. That's when he was released from a six-month prison term for fraud."

"What did he do?"

"I'm still waiting for further information, but it appears that he was some sort of con artist. He seems to have been very good at pretending to be things that he wasn't."

"I never would have imagined that he wasn't a proper vicar," Bessie said.

"Perhaps if he'd been here longer, people might have begun to suspect something. The more he had to do, the bigger the risk of his getting caught out. And over time, of course, people would have found out about Ms. Hamilton. That would have raised eyebrows and started talk."

"I suspect it would have started quite a lot of talk. I'm sure there would have been complaints to the bishop about her. Were they really sharing a bedroom?"

"According to Ms. Hamilton, no, they weren't. She can't explain why the second bedroom in the vicarage was full of boxes that covered the bed, though."

Bessie sighed. "If she's going to lie to you about everything, how will you ever work out who killed the man? Or is she the chief suspect?"

"She would probably be the chief suspect if she didn't have a solid alibi. She was in Douglas for the entire day, having lunch with some friends who are visiting from across. We actually have video footage of the entire party at one of the restaurants on the promenade. She didn't leave Douglas until after the body was found."

"Were her friends acquainted with Walter Gray?"

"She says not, and they concur. The women in question are here for a girls' weekend, and at this point, we've no reason to believe that they knew Walter Gray as himself, or as Reverend Doyle."

Bessie sighed. "Who did know the man was here? He must have been killed because he was Walter Gray, mustn't he?"

"That's part of the problem. We don't know if the murderer wanted to kill Reverend Doyle or Walter Gray. As far as we know at this point, no one on the island knew the man's real identity, with the possible exception of Ms. Hamilton."

"Why would anyone want to kill Reverend Doyle? He'd only been on the island for a short time, and he was a vicar. No one could possibly have had any reason to want him dead."

"We have to consider all possibilities," John told her, "but it seems most likely that the man was killed because of something that happened before he arrived on the island."

"And Ms. Hamilton is the only one who knows anything about his life before he came here?"

"As far as we know, she's the only person the island that may have that information, anyway. What we're trying to do now is track down Walter Gray's wife."

Bessie nearly dropped her teacup. "He was married?" she gasped.

"He was. At this point, I don't know anything more than the woman's name and where she was living when Walter last went to prison."

"Which was when?"

"About a year ago. He was in prison for six months, and he was released about six months ago. We know she isn't still at the same address, because that was the first thing we tried."

"How hard will she be to find?"

"Hopefully, not very. It being the weekend is complicating things, but I fully expect to locate her on Monday, if not before."

"It will be a shock to her, finding out her husband is dead."

"I'd like to find her before she finds out, but that may not be possible. As I said, Dan Ross has the story, and it will be in tomorrow's paper. I don't think it's likely that Walter's wife reads the *Isle of Man Times*, but you never know."

"Where were they living when Walter went to prison?"

"Liverpool," John replied. "Right now I don't know anything other than her name. It's possible she has some connection to the island, though. It's also possible that her husband did."

"I asked him, when we spoke once, if he knew the island at all. He claimed that he'd barely even heard of it before he saw the post advertised somewhere. He also said he was really pleased with what he'd found now that he was here."

"But he may well have been lying," John sighed. "He may have grown up on the island, for all I know."

"Surely not. Someone would have recognised him if that were the case. There was an article about him in the local paper the week he arrived, with photos of the man, after all."

"I didn't realise that," John said. "I'm afraid I don't always get the local paper. I don't suppose you've kept that issue?"

"I don't usually keep the papers for more than a day or two, but I have a small pile at the moment. A few months ago Grace asked me if I could start keeping the papers for her for art projects at school. She hasn't collected them from me for a few weeks. Now that I think about it, she's off for the summer. I don't know if she'll be going back to work in the autumn or not, with the baby on the way. I should ring her and see if she's still going to want the papers."

"But you think you may have the one with the article about Reverend Doyle?" John asked.

"Sorry, I do go on sometimes, don't I?" Bessie laughed. "Yes, I just might. Wait here a minute and I'll go and see."

She was keeping the newspapers in a box in her office upstairs. It only took her a few minutes to find the right paper.

"Here you go," she said when she got back to the kitchen. "The article is on page seven."

John flipped through the pages and then stopped. "I don't know if anyone would have recognised the man from his photo," he said.

Bessie looked over John's shoulder. "I didn't realise at the time that he was standing in the shadow of the church like that," she said. "It's a dramatic sort of pose, but it does rather hide his appearance."

"Indeed," John replied.

As he read the accompanying article, Bessie read it over his shoulder. When she finished, she sighed. "He's incredibly vague about everything, isn't he? It didn't strike me that way at the time, but reading it now, it seems like he was being evasive with every question."

"Yes, his answers are superficially fine, but they don't really tell us anything. He talks about his long and successful career and how excited he is to take on a parish of his own, without providing any information about where he'd been before or how long he'd been a priest."

"What happens next, then?"

"Tracking down his wife is our first priority," John told her. "I'm sure she'll be able to answer a great many questions about the man. Right now we've no idea why anyone wanted the man dead. I'm hoping she might be able to suggest a motive or two."

"Surely, she had a motive, if he'd run off with Ms. Hamilton and left her."

"Maybe she threw him out," John suggested. "Remember that Ms. Hamilton claims she only met the man a few months ago. She may not have had anything to do with the breakup of the marriage."

"Maybe it hadn't broken up," Bessie said. "Maybe Mrs. Gray didn't know her husband was even out of prison."

"I think that's unlikely," John told her. "He was only sentenced to six months, and it wasn't the first time he'd been in prison. The files indicate that they'd been married for several years, during which time Walter had been in and out of prison at least three or four times."

"So the case is at a standstill until you find her?"

"We're still doing everything we can on the case, but as Ms. Hamilton isn't cooperating, we're hoping Mrs. Gray will be able to fill in a lot of the blanks."

"That's just for motive, though, isn't it? What about means and opportunity?"

"The man was stabbed with an ordinary kitchen knife. We've checked, and there are at least three shops in Douglas that sell the exact knife that was used. It's also widely available across. Ms. Hamilton wasn't certain whether she recognised it or not, but it's entirely possible that the knife came from the vicarage's kitchen. It's of the same sort of quality as the rest of the utensils there."

"So just about anyone had the means," Bessie sighed. "What about opportunity?"

"As far as we can determine, Walter was home alone for most of the day. Ms. Hamilton went into Douglas quite early in the morning. She claims she'd told Walter that she wouldn't be back before dark. The coroner is still working out the time of death, but his current estimate is some time between midday and five o'clock. At this point, I doubt there are many people on the island who can prove exactly where they were during those five hours."

"Except Ms. Hamilton," Bessie said thoughtfully.

"Yes, conveniently for her."

"I don't suppose there's any chance that she's faked her alibi?"

"As I said, we actually have video footage from a security camera that shows her with her friends for nearly the entire period. She does disappear once or twice, but not for long enough to have driven to Laxey and back."

"Anyone could have rung the vicar and asked him to meet them in the graveyard," Bessie said speculatively. "I can't imagine him refusing."

"The killer might also have come across the man by chance," John pointed out.

"Did the killer take anything from the body?"

"Not as far as we can determine. Ms. Hamilton didn't think that he was missing anything. His mobile phone was in his pocket and so was his wallet. He had about fifty pounds in his wallet, and Ms. Hamilton said that was what he usually carried."

"Someone must have come over from across to kill him," Bessie said. "That's the only thing that makes sense."

"It's one possibility, but in order for that to have happened, the killer had to have found him. From what we can work out, Walter did a very good job of disappearing from his old life. If we can find out how the killer found him, I think we'll be a lot closer to finding the killer."

"Did Walter have enemies, then?"

"I'm still looking into his past, but anyone who makes their living running cons is bound to make enemies. Once I know more about his past, we'll be able to start tracking down the people he stole from, for a start."

"It's all a lot more complicated than it first appeared," Bessie sighed. "I wonder how Pete feels, leaving behind such an interesting investigation."

John laughed. "Pete loves a good investigation as much as anyone, but I'm sure he was more than happy to leave this one behind. He and his beautiful bride are going on the trip of a lifetime. I can't imagine any case that would make him want to miss that."

Bessie nodded. "They make such a lovely couple. I'm so very happy for them both."

"Yes, me too," John said, "which reminds me, I should be getting home. Doona has been looking after the children for long enough. Maybe if I hurry, they'll still be up and I can take them back to my house for the night. Tomorrow is Sunday; I can have a later start, if nothing new comes in between now and then."

As John got to his feet, his phone rang. He frowned and then answered it. Bessie watched his face as he gave monosyllabic replies. By the time he dropped his phone back in his pocket, she was sure something exciting had just happened.

"Has someone confessed?" she asked.

John shook his head. "No, but can you ring Doona and tell her that I'm still going to be working for several more hours, please?"

"What's happened?"

He looked at her and then sighed. "You can't repeat this, even to Doona, but we've found Dawn Gray."

"Walter's wife?"

"That's the one."

"And she's willing to talk to you?"

"I don't know about willing, but I'm going to go and find out."

"Go? As in you're going across to question her yourself?"

"Go, as in I'm going to walk down the beach and question her myself," John told her. "It seems she and her family are having themselves a nice holiday on the Isle of Man right now. They're staying in one of the holiday cottages."

"They're what?" Bessie stared at John. "That can't be a coincidence, can it?"

"I don't know, but I intend to find out," John told her.

Bessie walked the man to the door. "If I stay up, will you come back and tell me everything?" she asked in the doorway.

"I can't repeat what the woman tells me. Anyway, it's getting late, and you've already had a long day. I'll come and see you tomorrow and tell you what I can."

Bessie wanted to argue, but John was already walking away. She pushed the door shut and began to pace around the kitchen. If Walter's wife was staying in one of the holiday cottages, then she had to be a suspect.

With her mind racing, she rang Doona. "John asked me to ring and let you know that he's tied up on the case," she told her friend.

"That's fine. The children are ready for bed, anyway. We're just watching another movie in our pyjamas, eating popcorn and drinking fizzy drinks. He probably wouldn't approve of any of that."

Bessie laughed. "I'm sure he wants the children to have fun, and maybe what he finds out tonight will break the case."

"What's happened tonight?"

"He'll have to tell you about that. He just asked me to let you know that he'll be busy for a few more hours."

"I really don't mind having the kids here. They're both almost too well-behaved and polite, but I hate seeing John working so hard. He must be completely exhausted by this point. I don't think he slept last night, and he probably isn't eating, either."

"I gave him tea and biscuits. I should have thought about it and offered to make him something more substantial."

"At least he's had tea and biscuits," Doona sighed. "Now I'd better get back to the movie. James Bond is about to die a hideous death, and I don't want to miss seeing that."

"I suspect he'll find a way out," Bessie laughed.

"Yeah, it's an old one with Sean Connery. I'm sure he'll be fine."

Bessie put down the phone and headed up to bed. Once she'd washed her face and put on her nightgown, she curled up with the book she'd been reading when John had arrived. It only took her a few minutes to discover that the author had left out a great many things throughout the story. On the last page, it was revealed that the killer was someone completely unexpected. Bessie shut the book and climbed back out of bed. The book went straight into the box in her spare room for books she planned to donate to a charity shop.

Back in bed with a different book, she quickly got lost in another world. After an hour that seemed to fly past, she reluctantly put the book down. She was too tired to keep reading, even though she was enjoying the story. Yawning, she switched off the light and snuggled down under the covers. She was asleep as soon as her head hit the pillow.

As Bessie walked along the beach the next morning, she couldn't help but wonder which cottage was currently housing Dawn Gray. She had no idea what the woman looked like, but that didn't stop her from glancing into each cottage as she went, hoping to spot the woman. If she were honest, Bessie usually glanced into every cottage as she walked anyway, but perhaps with less interest.

By the time she'd reached Thie yn Traie, Bessie reckoned that she'd spotted at least three women who might have been the newly widowed Mrs. Gray. The beach was getting busier as she strolled towards home, and Bessie added another two possibilities to her mental list. As she reached Treoghe Bwaane, however, she changed her mind about all of them.

There was a large rock behind her cottage with enough room for two people to sit comfortably together. Bessie often sat there and watched the sea for hours on end. The woman who was sitting on the rock now, with tears streaming down her face, simply had to be Dawn Gray, Bessie decided, as she walked down the beach towards her. She was around the right age, maybe in her mid-forties, with long brown hair pulled into a ponytail. Her T-shirt and shorts were just right for the beach and showed off a slender figure.

"I'm sorry. Am I on private property?" the woman asked as Bessie approached.

"The beach is public," Bessie assured her. "You're welcome to sit there all day if you'd like. I just wanted to make sure that you were okay."

"I've been better," the woman said with a sigh, "but I'm sure you don't want to hear about my problems."

"I'm happy to listen if you need to talk to someone, actually, but it's entirely up to you. I'm Elizabeth Cubbon, by the way. Everyone calls me Bessie."

"It's nice to meet you, Bessie. I'm Dawn Gray. I've never really had a nickname, although I really always wanted one. There isn't a short form for Dawn, is there?"

Bessie thought for a minute. "I don't imagine there is, really," she said eventually.

Dawn shrugged. "Do you live in that cottage, then?" she asked, nodding towards Bessie's home.

"I do, yes. I've lived there since I was eighteen."

"It looks quite tiny. Do you live alone?"

"Yes, I do. I always have. It was even smaller when I bought it. I've added on to it twice since I've owned it."

"My goodness, I can't imagine. I mean, it's adorable, but it must have been quite claustrophobic before you added on to it."

"I didn't mind. It was just me, after all."

"Yes, I suppose so. Maybe that's what I need to do, buy a tiny little house somewhere and live on my own."

"Some people don't like living on their own," Bessie said, "but it has worked for me."

"I'm not sure how I'd feel about it, really. I haven't ever lived completely on my own."

"Maybe you should try it, then."

"Maybe I should, except right now I think I'd feel awfully lonely. My husband just died, you see."

"I'm terribly sorry," Bessie said. "Were you married long?"

"Six years, although to be fair, we were separated, and I suspect we would have divorced soon. In truth, I'm feeling far more emotional about losing him than I ever thought I would. It's very strange, really."

"Would you like to come inside for a cuppa?" Bessie invited the woman. She could hear John's voice in her head, shouting at her for inviting a murder suspect into her home, but she ignored him.

"A cuppa may well be exactly what I need," Dawn told her. She climbed carefully off the rock, avoiding the many puddles of water that surrounded it. Later, when the tide came in, the bottom of the rock would be submerged, but for now there was still patches of sand for her and Bessie to walk across.

"This is cute," Dawn said as Bessie let her into Treoghe Bwaane. "And it feels larger inside than I expected."

"Have a seat," Bessie suggested, gesturing towards the kitchen table. She filled the kettle with water and switched it on before piling her best chocolate biscuits onto a plate. She put the plate onto the table in front of the woman and handed her a smaller plate for her selections. A few minutes later, the kettle boiled, and Bessie made the tea and served it.

"Do you want to talk about it?" she asked as she sat down opposite the woman.

"Yes, no, I don't know," Dawn said with a strangled laugh. "I feel as if I've talked about it no end, but then I don't think I've really talked about it at all. Talking to a police inspector isn't the same as talking about it, is it?"

"A police inspector?" Bessie repeated. "Is this about the man who was found at the Laxey Church recently?"

"It is, yes. I suppose I shouldn't be surprised that you know about it. Laxey is very small, isn't it? I would imagine my husband's murder is the most exciting thing that's happened here in a great many years."

Bessie took a sip of tea. The past year had seen far too many exciting things happen in Laxey, but she didn't want to start telling the other woman about them. "I should tell you that I was there when the body was found," she said after a minute.

"You were? How very odd."

"I was with my friends who were getting married," Bessie explained. "We were looking for the vicar, and when we were walking through the churchyard, one of them spotted the body."

"How much more do you know?" the woman demanded. "Do you know that the man wasn't really who he claimed to be?"

"I do, yes. I talked to a police inspector about the case last night, and he told me that much. Apparently, that fact is going to be in today's local newspaper."

"I wish I knew why Walter was pretending to be a vicar. His father was a vicar. Maybe that's part of it. I simply don't know."

"I understand he'd been in prison until recently," Bessie said softly.

Dawn nodded. "He was a career criminal. I didn't know that when I met him, but it didn't take me long to find out. He was arrested just a few weeks after we met. That's when I found out his true identity. Before that, I thought he was the disinherited third son of a minor duke."

"My goodness."

"He was incredibly convincing, you know. After I found out who he really was, I loved watching him work. He could convince total strangers that he was anyone he wanted to be. It was amazing. Of course, I wanted him to find ways to use his talent for good, but he was addicted to the rush of making fast, easy money."

"Except he kept getting caught," Bessie pointed out.

"Well, yes, but it was never his fault. He kept getting betrayed by his associates. We were together for years, and one day I decided that I'd had enough. When he was sent to prison the last time, I told him I was going to file for divorce."

"I'm sure that was a difficult decision."

"The thing is, though, I never actually did it. I kept putting it off and, well, I don't know, maybe I was hoping he'd come back one day. I knew he was serving a six-month sentence, and I really thought he'd turn up on my doorstep when he was released. He didn't. According to the police inspector I spoke to last night, he was living here with another woman. He wouldn't give me any information about her, but I'd be willing to bet I know who she is."

Bessie bit her tongue. If John hadn't told the woman about Ms. Hamilton, it wasn't her place to do so.

"You can't trust other women," Dawn continued. "I never should have confided in Constance Hamilton. We were best friends, and I told her everything. I think she and Walter were sleeping together before he went to prison the last time, you know. And she suddenly disappeared right around the same time as he was due to get out. If he had a woman here with him, I'd bet that who it was."

"I hope you told the police inspector all of this," Bessie said.

"Oh, yes, every last bit," Dawn replied. "Walter was murdered, after all. No matter how many problems we had, I never wanted him dead. I still cared a great deal about him, even though I'd told him I wanted a divorce. I mean, look at me, sobbing my eyes out over him, when I hadn't even seen him in a year."

"I'm sorry," Bessie said softly.

Dawn nodded and then sniffled as tears began to stream down her face again. Bessie quickly found her a box of tissues.

"I shouldn't be crying," the woman said after several minutes. "If you'd have asked me yesterday morning about Walter, I would have told you that I was over him. I really think I am over him. It's all just such a shock, you know? I was planning to finally file those divorce papers once we all got back home. I was ready to move on."

"And once the shock wears off, you'll be able to do just that," Bessie told her.

Dawn nodded. A sharp knock on the door kept her from replying. Bessie crossed to the door, hoping it wasn't John or Hugh on the other side. She didn't want Dawn to know that she was close friends with members of the constabulary. She opened the door and gasped. The two men on the doorstep were both strangers, and they both looked angry.

"Where's Dawn?" the taller of the two demanded aggressively.

CHAPTER 6

"I'm right here," Dawn said from behind Bessie. "Having a nice cuppa with a new friend."

"I don't think that's a good idea," the man replied. "You don't know anything about her. She could be friends with the police inspector who questioned you."

"I don't mind if she is," Dawn said. "I don't have anything to hide, after all."

"I think it's time for you to come back to the cottage," the other man said. "We left you alone as you'd asked, but if you're feeling like you want to be around other people, you should be with family."

Dawn sighed deeply. "Ms. Cubbon, this is my father, Lucas Mason, and my big brother, Brandon. They mean well, truly they do."

"It's very nice to meet you both," Bessie said. "It's actually Miss Cubbon, but everyone calls me Bessie."

"Great, wonderful, whatever," Brandon snapped. "Dawn will be leaving now."

"No, she won't," Dawn said. "I'll be back at the cottage when I'm ready to come back, and not before. You two go and splash in the sea or something."

Brandon opened his mouth to reply, but his father held up his hand. "You have to deal with everything in your own way. I understand that, but I think Brandon is right. You should be with family now."

Dawn shrugged. "If it were just family, maybe I'd agree."

"We can send Mike and Horace down to the pub," Brandon told her. "They won't mind, and then you can relax."

"I'll be back soon," Dawn replied. "Truly I will. I'm just enjoying having some girl talk, that's all. I can't do that with you two, now, can I?"

Lucas flushed. "You know I've done my best," he began.

"And you've done a wonderful job," Dawn interrupted. "I'll just finish my tea and my biscuits, and then I'll come back to the cottage, okay? Just give me a few more minutes with Bessie."

"We'll see you back at the cottage soon, then," the older man replied.

The pair turned and walked away slowly. They were both almost as wide as they were tall, and from what Bessie could determine, their bulk was mostly muscle. Brandon's dark brown hair fell almost to his shoulders, in contrast with his father, who was nearly bald. Bessie watched them walk away until they disappeared into the crowd behind the holiday cottages.

"I'm sorry if they seemed intimidating," Dawn said as Bessie pushed the door shut. "They don't mean to be. They just worry about me. I'm the baby of the family, and my mother passed away when I was just five, you see."

"I'm sorry. That must have been difficult," Bessie replied as she sat back down in her chair.

"I didn't really realise what I was missing until I hit my teen years. Dad did his best to be both mum and dad to me, but he couldn't really explain about puberty and periods and whatever. And Brandon wasn't much help, either, as you can imagine."

Bessie's eyes met Dawn's, and then they both chuckled. "How much older than you is he?" she asked.

"Three years. He was eight when Mum died, and sometimes I think it was worse for him than for me. He remembers her a lot more than I do, and he missed her terribly for a long time. That was all many years ago, of course. We got through, and the only long-term effect seems to be that both my father and my brother insist on treating me like I'm still five all the time."

"I'm sure they mean well."

"They do, but it's frustrating. Sometimes, I think I only married Walter because they were both so opposed to the idea. I did care deeply for the man, but I probably wouldn't have married him, given his criminal tendencies, if my father hadn't told me that I couldn't."

"They must have been happy when you and Walter separated, then."

"Oh, yes, they were delighted. We didn't see much of each other during the years that Walter and I were together, well, except when Walter was in prison. I sometimes went and stayed with my father when Walter wasn't around, as I didn't have a steady source of income. And I know, I've only myself to blame for them treating me like a child when I kept relying on my father to help me out of every difficult situation."

"And now you're all here on holiday together?"

"Because of Brandon," Dawn explained. "He was coming over with a bunch of friends. They booked two cottages next to one another, and then one of the women had a big fight with her husband, and they ended up cancelling, and someone else suddenly had to work." She shrugged. "I'm not sure I know the whole story, but Brandon ended up with two holiday cottages for himself and only two friends. He invited Dad and me to come and use one of them. He and his friends are staying in the cottage next to ours."

"That sounds as if it could be fun."

"It could be, except I'm not enjoying the company very much," Dawn shrugged. "Mike is okay, but Horace is a bit of a pain."

"Oh?"

"He keeps asking me out and hinting that we should get together, and, well, I'm just not attracted to him. I was using Walter as an excuse, telling him that I couldn't get involved because I was still married, but now I'll have to come up with something else."

77

"You could tell him you're in mourning," Bessie suggested.

"Yeah, except that will just upset my father and brother. They don't understand why I'm upset about Walter's death. If I was going to file for divorce anyway, I mustn't still have been in love with him."

"Love it far more complicated than that."

"It is, yes," Dawn agreed. "Anyway, Brandon wants me to get together with Horace, and my father seems to like the idea as well. Horace has a good job, and he's dependable, unlike Walter, you see. I really just want to go home and leave them all here for the rest of the week."

"I'm not sure the police will want you leaving just now," Bessie said.

"They don't. The very lovely police inspector who came to talk to me said that I need to stay on the island, at least for a few days. He asked me loads of questions, but he thought he'd probably have more later."

"He'll be trying to work out who might have wanted to kill Walter. Unfortunately, I've been involved in murder investigations before. There are always more questions."

Dawn nodded. "I don't think I'll mind if that same inspector is doing the asking. He had the most gorgeous green eyes I've ever seen."

"Inspector Rockwell is actually a friend of mine," Bessie felt obliged to tell her. "He's very good at his job."

"That's good to hear. I hope he can work out what happened to Walter fairly quickly. It's such a horrible thing."

"The inspector will be looking for people with motives. I'm sure he asked you lots of questions about that."

"He did, but I couldn't tell him much. I hadn't seen Walter in over a year. Knowing him, he made at least a dozen people angry enough to want to kill him in that many months."

"Oh, dear," Bessie exclaimed.

"Walter could be incredibly kind and sweet when he wanted to be, but he was a con artist. You never really knew where you stood with him or when he was being honest. If I were the inspector, I'd start by looking at Constance Hamilton. If Walter was here with her, she should be the inspector's prime suspect, and if Walter was here with someone else, Constance should still be the prime suspect."

"He must have made a lot of enemies due to his crimes," Bessie suggested.

"No doubt, but I don't really know much about that. Walter never confided in me about his schemes. He had so many problems with his associates, I suppose that isn't surprising. Whenever he did think he could trust someone, they ended up betraying him. Sadly, he never really trusted me, and he could have."

"Perhaps one of those former associates found him on the island," Bessie mused.

"I believe most of them are in various prisons around the UK, but that's one possibility, maybe. I don't know. As I said, I hadn't seen the man in a year. I just think that Constance is involved somehow, whatever happened to him. Maybe that's just because I'm still bitter that he took up with her in the first place. As I said, she had been my friend once upon a time."

"Not a very good one."

"No, not at all. I wouldn't mind a friend like that now, though. Someone who could take Horace off my hands would be more than welcome." Dawn looked at the clock and then sighed and got to her feet. "I really do have to go before Brandon comes back with Mike and Horace and drags me away."

"It was lovely meeting you. I enjoyed our chat," Bessie told her, getting up from her chair. "I'm nearly always home or out walking on the beach. If you want to talk further, you know where to find me."

"I may just take you up on that. It's peaceful here, and you are awfully easy to talk to."

Bessie grinned. "Everyone tells me that," she replied.

As Dawn walked away down the beach, Bessie watched her. She felt oddly sorry for the woman, but she wasn't sure why. When Dawn was out of sight, Bessie shut the door and headed for the phone. She wasn't sure she'd learned anything interesting, but that was for John to decide.

"My goodness, you've had a busy morning," John said after Bessie told him all about her meeting with the new widow. "I'd like to sit down with you and talk everything through, but I'm not sure that meeting at your cottage is a good idea right now. I don't want Mrs. Gray and her family to know just how close we are. Maybe we could meet at Doona's?"

"That would be fine with me," Bessie told him. "I can walk up there."

"Or Doona can come and collect you," John said. "Let me ring her, and I'll ring you back."

Bessie walked around the kitchen a few times while she waited for the phone to ring. John rang back within minutes.

"Hugh will collect you a few minutes before six and take you to Doona's," he told Bessie. "I'll be bringing Chinese food, and Hugh will be bringing pudding."

"I'll see you later, then," Bessie replied. She put down the phone and walked around the kitchen again. It was nearly time for some lunch. Her unexpected visitor had taken up the morning. Having eaten more than a few biscuits while she'd been chatting with Dawn, Bessie wasn't particularly hungry. What she needed was a walk up the hill to the shop at the top. The local paper would be full of the murder. Bessie wanted to see if they knew anything she didn't.

The girl standing behind the counter talking on her mobile phone was a stranger to Bessie. She smiled, but the girl ignored her. Sighing, Bessie grabbed a basket and wandered around the shop, wondering if she needed anything other than the paper.

When she reached the till, Bessie unloaded the basket, shaking her head at the packets of biscuits and bars of chocolate that had found their way into it. She'd been so busy selecting treats that she'd nearly forgot the local paper. She'd just added it to her pile when the shop door swung open.

"Well, well, well, if isn't Mrs. Cubby," Brandon Mason said as he strolled into the shop. "I was going to visit your cottage later. You've saved me a trip."

Bessie stared at the man, who looked even larger in the small shop than he had in her doorway. "What did you want to talk with me about?" she asked, working to keep her voice level.

"I want you to stay away from Dawn," the man said. "She doesn't need any new friends."

"I think that should be Dawn's decision, not yours," Bessie told him.

"You think whatever you like," the man sneered. "Just stay away from my sister."

Bessie opened her mouth to reply as the shop door swung open again. The two men who walked into the building were both as tall and broad as Brandon, and they looked to be of a similar age.

"They have lager, right?" one of the men asked Brandon.

"Yeah, in the cooler on the left," he replied, his eyes still on Bessie.

"Great," the man said. He walked past Bessie and opened the cooler.

"That's twelve pounds, eighty-seven," the girl behind the till told Bessie.

Bessie took a deep breath and then turned her back on the angry man. She counted out the exact change and then took her shopping bags from the girl. "Thank you," she said softly.

"Is everything okay?" the girl asked, glancing behind Bessie.

"I certainly hope so," Bessie replied.

"I can ring 999 if you want me to," the girl offered in a very low voice.

"Thank you, but I don't think that's necessary," Bessie told her.

"Why don't you wait here until they've left," the girl suggested.

Before Bessie could reply, the man at the cooler started piling packs of lager on the counter. "You're done, aren't you, love?" he asked Bessie.

"I forgot something," Bessie said, "but you go ahead. I need to go and find it."

Bessie carried her bags with her as she walked back into the shop. She ducked down the first short aisle and then watched the three men who were now at the counter.

"Just the lager today?" the girl asked.

81

"Maybe we should get some crisps and stuff," Brandon said.

"How about popcorn?" one of the men suggested. "That microwave stuff is easy and would be good with a movie."

"Sure, Horace, grab some popcorn," Brandon told one of the men.

Bessie peeked around the shelf, eager to see which man was the one that Dawn had said was interested in her. As Horace went to find the popcorn, Bessie studied him. He was around the same height as the others, probably around six feet tall. His shoulders were broad, but his T-shirt was stretched around his stomach as well. Thinning brown hair topped a rounded head, and thick glasses covered his brown eyes. Bessie didn't consider him the least bit attractive.

"What about crisps?" the other man asked as Horace threw a box of popcorn at Brandon.

"Yeah, yeah, we'll get some crisps too," Brandon said. "No one wants you to miss dinner, Mike."

The men laughed as Horace added a bag of crisps to the pile on the counter.

"That's dinner and pudding," he told the others. "Unless your sister is cooking again tonight?"

"She's in mourning," Brandon said with a harsh laugh.

"For that idiot she was married to? She should be celebrating his untimely demise," Mike said. "They were separated, weren't they?"

"Yeah, but she says that doesn't mean she didn't still have feelings for him, or some such nonsense. I'm just hoping he left her something in his will, like maybe everything."

"That would be good. He had loads of money, did Walter," Horace said. "Of course, most of it was probably hidden away in accounts no one knew about, as it was all illegally acquired. Does Dawn know where to find the money?"

"She says not, but we'll see. I'm watching her closely," Brandon replied.

"Nothing new there," Mike muttered.

"Is there anything else?" the shop assistant asked.

"We should get a bottle of wine for your sister," Horace said. "She won't want lager, will she?"

"Nah, she's too classy for that," Brandon laughed. "Sure, get her a bottle of wine. Grab another six-pack of lager for my dad too. We can all get drunk toasting Walter Gray and his unfortunate end."

"If you aren't doing anything later, you should come and have a drink with us," Mike told the girl behind the counter. "We're down at the holiday cottages on the beach. You'd have fun."

"Thanks, but I have a boyfriend," the girl replied.

"He doesn't have to know," the man suggested.

"Come on, Mike, leave the girl alone," Horace said. "She's young enough to be your daughter."

"Not hardly," Mike snapped. "Think about it," he said to the girl. "We could have a really good time."

The girl gave him a tight smile and then rang up their purchases. Brandon put everything on a credit card. Both Bessie and the shop assistant sighed with relief when the trio walked out.

"That's it, I'm getting a new job," the girl said angrily as the door swung shut behind the men. "I don't mind dealing with customers all day, but I shouldn't have to put with them trying to pull me while I'll working. Especially not creepy old men like that guy."

Bessie wouldn't have classed Mike as an old man. He was probably in his late thirties or early forties by her estimate, but to a girl in her late teens, he may well have seemed old. "He was definitely too old to be harassing you," Bessie said. "He should know better."

"If I'm going to get all this hassle anyway, I should have gone for a job in a pub," the girl sighed. "It would be less lonely too. I hate being here all by myself all the time."

"Maybe the owner should have two people here."

"He'd only do that if he could pay each of us half our wage. When I asked him about getting more help, especially during busy times, he told me he can't afford to have more than one person here at any time. He claims he's barely breaking even as it is."

"Maybe he should take a few shifts," Bessie suggested.

The girl laughed. "Have you met the owner? He has like zero people skills. There wouldn't be any customers left if they all had to put up with him."

"Well, I'm sorry that you had to deal with those men. I'm a bit worried about leaving you alone in here, actually."

"I'll be fine. I really do have a boyfriend, and he does karate. I think I'll give him a ring and have him come and hang out with me for a while."

"I think that's an excellent idea," Bessie told her.

"That one guy, he was here a few days ago on his own, and he was bad enough then. I didn't realise he had friends."

"Which one?"

"The one who paid," the girl said.

Brandon, Bessie thought. "Which day?" she asked.

"Oh, the last time I was working nights. It would have been Friday night."

"What did he buy?"

"Lager, mostly, same as today."

Bessie wanted to ask her more, but she didn't want start putting ideas into the girl's head. She'd tell John what she'd learned and let him take it from there. She checked that she had all of her shopping bags and then headed for home, giving the girl one last reassuring smile before she went. She was already on her mobile phone, ringing someone, as Bessie walked away.

Back at home, Bessie put her shopping away and then sat down with a cup of tea and the local paper. The headline was certainly attention-getting. "Murdered Vicar Actually Con Artist," it read.

Bessie worked her way through the article and then the rest of the paper. She learned that Walter's middle name had been George, but not much else. The paper devoted a section to speculation on the legality of Walter's performing marriage ceremonies, concluding that anyone that he'd married would have to have a second ceremony in order to make things properly legal. Bessie wasn't sure if the paper was right or not, but she was grateful that Pete and Helen had avoided any such confusion.

When the phone rang, Bessie answered it.

"Bessie? It's Elizabeth, Elizabeth Quayle. How are you?"

"I'm fine, my dear. How are you?"

"Oh, I don't know," the girl wailed. "I was just reading in the paper about how anyone married by the fake vicar wouldn't be legally married, and now I'm rethinking my wedding planning business. What if he hadn't been murdered and he'd performed Pete and Helen's ceremony? They wouldn't really be married, and it would be all my fault since I suggested that they get married in Laxey."

"I don't think anyone could possibly have blamed you, if that had happened," Bessie said soothingly. "He managed to fool the bishop into hiring him, after all. If the bishop was convinced that the man was who he claimed to be, you'd no reason to suspect anything else."

"That isn't strictly true," Elizabeth replied. "I had a weird feeling about the man, you know. There was something not quite right about him. I thought that when I met him."

"Yes, I'm sure you did," Bessie said, knowing that everyone would say something similar now that the man had been unmasked.

Elizabeth laughed. "I know, I know. Hindsight is twenty-twenty and all of that, but I really did find him slightly creepy. He kept looking at me in a leering sort of way that didn't seem at all appropriate for a vicar. I'd just about convinced myself that I was imagining things, though, right up until I heard that he wasn't really a vicar at all. Next time I'll trust my instincts."

"I don't know how many people he did marry over the weeks that he was here," Bessie said thoughtfully. "I suppose the bishop will be stepping in to help them make things right."

"I don't know that he married anyone, actually. When we were planning for Pete and Helen, he said something about it being his first wedding on the island. Maybe it was going to be his first wedding ever."

"Perhaps, if he had done it, we all would have had a hint that he wasn't who he claimed to be," Bessie said. "It would probably have been harder to fake a wedding than a standard Sunday service."

"When I think back to our meetings, he did seem a little bit unsure about things, but it was the leering that made me uncomfortable, not that. I just assumed he was still working to settle into a new parish."

"I hope you won't seriously let this stop you from going forward with your plans for your business. I actually want you to plan an event for me."

"What sort of event?"

"A baby shower."

"Ooh, like they have in America, right? I saw them on some telly programme. This girl got like a million presents for her baby."

"Exactly like that," Bessie laughed, "for Grace Watterson."

"That's a great idea. Mum will be thrilled as well. She really likes Grace. They talk on the phone every week. Apparently, Grace is still grateful for what Mum did for their honeymoon."

"Grace and Hugh are both hugely grateful for that, but now they're trying to buy a house, and they have a baby on the way. I thought it would be nice to get some of Grace's friends together to help out with all of the things that babies need."

"Mum can take Grace shopping and find out what she really wants," Elizabeth said thoughtfully. "She wanted to buy a bunch of stuff for the baby, but she didn't know how to do so without Grace refusing."

"That was my thought exactly, but she can't get upset if we have a shower."

"When should we have it, then?"

"I was thinking maybe early November," Bessie said. "It sounds a long way off, but really isn't. I don't think they'll do much shopping until they get into the new house, which will take a while longer."

"When is the baby due?"

"Mid-December. I thought it might be nice to surprise Grace, but I don't know what you think."

"Surprises are incredibly hard work, but so much fun when they go right," Elizabeth replied. "Let's try anyway. I'm sure Mum will want to be involved in every bit of it. I hope that's okay."

"Of course it is, but I don't want to end up dumping all of the work on her again, like I did with the honeymoon planning. I want to pay you to do all the work instead."

"Oh, I won't let you pay me, not for Grace, but I'm happy to do the work. Again, it will be another event to help get my name out there. I wonder if the café in Lonan would be able to do a baby shower. They did such an amazing job with the wedding that I'd really like to use them again."

"It was the best wedding food I've ever had," Bessie told her. "I'd love it if they'd do the shower. I'll be paying all of the bills, though, so we'll have to talk about a budget."

"You'll have to fight with Mum on that one. I suspect she'll want to pay for some of it as well."

The pair agreed on the first Saturday in November, and Elizabeth promised to get started on planning right away.

"I know it's early, but I think once word gets out that the café will do events, it will get booked up quickly," she told Bessie. "We'll want a cake of some sort. Andy will be back across, won't he?"

"He will. Maybe we should see if Dan can do a chocolate sponge or something similar?"

"That sounds great. Then we just have to get a list of names from Grace, so we know who to invite."

"How can we do that if it's a surprise?"

"Oh, leave that to my mother. She can be incredibly sneaky when she wants to be."

Bessie laughed. "You've already volunteered her for finding out what Grace wants," she reminded the girl.

"She'll happily do both. She's a very bright and incredibly bored woman, you know. Dad doesn't want her to work, and she's too shy to get actively involved in too many charities. She'll love having the chance to be useful."

"Showers usually have games and all manner of silliness," Bessie told her. "We'll have to think about how much we want to emulate the American tradition."

"I'll do some research. I have American friends I can ask about it, and I'll talk to some of my friends in London. I understand a few people have had them there as well."

Bessie put the phone down feeling excited for Grace. There was no doubt in her mind that Elizabeth would do a wonderful job with the baby shower. As she only had an hour until she was due to be collected, Bessie decided that a short walk on the beach was what she needed. She walked slowly through the groups of people spread across the sand behind the holiday cottages, letting her mind wander as she went.

"Hello, Bessie," Dawn Gray called from the open sliding door at the back of one of the cottages.

Bessie waved to her but didn't stop. She could see the woman's father hovering behind her. The next cottage was clearly where Brandon and his friends were staying. It was a huge mess, with piles of beer cans all over the floor and sandy footprints everywhere. Bessie could only imagine what Maggie Shimmin would say when the men left, and she went in to clean the cottage.

Back at Treoghe Bwaane, Bessie combed her hair and added a touch of lipstick to her lips. That was more makeup than she normally wore and was more than enough for dinner with her friends. She was standing at her door when Hugh arrived a few minutes later.

"Hello," he called through his open car window as he drove into the parking area. He climbed out and crossed to Bessie as she locked her front door. "How are you tonight?" he asked as he offered her his arm.

"I'm fine, thank you," Bessie replied. "It does feel rather odd, though, going elsewhere for our little gathering."

Hugh shrugged. "John thought it would be for the best, since we don't really want your neighbours to know that we're all such good friends."

"What if they recognise you?"

"I haven't met any of the suspects, er, I mean, family and friends of the deceased," Hugh told her. "They won't know who I am."

Bessie nodded and then glanced down the beach. Brandon and his friends were standing on the patio behind their cottage. Bessie was sure that they were looking straight at her as she climbed into Hugh's car.

CHAPTER 7

oona answered Hugh's knock and ushered the pair inside. "John's in the kitchen," she told them. "Go on through."

Bessie led Hugh through the sitting room, stopping to say hello to Amy and Thomas.

"How are you both?" she asked them.

"We're okay," Amy shrugged. "Doona's been taking us all over the island and trying to make sure we have fun."

"And we have been," Thomas said quickly. "Doona's been great."

Amy nodded. "But it will be nice to go home with Dad tonight," she said, "even if he does have to work tomorrow."

"Why don't we go sightseeing tomorrow?" Bessie suggested. "Is there anywhere you'd really like to go?"

"We haven't been to either of the castles," Amy told her. "Mum was always going to take us when we were living here, but she never got around to it."

"Which would you prefer for tomorrow?" Bessie asked. "Castle Rushen is a beautiful medieval castle with lots of interesting displays inside. You can learn a lot about how the castle was used in many different ways. Peel Castle is mostly in ruins. Parts of it are older than Castle Rushen, and there's a crypt and a graveyard to go around."

The siblings exchanged glances. "Castle Rushen," Amy said as Thomas said "Peel Castle."

"I don't know that we'll have time to go to both," Bessie frowned. "If we do go down to Castletown, there are some other sites there that we could visit. And if we go to Peel, we can stop at the House of Manannan as well."

"Castletown," Amy said firmly. "A castle with walls and a roof is better than ruins."

"But think about the crypt," Thomas replied. "That sounds wonderfully creepy."

"I think it's meant to rain tomorrow," Hugh said, "if that changes anyone's mind."

"Maybe we should do Castletown, in that case," Bessie said. "Peel Castle isn't very much fun in the rain."

"As long as we can go to Peel Castle later in the summer," Thomas said.

"I'm happy to take you both all over the island," Bessie told him. "I didn't really think you'd be interested. Everything I read about today's teens suggests that they aren't interested in history or in spending time with adults."

"It's fun to spend time with our friends, but I think we're both interested in the island's history," Amy told her. "We didn't get much of a chance to learn about it when we were living here, but Dad has told us some interesting things."

"I'll collect you from your father's house at half nine," Bessie told them. "I'll be in a taxi."

"Bessie, if you'd like, I could see if Grace is busy tomorrow. She might be happy to have a day away from packing and worrying about the new house. I know she loves visiting the historical sites around the island," Hugh offered. "She'd be able to drive, which would make it all easier for you, as well."

"If she's not too busy, and she'd genuinely like to come, she'd be more than welcome," Bessie told him, "but I'm happy with taxis if it comes to it."

Hugh quickly rang Grace. When he ended the call, he was smiling.

"She's thrilled," he told Bessie. "She's packed as much as she can and she's bored to bits at home. She'll collect you around quarter past nine, and then you can collect Thomas and Amy and be away."

"Perfect," Bessie said. "I'll see you both tomorrow morning, then."

The children both nodded and then went back to the television programme they'd been watching when Bessie arrived. She and Hugh continued on their way into the kitchen.

"I was starting to think it wasn't you two at the door," John said from his place at the kitchen table. "Doona went to let you in ages ago."

"I stopped to talk to Amy and Thomas," Bessie explained. "If it's okay with you, Grace and I are going to take them to Castletown tomorrow to see the castle and whatever else we can find to do."

"They're perfectly capable of entertaining themselves for a few days," John told her. "That's what they would be doing if they were at home with their mother, after all."

"I'm sure they would be fine on their own, but I haven't anything else to do and you know how much I love talking about the island's history. They seemed excited by the idea, but maybe they were just being polite," Bessie replied.

"They've both told me that they'd like to see more of the island while they're here," John said. "I'm hoping they may come to like it as much as I do, eventually."

"Well, tomorrow they'll get to see our finest castle, the old schoolhouse, and maybe a few others things as well," Bessie told him.

"I really appreciate it," John said. "I hate that I've had to spend so much of my time on this case while they've been here. I've already told the chief constable that I'll be taking some time off once it's solved. Maybe I'll be able to show my children a few of the island's sites myself."

Bessie flushed. "I didn't think about that," she said apologetically. "Would you rather I didn't take them to Castle Rushen? Did you want to take them there yourself?"

"It's fine," John told her. "You're the expert on such sites, anyway. I don't know much about them. I'd rather take them to the parks and to play crazy golf and that sort of thing. Let's hope I'll get a chance before too much longer."

"First, we need to work out what happened to Walter Gray," Bessie said.

"But before that, we need to eat," Doona said from the doorway behind Bessie.

Doona had changed out of the jeans and T-shirt she'd been wearing when she'd opened her front door. A pretty flowered skirt with a white shirt made her look summery and cool. She'd combed her hair and added some fresh makeup to her face as well. Bessie wondered if she'd done it to try to impress John or for some other reason.

"There should be plenty," John said, gesturing towards the counter where several takeaway boxes were spread out.

"And I left pudding in the car," Hugh exclaimed. "I'll be right back."

Doona followed him to let him out and back in again. While they were gone, Bessie and John filled their plates. By the time Doona and Hugh returned, they were sitting at the table, ready to eat. It didn't take long for the other two to join them. Doona handed around cold drinks before she sat down.

"So, what shall we talk about?" she asked brightly as everyone began to eat.

"I could tell you all about running into Brandon Mason and his friends at the corner shop this afternoon," Bessie suggested.

"I'd like to hear about that," John said quickly.

Bessie told them all about her shopping trip and the unpleasant trio that she'd encountered. When she was finished, Doona shook her head.

"That poor girl. She isn't safe on her own in that shop, is she?" she demanded.

"Statistically the island is one of the safest places in the world," John told her. "I'm sure statistics don't make that shop assistant feel any better, though. I may have to have a word with the shop's owner. I'd like to know what safety measures he has in place for his staff."

"Those three sound as if they'll be trouble," Hugh said. "Maybe we should step up our patrols in the Laxey Beach area."

John nodded. "We always do at this time of the year anyway. We haven't had much trouble with the holiday cottages, but we have had some minor issues. I would be much happier if they'd only rent the cottages to families, rather than groups of single men or women, but I know they can't discriminate in that way."

"It would be easy enough to get around," Doona said. "Anyone can claim they're booking a family holiday, no matter what they're actually planning."

"Yes, I suppose that's true," John said. "And, as I said, we've had surprisingly little trouble with the cottages. I thought, when I first saw them, that they'd be very popular for stag and hen weekends, but they don't seem to attract that sort of thing, at least not often."

"I walk past them every day, and I can't remember ever seeing a stag or hen party there," Bessie said. "Now that you mention it, it is a bit surprising."

"Now that we've discussed it, they'll probably be a rush of them," John said. "Touch wood." He did just that, as did Bessie.

"I hope not," Bessie said. "This trio is bad enough."

When everyone had cleared his or her plate, Hugh sliced up the apple pie he'd brought. "I bought it at the bakery in Ramsey," he told them. "Grace and I went to look at baby things, and I ran out of time to make anything myself."

"That must have been fun," Bessie said.

"It was, well, I'm not sure fun is the word," Hugh shrugged. "It's hard to believe that something so small could need so much stuff. And none of it is cheap, either. I can buy clothes for myself a good deal cheaper than you can buy baby clothes."

Bessie nodded. "I've heard that," she said, "but I don't believe that you need everything you see in the shops to have a happy and healthy baby. As long as you have a car seat for getting them from place to place and somewhere for them to sleep, you've made a good start."

"I'm really excited about the baby," Hugh replied, "but I keep thinking we should have waited until we were more settled. Not that the baby was planned, exactly."

"It will all work out," John told him.

"I know, and I know we're very blessed. Grace has a good friend who has been trying for a baby for over a year now. She and her husband are getting quite desperate. Grace didn't even want to tell her our good news, although she took it really well and is being very supportive."

"I suppose I should be happy that I never really wanted children," Doona said. "I suspect I'm too old to have them now, even if I did finally find the right man."

"And it's slowly becoming more socially acceptable for women to not want children," Bessie said. "That's a welcome change from when I was younger."

"As much as I'm enjoying this conversation, I think we should talk about the murder," John interrupted. "I'd like to get the children home before it gets too late."

"Sorry," Bessie said, "but where do we start?"

"Motive, means, opportunity," Hugh told her. "Same as always."

"I don't suppose Constance Hamilton has been any more forthcoming," Bessie said to John.

"Not a bit. She's still insisting that she thought the man was a vicar. I understand the local paper is going to run the interview with her tomorrow. I suppose they thought they'd sell enough papers today with the headline they used," John sighed.

"I'd suggest that she had a strong motive, but you've already ruled her out, haven't you?" Doona asked.

"We haven't been able to break her alibi," John replied. "We've tried, but I'm afraid she's out, unless we get some new information that changes that."

"So that leaves us with the man's wife and her family," Bessie said, "assuming they had the means and opportunity. When did they arrive on the island?"

"Friday morning," John answered. "According to Thomas Shimmin, they arrived at the cottages around midday. The cottages aren't meant to be available to new arrivals until two, so Thomas told them to come back later. I'd very much like to know what they did with those two hours."

"What did they say when you asked them?" Doona wondered.

"That they went into Laxey and had lunch at the café near the Laxey Wheel," John replied. "I've checked, and they were there, but not for the entire two hours."

"It wouldn't have taken them long to walk from the wheel to the church," Bessie speculated. "The weather was fine. They may have gone for a stroll around Laxey."

"My thoughts exactly," John said, "which means they might have bumped into Laxey's new vicar on their travels. It's also possible that someone in the party already knew he was here, of course. In that case, it doesn't much matter what they were doing while they were waiting for the cottages to be made up."

"Were they all together all of the time?" Bessie asked.

"They all claim they were, but when I tried to pin down exact times that things happened, the stories all rather fell apart. I suspect everyone was coming and going as they pleased, and no one was paying any attention. As soon as I started asking questions, of course, everyone began to insist that they were all together all afternoon and evening."

"So let's assume they all had the opportunity to sneak away and murder Walter," Doona said. "Who wanted him dead?"

Bessie shrugged. "The widow seemed quite upset about it, really, especially considering that she'd been planning to file for divorce."

"Just because she's upset doesn't mean she didn't kill him," Hugh said.

"That's true, and maybe she's just a really good actress," Doona suggested.

"Maybe, but how did she know she should be acting in front of me?" Bessie asked.

"Anyone on the island might have told her about your connection with the police," John pointed out.

Bessie frowned. "Starting with Maggie Shimmin," she sighed.

"We'll leave her on the list then," Hugh said. "What about her father?"

"I don't know," Bessie said. "He barely said two words, but he seemed very protective of his daughter."

"If he raised her on his own, I can understand why," Doona said. "And Dawn told you that he didn't approve of her marrying Walter in the first place, didn't she?"

"She did tell me that," Bessie agreed.

"So maybe he'd decided that enough was enough," Doona said. "Maybe they were having a nice stroll around Laxey, and he spotted the vicar and recognised him. Maybe, as everyone else was settling into the holiday cottages, he dashed back up to the church and got rid of his daughter's annoying husband once and for all."

"That's certainly a possibility," John said. "He may even have known the man was here."

"Then there's Brandon Mason," Bessie said. "I really don't like him, although that's no reason to assume he's the killer."

"Actually, I consider you a good judge of character," John told her. "If you don't like someone, I tend to look at them a bit more closely. Having said that, I was already looking at Brandon quite closely because I didn't like him either."

"He seemed very protective of Dawn as well," Bessie said. "She told me that he didn't like Walter, either."

"Maybe the dad and the brother were in on it together," Doona suggested. "Maybe they agreed to give each other alibis to cover for one of them sneaking away and murdering Walter."

"Or maybe they did it together," Hugh said.

"What about Brandon's two friends?" Bessie asked. "I didn't get any surnames for them, but they are called Mike and Horace."

"Michael Osprey is the younger of the two men," John said. "Apparently, he and Brandon work together. He has a girlfriend who didn't come along for some reason."

"He has a girlfriend," Bessie echoed, remembering the man's behaviour in the shop.

"He does," John confirmed. "I was told she decided not to come when the married couple cancelled. I gathered that she has a couple of children from a previous relationship, and she wasn't keen to leave them at home for a week, either."

"And then there's Horace, who allegedly is interested in Dawn," Bessie said.

"That would be Horace Green. From what he said when we spoke, he's friendlier with Dawn than Brandon. I got the feeling he only came along this week once he knew Dawn was going to be here."

"Lucky Dawn," Bessie muttered.

"Maybe he thought that killing Walter would be a good way to win Dawn's heart," Hugh said. "It's certainly faster than waiting for a divorce to come through."

"It's not the strongest motive I've ever heard, but we all know people have been killed for far less," John replied. "At this point, I believe that everyone in that group had motive, means, and opportunity for the murder."

"So where does that leave us?" Bessie asked.

"With a lot of detective work to do," John replied, "or rather, it leaves me with a lot to do. Our technicians are going over everything meticulously. We're working to track Walter's movements on the day he died. We also need to determine exactly what the widow and her party were doing throughout that day."

"It's all just a lot of legwork at this point," Hugh added. "Questioning people about who they saw and when they saw them, checking mobile phone records, trying to track down sales of the murder weapon."

"Are you keeping Dawn and the others on the island until the case is solved?" Bessie asked.

"For now, we've asked them to stay on the island for the duration of their planned holiday," John told her. "I'm hoping that will give me enough time to solve the case, but if it doesn't, we may have to ask them to stay a little bit longer."

"What about Constance Hamilton?" Bessie wondered.

"She's been asked to remain as well," John replied. "She's perhaps understandably eager to get back to the UK, but she's agreed to remain for a short while anyway. The bishop has arranged comfortable accommodations for her for the time being."

"That was nice of him," Hugh said.

"As she's still claiming that she was taken in by Walter's lies, he may well feel obliged to help," John replied. "I've suggested to him that she's lying, but he's chosen to take her at her word."

"Dawn Gray told me that Constance and Walter were involved before he went to prison a year ago," Bessie said.

"And Constance says Dawn is lying," John replied. "There's no way Constance will be able to keep up with her story for much longer, but it's fascinating to watch her try."

"But surely if she'd tell the truth, you'd get closer to finding out who killed Walter," Doona said. "Doesn't she want the man's killer found?"

John shrugged. "I don't know. I have every intention of finding the killer, though, with or without her help."

"But we know she didn't do it," Bessie sighed. "It seems as if Dawn and her family and friends are the most likely suspects."

"At this point, we're certainly taking a good look at them," John told her. "There are other possibilities."

"Such as?" Bessie asked.

"Walter Gray was a career criminal. He was a con man who cheated a lot of people out of money. It's possible that someone he cheated decided to get revenge," John told her.

"So you have to look at everyone that he ever conned?" Doona wondered.

"We're looking into the crimes we know he committed. A lot of it was small-scale stuff, just getting a few pounds here and there, but the last time he went to prison, it was for a more serious and long-term con. The people involved in that could well still be angry. Much of the money that was stolen was never recovered."

"But how would anyone have found Walter?" Bessie asked.

"Like Dawn and her group, it's possible that someone who was involved simply stumbled across the man entirely coincidentally," John said. "We're trying to work our way through flight and ferry records, looking for any of the people who were involved in the case. It's something of a long shot, but having already found the man's wife and her family here, I wouldn't be totally surprised to find a few of his victims as well."

"It's like looking for a needle in a haystack, though, isn't it?" Doona asked.

"It is, rather," Hugh sighed. "I say that because I've been working on it, and I haven't found anything yet."

"We're going to put a few more constables on the job tomorrow," John told them. "We're also tracking down Mr. Gray's former business associates. It's possible, maybe even likely, that some of them had reason to be unhappy with Mr. Gray. We just have to work out whether they've been on the island in the last month or not."

"Did anyone know he was here?" Bessie asked. "I mean, of the people you've interviewed, his wife and her family and any victims or anyone, did any of them know he was on the island?"

"No one has admitted to knowing he was here," John replied.

"That must make Constance Hamilton an even more important witness," Bessie said. "You need to work out who she told about moving to the island."

"Believe me, we're trying," was John's reply. "She claims she's more or less alone in the world, though. According to her, she didn't tell anyone about Walter or about moving, aside from her friends that she was with the day of the murder. They're friends from her school days. We don't believe that they knew Walter at all."

"It was Dawn's brother or father," Doona said firmly. "You just have to work out which one."

"I'll be talking to both of them again tomorrow," John said. "We're trying to pin down exactly where they all were from the time they arrived on the island until the body was found. As I said, there's a great deal of confusion over that."

"Which is suspicious," Hugh said.

"Not necessarily," John countered. "They are here on holiday, but they couldn't get into their accommodations immediately. They went to get some lunch and then, eventually, moved into their cottages. It's

99

hardly surprising that no one was keeping track of where everyone else was at any given time."

"Well, I didn't like any of them, except for Dawn," Bessie said. "I'd be quite happy for you to arrest any or all of them."

John laughed. "I'm not sure about all of them, but I'll do my best." He glanced up at the clock on the wall. "And on that note, I should get the children home. I think we all need some sleep."

"Indeed," Bessie said. "They've a busy day in Castletown tomorrow."

"And I've a busy day at the station," John added, "and in the field. How much does admission to Castle Rushen cost?" he asked, pulling out his wallet.

"Don't worry about it," Bessie said with a wave of her hand. "I'm allowed to bring guests because I'm a lifetime member of Manx National Heritage."

"Here's some money for lunch, then," John said, handing Bessie a few folded notes. "I hope that's enough for you and Grace and the kids. It's the least I can do, as you and Grace are entertaining them for the day."

Bessie wanted to protest, but the look on John's face kept her quiet. She was sure he was disappointed that he wasn't going to be able to spend the time with the children. Letting him buy lunch was a small thing, but she hoped it would make him feel better. "What time do they need to be home?" she asked as she put the money into her handbag.

"I'll probably be at the station until half five or six," John said. "Thomas has a key, though, so you can drop them off at your convenience, or rather at Grace's convenience."

"How about if I take them back to my cottage after Castletown," Bessie suggested. "I can put together some dinner for all of us for six o'clock. You can join us if you get there in time, or have leftovers when you arrive."

"I don't want you to have to fuss," John protested.

"It's no bother at all. I have to eat anyway, and so do the children.

I'll make something easy, like spaghetti with garlic bread, and the children can run on the beach while it's cooking," Bessie replied.

"If you're sure you don't mind, that would be great," John said. "I was planning on taking the children grocery shopping today, but obviously we didn't make it. I don't think there's a lot of food in my house for dinner tomorrow night."

"Remind them that I'll see them at around half nine, then," Bessie told him. "Now go home and get some sleep."

John nodded. He stood up and started out of the room. Doona got up and followed him while Bessie began to clear the table.

"You and Grace are welcome to join John and the children at my cottage for dinner tomorrow," Bessie told Hugh as he got up to help her with the washing-up.

"Thank you, but we're having dinner with Grace's mother tomorrow night in Ramsey. Her father is out of town for work, so her mother offered to treat us to dinner at the Seaview," Hugh replied.

"How lovely," Bessie said. "I'm sure you'll have a wonderful time."

"It's too fancy for my taste, really, but it's where Grace and her mother want to go. The portions are generous, at least."

"Grace can drop the children and me off at Treoghe Bwaane whenever she needs to so that she can be ready for dinner, then."

"Oh, we aren't meeting Mrs. Christian until seven, so that shouldn't be a problem," Hugh assured her.

Doona walked back into the kitchen with a frown on her face. "I could have done that," she told them.

"Is everything okay?" Bessie asked her.

"I just feel funny about sending the children home with John. I know he's really busy with the case, and I hate the thought of him having to leave them alone if something comes up."

"They're old enough to be left alone for a few hours now and then," Bessie said. "I know what you mean, though. I'd have them both to stay at my cottage for a few nights if I thought John would agree."

"He's determined to do as much as he can by himself," Doona sighed. "He wants to prove to Sue that he can manage looking after them on his own. I think he's hoping she might let them stay on the island after she's back, if they want to."

"He did say she won't be back until the end of September, which complicates things for the new school year. I can't imagine she'd want to let them stay here for an entire year, though," Bessie said.

"Maybe she and Harvey will decide to stay in Africa," Hugh suggested. "Then John could keep the children for good."

"That would be a lot for John to take on," Bessie pointed out. "He's already struggling a bit due to this case, after all."

"Part of the problem now is the uncertainty, though," Doona said. "The children don't feel settled because they're meant to be going back to Manchester in September. If John did have custody, they'd have to learn to like the island, whether they wanted to or not."

"Or they'd have to talk John into going back to Manchester with them," Bessie said. "I suspect he'd do it if both children asked."

Doona frowned. "You're probably right," she said after a minute. "I know how much he misses them when they aren't around. I just hope he doesn't decide to move back there once Sue and Harvey have returned. I'd hate to see him leave the island."

Bessie finished washing the cups and plates, worrying about John and what he might do come September. Hugh chatted with her and Doona about his new house and the baby and all manner of things as they worked. Bessie was quite tired by the time the last plate was put away.

"I'll run Bessie home if you want," Doona told Hugh. "You must be eager to get home."

"I am, but Bessie is almost on my way," Hugh replied. "It won't take me more than a few minutes to drop her off."

Doona walked the pair to the door. Hugh offered his arm to Bessie, and they made their way down the short pavement to the street where his car was parked. It only took a minute or two for him to make the short drive to Treoghe Bwaane.

"Thank you for the ride," Bessie told him as he parked his car.

"You're very welcome. I'll just come in with you and make sure that everything is okay," he said.

"Everything will be fine," Bessie replied. "It's always fine. The island is one of the safest places in the world."

"Yes, it is, and I work hard to keep it that," Hugh replied, "but I'm still coming in with you to make sure. Doona would never forgive me if I didn't."

Bessie smiled. "I won't tell her if you don't. I know you're eager to get home to your lovely wife. Just watch me walk to my door, and then you can be on your way."

Hugh looked at her for a minute, hesitating, before he shook his head. "I'll just walk you to your door and peek inside," he said. "As long as everything is normal, I'll leave you to lock yourself in for the night."

Bessie thought about arguing further, but she didn't think it would do her much good. Hugh was determined, and she knew he was only doing what he thought was right. She sighed deeply and then opened her car door. Hugh was there to help her out of the car before she could move. She took his arm and let him lead her across the uneven soil that made up the parking area.

Her keys somehow always managed to make their way to the very bottom of her handbag. When she had someone with her, they seemed to be even more difficult to find. She finally dug them out and reached for the doorknob. The door swung open under her touch.

CHAPTER 8

"You need to wait in my car," Hugh said firmly. "I'm going to get backup before I go in."

"Maybe I just didn't shut the door properly when we left," Bessie suggested.

"I was with you. You shut it properly, and you locked it," Hugh said. "Let's go back to the car and wait for John."

"Don't bother John with this," Bessie said quickly. "He's only just taken the children home for the night. Ring another constable if you need to, but let John have some time with Thomas and Amy."

Hugh let Bessie back into the car and then slid behind the steering wheel. "I'm sorry, I truly am, but I'm going to ring John," he told her. "He'll never forgive me if I don't."

Bessie frowned but didn't argue any further. While she felt terrible about bothering John, if she was honest with herself, she really wanted the man there. Someone had broken into her cottage, and she was shocked and more than a little upset by that. Closing her eyes, Bessie took several deep breaths, doing what she could to remain calm. She could hear Hugh talking on the phone next to her, but she didn't pay attention to what he was saying. It might have been five minutes or twenty when he finally took her hand.

"John and Doona are on their way," he told her, "along with a crime scene team and probably half of Laxey."

Bessie forced herself to chuckle at his words. "But who will watch the children?" she asked.

"Grace is going over to sit with them at John's until John is done here," Hugh told her. "She reckons she can use the practice."

"Teenagers are very different to babies," Bessie said. "I'm sure Amy and Thomas will be much less trouble than your baby will be when he or she arrives."

"No doubt," Hugh replied. "Here's John." He nodded at the road outside the car window. John pulled into the parking area a moment later. "Stay here for a minute, okay?" Hugh asked Bessie.

"Sure," Bessie replied.

In the quiet emptiness of the beach, the men's voices carried back to Bessie as they talked at John's car.

"The door swung open a few inches when Bessie touched it," Hugh said.

"You didn't go inside?"

"No, sir. I didn't even look inside. Bessie and I went back to my car, and I rang you."

John nodded. "Let's go and see what we have, then," he said.

Bessie watched as the two men approached the cottage door. John pushed the door open and shouted something. After a moment, he and Hugh stepped inside. They were back outside only a minute or two later. Bessie climbed out of the car and walked over to them.

"Is it really bad?" she asked, her voice quavering slightly.

"It's a mess," John told her, sounding disgusted. "Someone tore open just about everything they could get their hands on and spread the mess throughout the kitchen. I don't know what's beyond that, as I didn't want to risk contaminating any potential evidence. The crime scene team will be here soon."

Doona was parked and out of her car almost before Bessie noticed her arrival. "Are you okay?" she demanded, pulling Bessie into a hug.

"I'm fine, but don't be too nice to me, or I'll break down," Bessie told her in a low voice.

Doona nodded and then released her. "What happened?"

"Someone broke in and made a mess," John replied. "We won't know what was taken until the crime scene team has been through."

"How much of a mess?" Bessie asked.

"The kitchen appears to be covered in flour," John replied, "and everything from the refrigerator and freezer has been dumped on the floor."

Bessie blinked back tears. "Who would do such a thing?" she demanded.

"Bored kids from the holiday cottages, maybe," Hugh suggested.

"Or bored adults," Bessie said grimly. "Brandon and his friends were watching me as I left with Hugh. They're at the top of my list of suspects."

"We'll be going door to door at the cottages, asking if anyone noticed anything," John told her. "It will be interesting to see what Brandon and his friends have to say."

A police van and two police cars pulled into the parking area. That pretty much filled the entire space. If anyone else arrived, they'd have to park on the road. John walked over and spoke to one of the men. Bessie looked over at Hugh.

"I want to see," she told him.

"We need to let the crime scene team do their job first," Hugh told her.

"At least let me look through a window," Bessie replied.

Hugh hesitated and then nodded towards John. "Ask the inspector," he told her.

Bessie frowned at the man's use of John's title, but she supposed it was justified. Her home, her little cottage that she loved, was now a crime scene. Blinking and swallowing hard, she worked to suppress the tears that threatened again. Now was not the time to cry.

"The team will work as quickly as they can, but it will take them several hours to do the whole cottage," John said when he rejoined Bessie and the others. "Why don't you go home with Doona and get some sleep?" he asked Bessie.

"I want to see the cottage," Bessie told him. "I'm not leaving until I've had a chance to see exactly how bad it is."

John shrugged. "I can't let you in until the technicians are finished."

"There are windows," Bessie suggested.

John glanced back at the cottage and then looked at Bessie. "Give me a minute to walk around the whole cottage. It's just possible that our intruders used the windows to check that the cottage was empty. Again, I don't want to risk destroying any evidence."

Bessie nodded and then watched as the man walked away. When he'd disappeared behind the cottage, she turned and stared at the sea instead.

"It's going to be okay," Doona told her. "I'll help you clean it all up, and anything that's been taken can be replaced."

"I don't even have anything particularly valuable," Bessie shrugged. "A few pieces of jewellery, but none that are worth much. They simply have sentimental value; that's all. Some of my furniture is probably antique, but only because I bought it new many years ago. I can't imagine they found much of anything to take."

"Maybe that's why they made such a mess," Doona said. "Maybe they were angry that you didn't have chests full of silver and gold."

Bessie gave her a bleak smile. "You know I would count my books as my most valuable possessions. I just hope they didn't have the time or the inclination to destroy them." Movement caught her eye, and she watched John as he crossed the parking area to her side.

"Okay, let's take a walk around," he told Bessie. "You can't get too close, but the techs have lights on everywhere. You should be able to get some idea of what you're going to have to deal with."

"What we're going to have to deal with," Doona reminded her. "We've already been through a lot together. We'll get through this as well."

"Yes, I know," Bessie replied. Doona took her hand, and John offered his arm. Together the trio made their way closer to the cottage. When standing behind it, she got a good view into her kitchen.

"My goodness," she exclaimed when she saw the mess that had

been made there. "I'm awfully glad you warned me, but even so, I wasn't, that is, my goodness. I've never seen such a mess."

Bessie could see puddles of milk and other liquids all over the floor. Containers of soup and spaghetti sauce from her freezer had been opened. The containers had been dumped on countertops and on her kitchen table. Crackers and biscuits had been taken from their packages and seemingly thrown in every possible direction. The entire room appeared to have a fine layer of flour over the top of everything else.

"We'll get someone in to clean it all up," John said.

"I don't know about that," Bessie replied. "I'm not sure I'd be comfortable with having someone else doing the cleaning. I'm not sure I want any more strangers at Treoghe Bwaane."

"The sitting room doesn't look as bad," Doona said. She'd taken a few steps further along the beach. Bessie joined her there.

"It hardly looks touched, at least in comparison to the kitchen," Bessie said, feeling relieved. A few books had been taken off their shelves and dropped on the floor, but otherwise the room looked much like it always did, aside from the dusting of flour that Bessie could see in the doorway between the sitting room and the kitchen.

"I've spoken to Matthew, the head technician. He says the rest of the house is much like the sitting room. A few things have been tossed around, but nowhere near as badly as the kitchen," John said. "He reckons whoever it was didn't spend long upstairs. Obviously, he can't say whether anything has been taken or not, though."

Bessie blew out the breath she'd been holding. "Overall, it isn't as terrible as I thought it would be," she told her friends. "I mean, the kitchen is horrible, but if the rest of the cottage is okay, then it shouldn't take too long to put it all right again."

"Which is a job for tomorrow," Doona said. "For tonight, come home with me. You can sleep in my spare bedroom now that the children have gone to John's."

"Who also needs some sleep," Bessie said, looking pointedly at the man in question.

John nodded. "I think I'll go home now, actually. The team doesn't need me underfoot. I'll get a full report from them in the morning and then come and talk to you about what they found," he told Bessie.

"When can I get inside?" she asked.

"Probably in the morning. We'll want you to go through it as early as possible, so we can get a complete list of what's missing. The sooner we have that list, the sooner we can start looking for the items," he replied.

"So we'll see you in the morning," Doona said. "I have to work at nine, but Bessie is welcome to stay at my house until you get there."

"I should be there before nine," John told her. "A lot will depend on how the team does here, of course."

"But I'm meant to be taking the children to Castletown tomorrow," Bessie remembered. "I don't want to disappoint them, but if I have to go through the house..." she trailed off.

"The children will survive," John said. "They need to find ways to entertain themselves."

"Maybe they can come down and spend some time on the beach while I'm cleaning," Bessie suggested.

"Let's work on one thing at a time," John said. "You go with Doona now and get some sleep. I'll be over to talk to you in the morning. If the techs are done here, I'll bring you down to go through the house to see what's missing. Cleaning can wait until both of those things are done."

"The milk will sour, and the floors will be ruined," Bessie objected.

"One thing at a time," John replied. "I'll get someone to mop up the worst of the puddles on the floor before they go. The rest can wait a short while."

Bessie wanted to argue, but she was too tired and upset to do so. Doona led her to her car and bundled her inside. "Try not to fret," Doona said. "We'll get it all sorted in a day or two."

While she nodded, Bessie wasn't sure it was going to be that easy. Her brain kept replaying the shocking mess that had been her much-loved cosy kitchen. Whenever she tried to think about something else, she started to worry that the intruders might have inadvertently stolen something that she held as valuable. The locket that Matthew

Saunders, her lost love, had given her was probably only worth a few pounds, but it had huge sentimental value. The thought that someone might have taken it made Bessie feel physically ill.

"Come on, now," Doona said coaxingly after she'd parked in front of her house. "Stop thinking about it. There's nothing you can do tonight except rest. Tomorrow is another day."

Bessie followed Doona into the house and then into Doona's spare bedroom. While Doona found a nightgown and a spare toothbrush for her, Bessie sat on the edge of the bed feeling numb.

"I have some tablets that will help you sleep," Doona told her.

"No, thank you. I'll be fine," Bessie said, fully aware that she wasn't telling the truth.

"You won't, but you're too stubborn to give in," Doona replied. "I'll leave a sleeping tablet in a glass by the sink in the loo. If you decide you want it, it will be there."

Bessie nodded. As soon as Doona shut the door, she climbed into the borrowed nightie and then crawled under the covers. Squeezing her eyes tightly shut didn't stop the tears that began to flow. Bessie was shocked the next morning to discover that she'd cried herself to sleep.

Doona's house was quiet when Bessie awoke. It was right around six, and Bessie knew she'd never get back to sleep at that hour. While she wanted a shower, there seemed little point in having one, as she'd only be putting back on the same clothes she'd worn the previous day. After helping herself to a bowl of cereal, Bessie let herself out and began a brisk walk along the pavement that ran the length of the street.

She walked from Doona's to the far end of the road and then back again. The fresh air and exercise helped to wake her up and even improved her mood, at least slightly. She was still feeling shocked and saddened by what had happened, but in the cold light of morning she felt more ready to cope with it.

Doona was up when Bessie got back. "I was only a little bit worried when you weren't here," she told Bessie as Bessie let herself back into the house.

"I left you a note," Bessie told her. "It's under the kettle."

Doona laughed. "I didn't even go into the kitchen. I peeked in on you, and you were gone, so I came in here to look outside and see if I could see you. You walked back in before I even got to the door."

"I just had a walk up and down the street. It isn't the same as walking on the beach, but it was the best I could do," Bessie explained.

"You should leave a change of clothes here," Doona suggested, "just in case you ever have to stay over again."

"I hope nothing like this ever happens again," Bessie told her.

"I do too, but maybe it would be good to be prepared."

Bessie shrugged. "You don't have spare clothes at my house," she pointed out.

"No, but maybe I should," Doona retorted. "I'm going to shower and get dressed. I'd like to be presentable when John gets here, and I do have to go to work before too much longer as well."

Bessie curled up with a book that she borrowed from Doona's shelves. She had trouble getting into the story, but was just starting to find it interesting when someone knocked on the door.

"John, good morning," she said as she let the man in.

"Good morning," he replied.

Doona walked into the sitting room as John dropped onto the couch. "Good morning," she told him.

"Good morning. The crime scene technicians are finished with the cottage," he told Bessie. "Most of the mess was confined to the kitchen, and they cleared the worst of the puddles on the floor before they went. The next thing we need is for you to go through and see what's missing."

"Did they get any fingerprints?" Bessie asked.

"They got a great many fingerprints, or partial prints," John replied. "I suspect the vast majority of them will belong to legitimate visitors, though. I suppose it's lucky that Hugh, Doona, and I all work for the police. They already have our prints to compare with the ones they found on the scene. Can you suggest anyone else who has been there lately who should be eliminated?"

"Helen," Bessie said, "but she's on her honeymoon. They'll have to wait until she's back to get her prints."

"I'm sure if I ring Pete, he'll be able to find someone in the US to take her prints and send them to us," John said.

"No, don't do that," Bessie said. "I don't want to bother them during their honeymoon. It can wait until they get back."

John looked as if he wanted to disagree, but after a moment he nodded. "Anyone else been at the cottage lately?"

"Dawn Gray," Bessie said thoughtfully. "She never went any further than the kitchen, though. If her prints turn up anywhere else, that could be interesting."

"I'll have Hugh visit her today and ask her to let him take her prints," John said.

"What if she refuses?" Doona asked.

"We can't make her cooperate, but I can't see any reason why she'd refuse. Surely, she'll want to do what she can to help," John said.

"Yeah, right," Doona muttered.

"Were her brother or father ever actually inside the cottage?" John asked.

"No. They never got past the door," Bessie told him.

"I'm going to have Hugh ask them for their prints anyway," John said. "We can tell them that we found several prints on the door itself and that we want to eliminate theirs. They might be more reluctant than Dawn, however."

"Especially since I'm sure it was Brandon who broke in," Bessie said.

"I haven't seen the notes from the constable who interviewed them last night yet, but I'm sure if Brandon did or said anything suspicious, it would have been brought to my attention," John told her.

Bessie shrugged. "Until you catch whoever did it, I'm going to believe it was Brandon," she told John. "Is there anything else for now, or can we go and see it for ourselves?"

"Let's go," John said, getting to his feet.

Bessie stood up and squared her shoulders. This wasn't going to be pleasant, but she was tougher than she looked, she reminded herself.

"I have to get to work," Doona said, glancing at the clock. "Are you going to be okay on your own?"

"Grace is going to be with us," John said. "She's going to meet us there. She's bringing the children, so they can run on the beach while we go around the cottage."

"You go and work," Bessie told Doona. "I'll talk to you later."

"Promise me you won't start on the cleaning until I get there," Doona said, taking Bessie's hands. "Promise?"

"There's so much to do," Bessie said. "I promise I won't get it all done before you get there."

"Don't even start," Doona said firmly. "There's far too much for you to do on your own, and you'll only get discouraged if you try. I'm going to see if I can't get a few helpers together for tonight. Just leave it all until then."

"She won't do anything," John told Doona. "I'll make sure of that, even if I have to arrest her and take her down to the station for the day."

"It's my cottage," Bessie said crossly. "If I want to clean it, I can."

"Doona is right," John said gently. "It's going to be a huge job. Let Doona come and deal with the heavy lifting and the difficult parts."

Bessie was too overwhelmed by it all to argue any further at that point. What she really wanted to do was see what was missing. The more time she spent arguing with John, the longer it would be before she could do that.

"Let's just go and see what's been taken," she said, aware that she sounded defeated.

"The team didn't notice any obvious gaps anywhere," John told her as they walked to his car. "It may just have been criminal mischief rather than burglary."

Bessie was silent on the drive. When they pulled to a stop in front of her cottage, she stared at it for a moment. It almost didn't look the same to her. It didn't really seem to be her safe, cosy home at the moment.

"It will get better," John told her. "You'll have to give it some time, though. For now, it's normal to feel as if it isn't home anymore."

Bessie nodded and blinked back tears. "Let's go," she said in a low voice.

Grace was standing on the beach, watching John's children as they splashed in the sea. She pulled Bessie into a hug when they reached her. "I'm so sorry," she whispered.

Bessie took a step back and then smiled at her friend. "My goodness, when did that little bump appear?" she asked.

Grace grinned and rubbed her tummy gently. "I'm still getting used to it being there, although I understand it's going to get quite a bit larger," she said. "It isn't much of a bump yet, really, but I'm ever so fond of it."

"Thank you for coming over this morning," Bessie told her. "I'm sure you have better things to do."

"We were going to go to Castletown," Grace reminded her. "With that off the cards, no, I really didn't have anything better to do. I'm a teacher on summer holidays. My days are long and lazy, and coming over here was better than sitting at home and worrying about the new house and the baby."

"Let's go, then," John said. He led Bessie up to her door and then removed the police tape that was stretched across it. "I may need to put this back up once we've been through," he told Bessie. "It depends on what you find. If things are missing, we may need to get a tech back here to take a closer look at some things."

Bessie nodded and then took a deep breath and followed John inside. Grace was right behind Bessie, holding tight to her hand.

"It isn't as bad as I feared," Bessie said after glancing around the kitchen. Someone had done a good job of clearing up the mess on the floor and had also cleared away most of the spills on the countertops and table. The air felt dusty as Bessie breathed in, no doubt from all of the flour that was still liberally covering everything.

"Can you tell if anything is missing in here?" John asked.

Bessie glanced around the room and then shook her head. "They could have taken a few spoons or an odd cup or two, but I can't tell from just a quick look."

"I went through here last night, and I couldn't think of anything that might be missing," John told her. "All of the drawers and cupboards were left open, but they all seem to be full, aside from the ones that had had food in them."

"Those are all empty, but we know where the food went," Bessie said, glancing around again. "They might have taken some boxes of biscuits, I suppose. I don't want to try to work out exactly what's been thrown around in here."

"Let's move on," John suggested, "unless you had any secret hiding places in your kitchen?"

"Secret hiding places?" Bessie repeated.

"Some people keep extra money inside an empty tin can or something like that," John explained.

"It seems a good idea, really," Bessie said, "but I don't have anything like that in the kitchen."

Aside from books on the floor, Bessie couldn't find anything out of place in the sitting room or the dining room. When they got upstairs, she again found that many books had been pulled from their shelves and dropped to the floor, but nothing appeared to be missing.

In her bedroom, she frowned at the books from her nightstand that had been scattered across the floor. She carefully picked up the *Complete Works of Shakespeare* that was always at the bottom of the pile.

"Oh, thank goodness," she exclaimed as she opened the book and found that her small collection of jewellery was still in place in the hollowed-out centre of the book.

"They missed that, then," John said.

"None of it has any real value," Bessie told him, "but it all has sentimental value."

"They'd have taken it anyway, if they'd found it," John said.

"I'm awfully glad they didn't," Bessie sighed. "As far as I can tell, nothing was taken."

"They may have been looking for money or medication," John said. "I assume you didn't have either in the house."

"I don't keep money lying around," Bessie said. "I have credit cards and debit cards for shopping. Any notes I have I carry with me in my handbag."

"And medication?" John asked.

"I don't take anything other than over-the-counter medicines, and those are all in their usual place," she replied.

John nodded. "Perhaps, then, whoever it was became upset because they didn't find anything to steal. That may be why they destroyed your kitchen."

"I still think it was Brandon," Bessie told him. "Maybe he thought he could scare me away from my home or something."

"If it was Brandon, I'm not sure what he was hoping to accomplish," John said, "which is one reason why I'm more inclined to think it was someone else."

"Who else would break into my cottage?" Bessie asked.

"As I said last night, kids from the holiday cottages," John replied. "They might have just been bored, or they might have been looking for drugs or money. While this sort of thing doesn't happen on the island very often, it wouldn't be the first time teens on holiday behaved badly."

"And you think that's a more likely explanation than Brandon?" Bessie wondered.

"At this point, yes," John replied. "I simply can't see what he'd feel he might gain from breaking in here."

Bessie didn't argue. She didn't have any logical reason for suspecting Brandon; she was simply going with her gut instinct. It rarely steered her wrong, but that didn't prove anything.

"I think we're done here," John said as Bessie dropped her jewellery pouch into her handbag. "Let's just walk back through slowly, so you can have another look."

Bessie took her time going back through the house, checking on little things here and there. When they got back to the sitting room, she stopped. "There might be a few books missing," she told John. "I won't know for sure until I get everything back on the shelves, and even then I won't be certain exactly what's missing. I'll just know if there are spaces left because the shelves were pretty packed before."

John nodded. "None of the books are valuable?" he asked.

"All of the books are valuable," she retorted. "Only inasmuch as they're all capable of taking you on an adventure. I don't have any first editions or autographed copies or anything like that, if that's what you mean. I don't even often get hardcover books. Nearly everything I have is in paperback, and they've all been read, sometimes many times over."

"Maybe we should go out the other door," Grace said. "Then we don't have to go back through the kitchen."

Bessie shrugged. "I'll have to face it sooner or later," she said. "I really should get started on the cleaning."

"Except you promised Doona you'd wait for her to help," John told her.

"I don't think I promised," Bessie argued.

"Let's go and take the children to lunch," Grace suggested. "It's getting close to that time anyway. Maybe we could go into Douglas, get lunch, and then do a bit of shopping. I need a few new books to help me fill up my summer holiday. You wouldn't mind a trip to the bookshop, would you, Bessie?"

Bessie chuckled. "You're a very clever girl, but I can see what you're trying to do. You want to keep me busy until Doona's done at work and can help with the cleaning."

"I want to give you something to do so that you can forget about this mess for a few hours," Grace countered. "And I want to have some lunch. I'm always hungry these days, and although my midwife keeps telling me I don't need twice as many calories as normal, I definitely feel as if I want at least twice as many calories as normal."

"Let's go and get lunch, then," Bessie said, glancing at her watch. "By the time we get into Douglas, I should be hungry."

"And I'll bet Thomas and Amy are hungry already," Grace said. "Especially Thomas. He reminds me of Hugh."

"You don't have to entertain my children all day," John said. "They can go home and entertain themselves quite happily."

"I know they can, but as I have the day free, and I'd like to keep

Bessie busy, they're the perfect excuse," Grace replied. "We'll have to leave Castletown for another day, though."

"Maybe one day next week," Bessie said, "after I've had time to get the cottage back in order."

It didn't take them long to find the children. Thomas was racing another teenaged boy up and down the sand, and Amy was building a sandcastle with two toddlers under the watchful eye of their mum.

"How about lunch and some shopping in Douglas?" Grace asked them.

"Sure," Thomas shrugged.

"I need a few things, actually," Amy said, "and I'm starving."

John gave them each a few notes. "I'll be back later to help with the cleaning," he told Bessie. "I may even make the kids help."

"We can," Amy said. "We'd be happy to help."

"Yeah," Thomas said with a marked lack of enthusiasm.

"Let's go and get some lunch for now," Grace said. "I don't know about anyone else, but the baby is hungry."

CHAPTER 9

$\mathcal{T}$he drive into Douglas didn't seem to take long. Thomas and Amy chatted easily with Grace, keeping up a running conversation that kept Bessie's mind off the break-in at her cottage.

"Italian?" Grace asked as they all walked out of the car park in the town centre.

"That sounds good," Thomas said.

"Baby seems to have a liking for pasta and garlic bread," Grace said with a grin, "or rather, I seem to be craving both nearly all the time, even at six in the morning when I first wake up."

Bessie suggested her favourite Douglas restaurant, which was only a short walk away. "They do the best garlic bread on the island, as far as I'm concerned," she told Grace.

"I won't argue," Grace replied.

The restaurant was busy. Bessie added their name to the waiting list, and then they all settled in on couches in the small waiting area.

"I hope we don't have to wait long," Grace said. "I can smell the garlic bread from here and it's driving me crazy."

"He said it would only be fifteen minutes," Bessie assured her. "Let's talk about something other than food while we wait."

"Dad said that someone broke into your cottage," Amy said. "I hope they didn't steal anything valuable."

Grace frowned, but Bessie smiled at the girl. "It doesn't appear as if they took anything at all," she said. "They just made a huge mess, really."

"That's mean," Amy replied. "We could see your kitchen when we were on the beach. It looked like a bag of flour exploded everywhere."

"It does, yes," Bessie told her. "I suspect I'll be finding flour in unexpected places for weeks."

"Thomas dropped a bag of icing sugar once and it went everywhere," Amy told her. "Mum nearly killed him."

"It was an accident," Thomas said. "Anyway, Mum wasn't nearly as upset as Harvey was. I thought he was going to hit me, really."

"He did get really mad," Amy giggled. "I don't think he's used to children. Mum told me that's one of the reasons why they split up in the first place. She wanted to have a family and he didn't."

"Well, he has one now," Thomas said, "and I don't think he's overly happy about it."

"It will be strange for him, becoming a parent to two teenagers almost overnight," Bessie said, feeling as if she ought defend the man she'd never met. "I'm sure he'll get better at it as time goes by."

"We can help you clean up," Amy said. "Thomas and I cleaned up all of the icing sugar, and that was sticky and awful. Flour shouldn't be as bad."

"No, I suppose it shouldn't be," Bessie agreed, "but you're meant to be on holiday. You shouldn't have to clean someone else's house. I'm sure your father would much rather you cleaned his."

Amy laughed. "Dad must have spent ages cleaning before we got here. His house is almost too clean. It doesn't really feel lived in, though. I'm sure he works too hard."

"You're right about that," Bessie told her.

"I don't want to wait," a loud voice said in the doorway.

Bessie was sure she recognized the voice. She looked up and then touched Grace's arm. "Brandon and Dawn," she mouthed to her friend.

"I'm told the food is very good here," Dawn replied to her brother. "Anyway, it will take ages to find somewhere else to go. Let's just wait."

"I'm sure there are restaurants all along the promenade," Brandon said. "Come on."

"Let me see how long the wait is," Dawn said in a placating tone. "Just give me a minute."

"Table for five, remember," Brandon called after her as Dawn headed for the hostess station. When she turned back around, she glanced around the room and then headed towards Bessie.

"Miss Cubbon, this is a surprise," she said, quickly dropping onto the couch next to Bessie. "There's a fifteen-minute wait for a table, and if I tell Brandon that, he'll make us go elsewhere. Can I just sit here with you for a few minutes?" she asked in a whisper.

"Of course you can," Bessie said. "The food here is well worth the wait."

"That's what I've heard. I love Italian food, but Brandon isn't as fond of it. Dad and Mike and Horace are meeting us here, though. If we go somewhere else, they'll never find us," Dawn told her.

Bessie introduced the woman to Grace and the children, taking care not to mention the children's surname. It seemed unlikely that Dawn would make the connection between them and the inspector who had questioned her about her late husband's murder, but Bessie didn't want to take any chances.

"But what happened at your cottage last night?" Dawn asked after the introductions were complete. "I saw flashing lights and a bunch of cars over there when I was going to bed."

"Unfortunately, someone broke in," Bessie replied.

"I hope nothing valuable was taken," Dawn said.

"I don't have anything valuable to take," Bessie told her with a wry grin. "I suppose I'm lucky in a way that I've always had to live very frugally. I've never accumulated valuable jewellery or expensive trinkets."

"Do such things happen often on the island?" Dawn asked.

"No, not at all," Bessie replied. "I've lived in that cottage since I was eighteen and this was the first time anyone has ever broken in. As far as I know, no one has ever broken into any of the holiday cottages, either." Aside from the one time that someone was murdered in one, but Bessie didn't bother Dawn with that information.

"That's good to hear," Dawn said. "Although we've nothing of value in our cottage, either. I left all of my good jewellery at home, and I don't collect trinkets, valuable or otherwise. Have the police made any arrests yet?"

"No arrests, but I understand they have a suspect in mind," Bessie told her. When Dawn immediately glanced at her brother, Bessie was suspicious.

"I hope they can work out who did it quickly," she told Bessie. "Someone came by last night to ask us if we'd seen anything, but we were busy having dinner and drinks on the beach. Someone probably could have pulled a removals van up to your door and emptied your cottage without us noticing."

"I hope not," Bessie exclaimed.

"Dawn, we're not waiting all day," Brandon shouted from his place by the door. When Dawn didn't move, he crossed the room to join them. "Let's find somewhere else," he said. "I'll text the others from wherever we end up."

"I suspect most places will have short waits at this time of day," Bessie told him coolly. "You're probably better off just waiting here."

"Maybe you'd be better off minding your own business," Brandon snarled at her.

Bessie stared up at him with a level gaze. "I was just trying to help," she said. "You're strangers here, and I know the island well. During the summer, Douglas gets quite busy, you see."

Brandon's eyes stared into hers. "You seem to have lots of friends in the police," he said. "It looked as if you were having a party last night."

"Sadly, I wasn't," Bessie said. "Someone broke into my cottage. The police were there to investigate."

"Nothing taken, I hope," the man said.

"A few things, but nothing that can't be replaced," Bessie replied.

Brandon opened his mouth and then snapped it shut again. He looked over at his sister. "Let's go," he said sharply.

"It must be nearly time for our table to be ready," she argued. "Anyway, there's Dad." She waved at the man who was standing in the doorway, looking around.

"Mike and Horace aren't going to want to wait," Brandon told her as Dawn got to her feet.

"Horace will wait if I ask him to," Dawn replied, "besides they aren't even here yet."

"Miss Cubbon? Your table is ready," the young hostess said softly to Bessie.

"Good, thank you," Bessie said. She and the others got to their feet and began to follow the girl into the restaurant.

"Don't forget to keep your doors locked," Brandon said in a menacing tone as she walked past him. When she turned to look at him, he gave her a nasty grin. "Just sharing some advice of my own," he told her.

Bessie shivered and then walked quickly away. She and her friends were seated in a quiet corner of the large restaurant, and Bessie was happy to settle in. "I hope they leave," she told Grace in a low voice.

"If they do stay, I hope they end up sitting on the opposite side of the room," Grace hissed.

"Garlic bread?" the girl asked after she'd handed them all menus.

"Oh, yes, we'd better have two," Bessie told her.

She nodded and then walked away. Their waiter was there a moment later to get drink orders. By the time they were ready to order their meals, the garlic bread had already been delivered.

Bessie was relieved to see Dawn and her group seated on the opposite side of the room. That didn't stop her and probably everyone in the restaurant from hearing everything that Brandon said as he ordered himself a pint of lager and complained about the menu options.

"It's all Italian food," he shouted.

"It's an Italian restaurant," Mike said in a voice nearly as loud. "Just order some spaghetti Bolognese and shut up."

"I don't like Italian food," Brandon told him.

"Then go back to the cottage and eat some of the crap you've stashed all over the place," Mike suggested.

"Dawn wanted to come here, and I think it's very nice," Horace said, raising his voice to be heard over the others.

"You think anything Dawn likes is very nice," Brandon snapped. "Because you want to get in her pa..."

"That's enough," Lucas Mason barked. "Brandon, find something to eat or simply sit there with your mouth shut while the rest of us eat. I don't want to hear another word out of you."

Bessie hid a grin as she sipped her drink. It wasn't often you heard a father shout at his son when the son was in his forties. Brandon didn't look nearly as amused as Bessie felt. He downed half of his drink in a single swallow and then waved to their waitress for another.

"Brandon is the man you think broke into the cottage, right?" Grace whispered.

"Yes. The older man is his father, Lucas. The woman is Dawn Gray, Walter's wife," Bessie replied.

"Brandon is thoroughly unpleasant, anyway, even if he didn't have anything to do with your break-in," Grace said. "Who are the other two men?"

"They're both Brandon's friends, although I gather Horace would like to be more than friends with Dawn," Bessie said. "Now let's talk about what we're going to do after lunch."

The little group quickly agreed that the local bookshop was their main priority.

"I need some shampoo and a few other things," Amy said, blushing lightly. "Dad doesn't have the right things."

Grace smiled. "I'm sure he had no idea what to buy for you," she said. "My father is totally lost when it comes to the sorts of products that women use."

"I didn't think to bring anything with me because, well, when we all lived together everything I needed was there. I never stopped to think that it was Mum who was doing the shopping in those days," Amy told them.

"There's a ShopFast just down the road," Grace said. "You and I can pop in there while Bessie and Thomas have a stroll on the promenade. Then we can all meet in the bookshop before we go for ice cream."

"Ice cream?" Thomas grinned. "That's the best part of the plan by far."

With ice cream on the cards, they decided to skip pudding at the restaurant. Bessie used the money John had given her to pay for lunch, adding the tip herself. "You did the driving," she told Grace.

"Dad gave us some extra money," Amy said.

"Save that for the shops," Bessie told her.

They were making their way back through the restaurant when Bessie saw a familiar face. She stopped as Constance Hamilton strolled into the room. As Bessie glanced over at Dawn, Brandon spotted the new arrival.

"Well, well, well, look who's here," he said loudly.

Dawn looked up and flushed. "Constance?" she said softly.

Constance turned and looked at Dawn. "Oh, dear," she exclaimed.

"Oh, dear?" Dawn echoed. "Oh, dear? Is that really an appropriate greeting, do you think?" Dawn got to her feet and advanced towards the other woman.

Bessie took a few steps backwards, guiding the children and Grace behind her. It would probably be best if they didn't witness the argument that Bessie was sure was about to begin, but Bessie was determined not to miss it.

"Dawn, hello," Constance said in an artificially bright voice. "I wasn't expecting to see you here."

"No, I'm sure you weren't," Dawn replied. "I'm sure you were hoping you'd never see me again after you ran off with my husband."

"It wasn't like that," Constance protested. "I didn't realise, I mean, I didn't know anything about him."

Dawn laughed. "I saw the article in the paper where you talked about how you were taken in by Walter's deception," she said. "You had the nerve to claim that you actually thought he was a vicar."

"He was very convincing," Constance replied.

"Except you'd already known him for what, three years, maybe four, before he moved over here as Reverend Doyle," Dawn said. "Or are you claiming that you thought he was really a vicar all along and just pretending to be Walter Gray?"

"It's all very complicated," Constance protested.

"It's complicated by the fact that you lied to the police and to the newspapers," Dawn said. "That's making it harder for the police to work out who killed Walter. The reporter from the local paper might have believed your lies, but I can promise you the police do not. I've told them all about you and how you wormed your way into my husband's affections and stole him away from me."

"I did no such thing," Constance snapped. "He got tired of you and your constant demands. You were never happy, and every time he got into any trouble, you ran back to your daddy and got him to look after you. Walter had had enough of trying to compete with your father, that's all."

"He wasn't half the man my father is," Dawn said. "I should have listened to Dad when he told me not to marry Walter in the first place."

"Yeah, you should have," Constance agreed. "You two were all wrong for each other."

"And you were better for Walter?" Dawn asked.

"I was a lot better for him. I helped him with whatever he needed to do," Constance replied. "I was even willing to come over and hide out with him in that tiny house while he pretended to be a vicar. You never would have done that."

"No, I wouldn't have," Dawn agreed. "I never supported him in his criminal endeavours."

"This wasn't a criminal anything," Constance told her. "This was just about staying safe. There were some very scary people looking for Walter."

"And if you'd tell the police about them, maybe they'd be able to work out who killed him," Dawn pointed out.

"Yeah, but I'm afraid of them as well," Constance said. "I don't want to be the next victim."

"Who was Walter hiding from?" Dawn demanded.

Constance shrugged. "I don't know, really. When he got out of prison, he and I started doing some travelling. At some point something happened, but I don't know what, and I'm not sure where it happened. I only noticed over time that Walter was being increasingly secretive. Then, about six weeks ago, he decided we should move to the Isle of Man. He'd found out that a vicar was needed and he'd found a way to put himself forward for the position. I don't know exactly what he did, but a short time later he told me that we were moving."

"You really need to talk to the police," Dawn said steadily.

"I don't want to," Constance said, making a face.

"How about I make you?" Brandon asked, getting up from his chair.

Constance looked at him for a moment and then smiled. "Hey, Brandon," she said softly. "You don't really want to get me into any trouble, do you?" she cooed.

Brandon flushed and looked down at the ground. "Maybe she doesn't need to talk to the police," he said to Dawn.

"That's right, before you stole my husband from me, you were sleeping with my brother, weren't you?" Dawn asked. "I can't believe we were ever friends."

"Brandon and I are both single. Who we sleep with isn't anyone else's business," Constance retorted.

"What's your excuse for sleeping with my husband, then?" Dawn demanded.

"You left him," Constance replied. "You went back to live with your father and left him."

"He went to prison," Dawn said. "I couldn't very well go with him, could I?"

"You didn't even visit. He told me, when I visited, that you'd told him you wanted a divorce," Constance answered.

"I told him I wanted to talk about a divorce when he got out," Dawn argued, "but when he got out he ran off with you instead."

"We fell in love," Constance told her, pulling a tissue from her pocket and dabbing at her eyes. "I never meant for it to happen, but it did. I never wanted to hurt you, you know that."

Dawn laughed. "So touching, and almost believable. I know better of course, but by all means keep up the pretense. Other people might even feel sorry for you."

"I feel sorry for you," Constance snapped. She took a step closer to the other woman. "You lost Walter and now you're sad and bitter about it. He didn't love you anymore. Maybe it was you that he was hiding from, did you ever think about that?"

"He had no reason to hide from me," Dawn said steadily. "If he wanted a divorce, all he had to do was ask. I was going to file soon anyway."

"Yeah, that's what you say now. Maybe you're just telling people that to hide how much you hated him and how angry you were that he left," Constance suggested. "Maybe you're just trying to divert suspicion since you killed him."

Dawn closed the distance between herself and Constance. "How dare you," she hissed, her face only inches from Constance's. "I loved Walter, and as much as I hate to admit it, I would have taken him back in a second if he'd asked. I'm not proud of that, but that's how much I loved him. You were just a passing fancy, like all of the other women before you. He was my husband, and he would have come back to me if he hadn't been brutally murdered."

"You tell yourself that if it helps you feel better," Constance said mockingly. "I know the truth. I was the one on the island with the man, not you. I was the one who shared his very last kiss with him."

"You reckon? Maybe you did, but maybe he had another woman," Dawn said. "Maybe he was seeing someone behind your back and that's what got him killed. He wasn't the faithful type, but I don't have to tell you that, do I?"

Movement in the doorway silenced both women. Bessie didn't

recognise the man who walked into the restaurant with two uniformed constables on his heels.

"Ladies, I'm sure you aren't meaning to disturb everyone's lunch," the man said in a low, firm voice. "Let's take this conversation elsewhere, shall we?"

"I'm not going anywhere," Constance snapped. "I'm going to have some lunch. Please take her away, though. She was saying horrible things to me."

The man shrugged. "I'm sorry, but you're both going to have to come with me. We'll sort everything out at the station."

"I'm not finished eating yet," Dawn protested.

"I'm sure the restaurant can box your meal up," the man said. "You can finish it later."

"My sister should be allowed to finish eating," Brandon said loudly. "I don't know who you are, but you can't just drag her out of here like this."

"I'm Inspector Davidson with the Douglas CID," the man replied. "I don't want to have to arrest anyone, really, but if people don't want to cooperate, I will."

"You can't arrest my sister. She hasn't done anything wrong," Brandon shouted.

"Brandon, sit down," Lucas Mason said sharply. "Inspector Davidson, I'm sure my daughter didn't mean to cause a scene. She's had a difficult few days, learning that her husband had been murdered and then finding out that he'd been living with a woman whom she'd once considered her closest friend. I'm afraid when she saw that former friend in here she simply couldn't keep quiet. If you'd like to discuss the matter with her elsewhere, I'm sure she'll cooperate."

The inspector nodded. "Thank you. If you'd both come with me, please," he said to Constance and Dawn.

Dawn looked at her father and then sighed deeply. "I'll just get my handbag," she said in a defeated tone.

"I'm not going," Constance said. "I've told the police everything that I intend to tell them."

"You lied to them," Dawn said. "You told them and the local paper a whole host of lies. They should lock you up and throw away the key."

"I may have omitted a few things from my statement," Constance countered, "but I didn't exactly lie."

The police inspector looked from one woman to the other and then shook his head. "I can see we're going to have a lot to talk about," he said. "I may have to invite John Rockwell to join us."

Bessie was happy to hear him say that, as she'd been trying to work out a way to suggest that very thing to the man. Constance protested a few more times, but in the end she and Dawn were both escorted out of the building by the uniformed constables.

"I should go with her," Brandon said as they left.

"No, you shouldn't," his father said firmly. "Dawn will be fine. She knows when to keep her mouth shut. You, on the other hand, well, you don't."

Bessie thought Brandon might argue, but instead he resumed eating. A moment later the rest of his party did the same.

"That was interesting," Grace said in Bessie's ear as they continued on their way to the exit.

"That's one word for it," Bessie replied. "I hope the inspector does include John when he questions the women. We need to tell him what we heard, as well."

"I rang Hugh when Constance walked in," Grace told her. "Then I put the whole thing on speaker on my mobile. Hugh and John were listening in. They were the ones who sent Inspector Davidson over to break up the fight."

"What a very clever thing to do," Bessie exclaimed.

Grace blushed. "It was Amy's idea," she admitted.

Bessie smiled at the girl. "It was a wonderful idea," she told the teen. "I'm sure your father will be very proud of you for thinking of it."

"Dad hasn't told us much about the case, but I know a little bit, and I read more in the local paper. I thought I recognised the woman when she came in as the one who'd been interviewed about the case. I knew the other woman was the victim's wife, because she was on the front page of the paper, too," Amy replied. "If I can do anything to help Dad, I want to do it. Then he'll have more time to spend with us, and a killer will be behind bars."

The little group was making their way down the promenade as Amy spoke. "I'm sure your father will appreciate that you want to help, but you also need to be careful. Investigating murders can be a dangerous job," Bessie said.

"Dad says it isn't dangerous if you do it right," Thomas interjected.

"I'm sure he's right, but he's with the police. It can be dangerous for other people when they stick their noses in," Bessie said, something she knew only too well from her own experiences.

"Let's talk about something pleasant," Grace suggested. "Which shops do we want to visit?"

It turned out that the children weren't terribly interested in shopping. Grace took Amy off to ShopFast for her essentials while Bessie continued down the promenade with Thomas.

"Are you liking the island more now, then?" she asked the boy as they walked.

"I liked it okay the first time," Thomas told her. "I made some friends, and I liked the school in Ramsey. Mum hated it so much that, well, I felt as if I had to act like I didn't like it, too. If I'd known then that she just wanted to get back to Manchester to be closer to Harvey, I wouldn't have gone along."

"Have you been able to see some of your friends now that you're back?" was Bessie's next question. She wanted to avoid talking about Sue and Harvey if at all possible.

"Yeah, we met up once and are planning to do some other things later in the summer. Most of them do lots of sports, though, so they don't have as much free time as I do."

"Maybe you should talk to your father about putting you into some sort of sport," Bessie suggested.

"We're leaving in a few months. It doesn't really seem worth it."

"And you want to join the police when you finish school?" Bessie asked.

Thomas shrugged. "I don't know. It seems like an interesting job.

No day would ever be exactly the same, which seems desirable, but it doesn't pay much, really, not for all the long hours that go along with it. I like telling Mum I want to, though, because it makes her cross. No matter how hard she pushes me, I'm never going to become a doctor like Harvey."

"That's another job that must be interesting," Bessie said. "I can't imagine any two days are alike there, either. And, of course, it does pay rather well, or so I'm told."

"Yeah, I might even be tempted by the idea if it weren't for Harvey," Thomas told her. "It isn't even Harvey, really, it's Mum with Harvey. If I decided to study medicine, she'd insist on telling everyone that I was following in Harvey's footsteps. She'd use it to justify leaving Dad and breaking up the family."

Bessie nodded. Thomas was clearly still upset about the divorce and Bessie could understand how he felt. "I suggest you stop worrying about what your mother will do and focus on what you want," she told the boy. "If you genuinely want to study medicine, you should do so, no matter what your mother thinks."

"We'll see," Thomas replied. "I'm doing all the right GCSEs, anyway. I don't have to make any real decisions for a few more years."

The pair walked in silence for a few minutes and then chatted about the weather and the people on the beach for a while. When Bessie's phone buzzed they were nearly back to the centre of Douglas.

Bessie pulled out her phone and read the text message. "Grace and Amy are waiting for us at the bookshop," she told Thomas.

"Great. I hope they have new stuff. A few of my favourite authors are meant to have new books out," he said happily.

Bessie was relieved to hear that the young man enjoyed reading. It seemed to her that fewer and fewer children were being encouraged to read books these days. Electronic devices were taking over their lives and Bessie didn't feel that was an improvement.

The foursome spent a happy half hour browsing the shelves. Thomas found three books he wanted and Amy found four. Bessie found about a dozen, but she limited herself to two paperbacks. She had a great deal of cleaning and tidying to do at home. Time for reading would be in short supply for a few days, anyway. Grace bought several books on pregnancy and baby care, which made Bessie smile.

"I know," Grace said as she took her bag from the shop assistant. "No matter how much I read, I'll still be totally unprepared. I feel as if I'm studying for a French exam but that when I sit down the entire paper is going to be written in Japanese. Having said that, I still can't resist buying more and more books."

"I'm sure you'll get many helpful tips from the books," Bessie told her. "Just don't forget to trust your instincts. People have been bringing up babies quite successfully for many years. You'll be just fine."

"My mum laughs at me when she sees all the books I already have," Grace said. "She didn't have any books and she reckons I turned out okay."

Bessie chuckled. "Now who wanted ice cream?" she asked.

Thomas and Amy got two scoops each, in different flavours. Bessie and Grace opted for single scoops instead.

"I'm still feeling quite full after that delicious lunch," Grace said as they walked out of the ice cream shop.

"The food is always good there," Bessie said. "I couldn't say no to ice cream either, though."

When the sweet treats were all gone, the group piled back into Grace's car and headed back towards Laxey. For perhaps the first time ever, Bessie wasn't looking forward to going home to Treoghe Bwaane.

CHAPTER 10

"**I**'m not sure where to park," Grace said as she approached Bessie's cottage.

Bessie shook her head. "People from the holiday cottages sometimes use my parking area, as it's always less busy than their car park. I'll have to ring Thomas or Maggie and ask them to get people to move their cars," she sighed.

"That one is Doona's, anyway," Grace said, "and I think I see John's car as well."

"You'll have to park on the road," Bessie told the girl. "Although you don't have to park. You can just let me and the children out and then you can get home."

"I'm going to park," Grace countered. "I told you that I'd come in and help you with the cleaning that needs doing."

"It looks as if John and Doona have already started," Bessie muttered as Grace pulled her car off the road as far as she could.

She was out of the car and walking briskly towards her cottage before Grace could unbuckle her seatbelt. While Bessie appreciated that her friends wanted to help, she felt odd about them working on the cleaning while she wasn't home. The front door to the cottage was standing open, and when Bessie stepped inside she simply stopped and stared.

"Grace was meant to keep you busy for another hour," Doona said from where she was standing behind Bessie's cooker. "We'd have been done by then."

Bessie looked around the room slowly. "It looks as if you're nearly done anyway," she said, shaking her head. "It must have taken you hours."

"Not at all," Doona replied. "I had a lot of help." She turned her head and looked over towards the dining room. "Bessie's home," she called loudly.

A few moments later Bessie heard what sounded like a herd of elephants tramping through her house. John was the first to join her and Doona in the kitchen.

"Ah, Bessie, I thought Grace was going to keep you out for a while longer," he said. "We've just finished tidying the upstairs."

"We?" Bessie echoed softly.

"Hello, Aunt Bessie," Hugh said brightly. "Doona wanted to handle the kitchen herself, so John and I worked on putting books back on shelves and that sort of thing."

Bessie nodded. "Thank you," she said.

"I helped in the kitchen," another voice said, "or rather, Mum and I did."

"Andy? But surely you had better things to do," Bessie said to the young man who was back on the island on summer break from culinary school.

"I couldn't think of anything I'd rather do today than help clean Treoghe Bwaane," he said cheerfully. "After all the time I spent here in my teen years complaining about my mum and all, it was the least I could do."

"You never complained about me, really," Anne Caine laughed from where she was standing behind her son. "I was an awesome mum."

"You were, all things considered," Andy agreed. "Anyway, when I heard what had happened here, I rang the police to find out if I could help. Doona was kind enough to let Mum and me come over and do a few things."

"I've made a list, actually," Doona said. "There have been about twenty different people here throughout the day. The phone at the station didn't stop ringing with people who wanted to come and help, and some of them simply showed up at your door. As I said, in another hour we'd have finished the job."

Bessie felt tears welling up in her eyes. "I can't begin to thank you all," she said, stopping because she felt completely overcome.

"We were happy to do it," Hugh said. "With so many people helping, it didn't take long, anyway. Once Andy vacuumed up most of the flour, there wasn't that much else to do."

"There was lots to do and I'm immensely grateful to all of you and to the others on the list who helped," Bessie said. "I don't know how to thank you. I wasn't looking forward to coming back here this afternoon, but you've made the cottage feel homey again."

Grace put an arm around Bessie. "I hope you couldn't tell that I was dragging my feet and trying to keep you away," she said. "Doona didn't want you back until five at the earliest."

"I was dragging my feet too," Bessie replied. "I didn't want to come back and deal with the mess."

"I've finished the dining room, although there wasn't much to do in there," Bessie's friend Bahey Corlett said as she walked into the room. "Joney wanted to come and help, too, but I think it's best that she didn't. There isn't any more room to park, and I think we've done nearly everything anyway."

"I just need to move the cooker back into place and give the kitchen a final polish," Doona said. "Mary and Elizabeth should be back by the time I've done that."

"Mary and Elizabeth?" Bessie echoed.

"Your neighbours from Thie yn Traie," Doona said. "They've just gone to run a few errands."

Bessie was afraid to ask what those errands might entail. Everyone insisted that Bessie sit down at the kitchen table while John and Hugh slid her cooker back against the wall. Doona gave everything one final wipe with her duster, and then she went and stood in the middle of the room.

"I think it looks pretty good," she said as she slowly turned and surveyed the kitchen.

"I think it looks better than it has in a long time," Bessie replied. "I can't remember the last time I moved the cooker out to clean behind it."

Doona laughed. "It needed doing because of the flour," she explained.

Bessie nodded. She could only imagine how difficult it must have been, cleaning up all of that flour. "How can I ever thank you?" she asked.

"That's what friends are for," Bahey told her. "We were all happy to help. Now we should get out of the way."

Bessie gave her a hug before she left. Anne and Andy were the next to go. "Ring me if you need anything," Anne said in her ear.

As Bessie let them out of the cottage, Mary Quayle's expensive car slid into the parking area. Elizabeth jumped out of the passenger seat as soon as the car stopped.

"We were hoping to be here before you got home," she told Bessie. "At least now you can make sure we put things in the right places."

Hugh and John helped the women carry in dozens of bags of groceries. Bessie's cupboards were all completely full when they were finished unpacking, and a few boxes of biscuits and crackers ended up on the kitchen table because there simply wasn't any more room in the cupboards.

"I hope we've managed to replace everything," Elizabeth said.

"I've never had this much food in my cottage at one time before," Bessie told her. "Not even at Christmas. I'll never manage to eat it all before it starts going out of date."

"I'm sure you'll have lots of help," Elizabeth replied. "Everyone you know will want to visit to make sure you're okay."

There was some truth to Elizabeth's words, but Bessie wasn't convinced that, even with help, all of the food would get eaten.

"We won't stay," Mary told her. "I'm sure you'd like some peace and quiet after all of the upset."

"Thank you so much," Bessie replied. She hugged both mother and daughter as they headed for the door.

"Bessie, sit down," Grace suggested as Bessie shut the door behind the Quayles. "It's been a long day after a late night."

Bessie wanted to argue, but Grace was right. She was exhausted. It would be lovely to sleep in her own bed later, she thought, blocking out the immediate rush of fear that followed the idea. Her cottage had always felt safe and secure, and now it didn't.

"If you're okay, I think I'll take the children and go home," John said. "Maybe we could have another gathering tomorrow to talk everything through."

"That would be good," Bessie replied, "but I'm not sure I want to go out and leave the cottage empty again in the evening."

"We'll find someone to watch the cottage," Doona told her. "I suspect Brandon is well aware of your connection with John by now, though."

"So you may as well all come here," Bessie suggested. "Goodness knows I have plenty of food for everyone. I'll cook something and we can each eat our own body weight in biscuits for pudding."

"I might just be able to do that," Hugh said with a chuckle.

"Especially now that he's eating for two," Grace teased.

Hugh flushed. "I have been incredibly hungry since Grace found out she was pregnant," he said.

"You're always hungry," Doona countered.

"I know," Hugh shrugged.

Bessie walked John and the children to the door. "Thank you for spending the day with me," she told Thomas and Amy. "You helped keep my mind off of my cottage."

"It was fun," Thomas told her.

"But next time we go to a castle," Amy said firmly. "Just not tomorrow."

"What's tomorrow?" John asked.

"I told you, I'm meeting Maddie and Sue in Ramsey. We're going to go shopping and maybe go to the park," Amy replied. "Doona said she could take me."

"That's good of her," John replied.

"I thought I'd have her take me as well," Thomas added. "There's more to do in Ramsey than there is in Laxey."

The trio were still talking about their plans for the next day as Bessie shut the door behind them. Hugh and Grace were talking quietly together when Bessie turned around.

"We're going to go too," Hugh said. "Grace needs to put her feet up for a while."

"I'm sorry," Bessie replied. "You must be tired after everything we did today."

Grace shook her head. "I'm fine. Hugh just likes to fuss. I'll let him make dinner while I curl up with one of my new books, to make him feel important."

"I can hear everything you're saying," Hugh pointed out, "and I don't need to feel important. You can make dinner if you want."

"I am a little bit tired," Grace said, winking at Bessie.

Bessie chuckled. "Off you go. Hugh, make something lovely for your beautiful bride. You won't get to spoil her in the same way if you have more children, you know. Once the first one arrives, the world suddenly revolves around him or her."

Hugh held Grace's hand as they walked to the door. Bessie watched them walk to Grace's car. Hugh carefully tucked Grace inside and shut her door. He watched her drive away before he climbed into his own car and followed.

"Those two are sweet together," Doona said.

"They are. That baby is very lucky."

"You're right about that. And now that everyone else is gone, why don't you take a walk through the cottage and make sure that every-thing is the way you want it? Then we can think about dinner."

Bessie nodded and then took Doona's advice.

"So how did everyone do?" Doona asked when Bessie walked back into the kitchen a few minutes later.

"It looks almost exactly the same as it was," Bessie told her. "I suppose a few books might be in different places, I didn't look all that closely, but everything else is just right."

"There were a lot of people here helping out. Everything in the kitchen that was moveable was taken outside and cleaned. The floors were scrubbed and then polished. Jasper from the Seaview brought an industrial-strength vacuum cleaner and he and Andy tackled the worst of the flour, sugar, and spices that had been spread everywhere."

"I shall have to ring him and thank him," Bessie said.

"As I said, I have a list for you of everyone who helped. I really did have to turn people away, you know. You have a great many friends on this island."

"It's been my home for more years than most people have been alive. But even so, I never expected, that is…" Bessie trailed off and swallowed the lump in her throat.

"We were all happy to help," Doona told her. "What about dinner, then?"

"I had a large lunch. Maybe just sandwiches?" Bessie suggested.

Doona nodded. "That's fine with me. I know Mary and Elizabeth brought bread and sandwich meats and cheeses."

They pair ate sandwiches with crisps and fizzy drinks, and then followed the meal with some chocolate-covered biscuits. "I know these must have been really expensive," Bessie said as she put them onto a plate. "I've never even seen them before."

"They taste expensive," Doona told her a moment later, "and oh, so good."

Bessie couldn't argue. The biscuits were delicious. She just wished that Mary would have let her pay for the food that she and her daughter had purchased.

"You haven't had a proper walk today, have you?" Doona asked as she finished the washing-up. "Why don't you go and walk on the beach while I curl up with a book."

"You don't have to stay," Bessie told her.

"I don't want to leave your cottage empty, and I don't mind curling up in your sitting room with a book, anyway. Your cottage is much cleaner than my house."

Bessie laughed. "My cottage is much cleaner than it's ever been," she countered, "especially the kitchen."

Now that Doona had mentioned it, Bessie was suddenly eager to get out and take a walk on the sand. She put on some shoes and headed out the back door, leaving Doona happily looking through Bessie's shelves for something to read. The fresh sea air tasted just right as Bessie breathed in deeply.

It was dusk, and there were still several families spread across the sand behind the holiday cottages. As the tide was out, however, there was plenty of room for Bessie to stroll along the water's edge. She kept her eyes on the sea, ignoring the people around her. At Thie yn Traie, she stopped and stood at the foot of the stairs, looking back down the beach.

Dawn and her father were sitting together on the patio behind their cottage. From what Bessie could see, the cottage next to theirs, where Brandon and his friends were staying, was empty. Bessie strolled slowly back down the beach. Dawn called to her as Bessie walked behind their cottage.

"Miss Cubbon, Bessie? How are you?"

"Good evening," Bessie replied. "I'm well, thank you. How are you?"

Dawn got up from her chair and joined Bessie on the sand. "I've been better, but at least I'm not Constance. She's still talking to the police, or she was, the last I knew."

"I'm surprised she'd trying lying to the police about something so easily disproven," Bessie said. "There must be dozens of people who know when she met your husband."

"Yeah, but none of the rest of them are on the Isle of Man. She didn't know I was here when she first talked to the police. I suspect she might have managed to get away with it if I hadn't been."

"But once she learned that you were here, she must have realised her mistake."

"And she probably decided to just brazen it out," Dawn said. "Knowing her, she never considered going to the police and telling them she'd lied. She'd have rather been caught in the lie than actually admit to it."

"And now she has been."

"Indeed. And I have to admit I'm feeling smugly satisfied about that. Now maybe the police can find out what happened to Walter."

"What do you think happened?"

"He must have been caught up in something that was over his head," Dawn shrugged. "He was a good con artist, but he was terrible at choosing associates. Knowing him, he found out he was involved in something much bigger than he'd realised and he decided to run away. Hiding here probably sounded like a good idea, but he probably should have tried Canada or New Zealand or somewhere. The island is just too close to the UK. Whoever he was hiding from must have found him and eliminated him."

"But you don't know who that might have been?"

"I've told the police everything that I know," Dawn replied "I gave them a list of all of his former associates, the ones I knew about, anyway. I'm pretty sure none of them were involved, though. I think I would have heard about it if he were working with anyone I knew."

"It's scary to think that someone like that is on the island."

"They probably aren't still here. He or she would have come across, taken care of Walter, and then gone home and carried on as normal."

"I just hope the police catch him or her."

"If I were Constance, I'd be worried," Dawn added. "She has to know what Walter was mixed up in. It seems as if she could well be the next victim."

"Maybe the police should lock her up to protect her."

Dawn laughed. "I love the idea of her being locked up, whatever the reason," she said. "Maybe I'll ring that nice Inspector Rockwell and suggest that very thing."

"Dawn, I thought you weren't going to talk to the nosy neighbours anymore," Brandon's voice carried across the beach.

She looked up at the man who was walking towards them. "Just saying hello," she replied lightly. "Not that it's any of your business."

"I thought you'd be cleaning up your cottage all day today," Brandon said to Bessie, "but first we saw you in Douglas and now you're out having a stroll as if you haven't a care in the world."

"Some dear friends of mine did most of the cleaning for me after the police were finished going through the cottage," Bessie told him. "I dare say it's in better shape now than it was before the break-in."

"Really? Interesting," the man replied. He looked at his sister. "We brought back beer and snacks."

"Same as every night," Dawn sighed. "I think maybe I'm going to head to bed."

"Oh, come on. You need to come and have a drink or two with us," Brandon replied. "Horace bought more of that wine you like."

"The wine, I like. Horace, not so much," Dawn said. "Okay, one drink," she added quickly as Brandon gave her an angry look. "Good night," she said to Bessie. "I'm glad your cottage is okay."

"Thank you," Bessie replied. "Have a nice evening," she told the siblings.

Brandon gave her an icy stare and then turned and stalked up the beach with his sister right behind him. With a sigh, Bessie continued on her way back to Treoghe Bwaane.

Doona jumped up as Bessie walked back into the cottage. "I was starting to worry about you," she said. "I didn't think you'd walk for that long."

"I was talking to Dawn and Brandon."

"Oh, dear. What did they have to say?"

Bessie repeated the conversation as fully as she could. When she was finished, Doona frowned. "You need to ring John and tell him all of that."

"I should have done that in the first place," Bessie sighed. "You could have listened in on the conversation and I wouldn't have had to repeat myself."

"Thank you," John said when Bessie was finished recounting the conversation again.

"You're welcome. I don't imagine you'd like to return the favour by telling me what Constance said when she was interviewed today?" Bessie replied.

"I would if I could, but you know I can't repeat what I'm told in interviews. Let's just say it was an interesting conversation, but I'm not sure we're any closer to finding Walter's killer as a result."

"That's disappointing," Bessie sighed. "I was hoping you'd have the case wrapped up soon. I think I'll feel better when Brandon and his friends are off the island."

"We're still processing the evidence from your cottage, but at this point we haven't found anything that points to Brandon or anyone else involved in the murder investigation."

"I still think it was Brandon," Bessie said firmly.

"All I can tell you is that I'm looking at him very closely," John said. "Along with several other people."

"It's getting late. We can talk about all of this tomorrow night," Bessie suggested.

"Great. See you tomorrow."

Bessie put the phone down and turned to look at Doona. Part of her wanted to send her friend home so that they could both get some sleep, but part of her didn't want to be alone in the cottage. She opened her mouth to say something, she wasn't sure what, when someone knocked on the door.

Doona was on her feet and at the door before Bessie could even stand up.

"I assume you aren't expecting anyone," she said to Bessie.

"No, not at all."

"Maybe we should ring John back."

"It's probably another friend who wants to help with the cleaning," Bessie suggested. "Or someone who just wants to check on me. I'm sure it's fine."

She walked over to join Doona at the door. When she reached for the knob, Doona stopped her hand.

"Take a step back," she told Bessie, "and be ready to ring 999."

"Don't be silly. I'm sure it's fine," Bessie replied with more confidence than she actually felt.

The visitor knocked again. Doona sighed and then slowly opened the door. Bessie stared at the man on the doorstep. He looked to be in his late fifties or early sixties, with short grey hair and thick bifocals. He was wearing a pair of dark grey trousers with a lighter grey polo shirt and black leather loafers. As he smiled, Bessie noted that he wasn't much taller than her own five feet three.

"Ah, good evening," he said in a pleasant voice. "I'm sorry for visiting so late, but your lights were still on. I hope I'm not imposing."

"Not at all," Bessie replied, wondering who the man was and why he was calling on her at all.

"That's very kind of you," the man said. "I was told that if I wanted to know anything about Laxey or the island that I should visit Aunt Bessie at Treoghe Bwaane."

Bessie flushed at the unexpected compliment. "You did well with the Manx," she told her visitor. "I'm Elizabeth Cubbon. Everyone calls me Aunt Bessie."

The man gave her a small bow. "And I am Reverend William Doyle," he replied.

Bessie and Doona both gasped.

The man grinned at them. "I've been getting that reaction a lot over here," he said.

Bessie nodded. "That's hardly surprising," she said, "but please come in."

Doona shot Bessie a worried look, but Bessie ignored it. The man was a priest, after all, or so Bessie hoped.

"I can put the kettle on," she offered.

"Oh, no, I don't want to be any bother," the man said quickly. "I really just wanted a few minutes of your time."

"Certainly, have a seat," Bessie suggested, gesturing towards the kitchen table.

Reverend Doyle sat down and Bessie joined him at the table. Doona remained standing near the door. Bessie noticed that her friend had her mobile in her hand as she watched the guest closely.

"What can I help you with, then, Reverend Doyle?" Bessie asked.

"Do call me William," he replied. "You see, it came as something of a shock to me when the police turned up at my home to question me about the man who'd recently died on the island. I had no idea that he'd, well, let's say borrowed, my identity."

"I'm sure it must have been a huge shock," Bessie said.

"Yes, it was, actually. I've been more or less retired for a few years now. I suffered from some ill health and couldn't continue to carry out my duties at my last church, you see. I live very simply and quietly on my own. It suits me."

"I'm in a similar position," Bessie told him.

"Living alone is very peaceful," the man told her. "After the demands of running a vicarage for many years, well, I really enjoy the peace."

"I'm sure," Bessie murmured.

"As I said, I was completely unaware that my name, and indeed, my credentials, were being used elsewhere. It seems that Mr. Gray managed to get his hands on a copy of my CV, which he then copied and used as his own."

"Do you know how he managed that?" Bessie asked.

"The police asked me that as well. I suspect he may have been the person who advertised for a position for which I once applied. It would have been some years ago now, before I fell ill, but it wouldn't have been difficult for him to find out where I'd been since," William explained.

"So he started using your identity years ago?" Bessie wondered.

"I don't believe so, but he may have done," the man sighed. "I believe he simply kept the CV so that he had it ready when he decided to use it."

"That's a lot of advance planning," Bessie said.

"The police inspector with whom I spoke said that such advance planning would not have been out of character for the man. Apparently he was very good at hiding who he was and at building new identities slowly and carefully."

Bessie nodded. "So he had your CV and he used an updated copy of it to apply for the job here?"

"Yes. I've seen the CV he sent in to the bishop here. It's an exact copy of mine, with a few changes to bring it up to date. The bishop rang a few of my former parishes, as you would expect, but they all thought he was asking about me and gave me adequate references."

"I've been told that the man was very good at what he did," Bessie sighed. "It sounds as if he planned very carefully for his move over here."

"It's a lovely island, actually. I've never been before and the scenery is stunning. If my health were better, I'd be tempted to talk to the bishop about the position that's available."

Bessie nearly shuddered at the thought of the man taking Walter's place. It would be odd having Reverend Doyle replace the imposter. "Perhaps you should consider spending some time on the island as you recover," she suggested. "I'm sure the sea air would do you good."

"I'm staying with the bishop for a few days. He offered that when he rang to talk to me about what had happened here. I've only been here a few hours, actually, and I am already thinking that I'd like to stay longer. I'm not sure that I'll want to stay with the bishop for any length of time, however."

Bessie grinned. "There are hotels, bed and breakfasts, and holiday cottages all over the island. I'm sure, if you try, you'll be able to find somewhere to stay, even during the busy summer months.

"We shall see. Tomorrow I plan to do some sightseeing. I studied history at university and I understand you have many interesting historical sites."

"If I start talking about those, we'll need tea," Bessie laughed. "I'm an amateur historian with a deep love of the subject."

William glanced at the clock and shook his head. "I mustn't stay much longer. I've promised the bishop that I'll be back before ten."

"But you have some questions for me?" Bessie asked.

"As I said, I was told you know Laxey better than anyone. I suppose I'm simply curious as to how this Walter Gray performed as vicar. It's odd, but I feel as if his behaviour reflects on me in some way. I'm hoping you'll tell me that he was doing his job well before he died."

"I didn't have any complaints about him," Bessie replied. "Some parishioners felt that he went through the service too quickly, or that his sermons were too short, but neither of those things bothered me."

William chuckled. "I must say, no one has ever accused me of giving a sermon that was too short. I think I'd like to meet some of the parishioners in Laxey."

"Perhaps the bishop would let you officiate at a service while you're here," Bessie said. "If your health would permit."

"That's not a bad idea," the man said thoughtfully. "I'm sure he'd appreciate the help and I'm just about capable of handling a service or two over a weekend. It's the day-to-day demands of being a parish vicar that I'm not able to manage at the moment."

The pair chatted for a few more minutes about Laxey and the island. Doona remained at the door, watching the man closely. After a while, he glanced at the clock again.

"I really must go," he said. "I'm not sure that I asked you everything that I wanted to ask, but I feel better for having spoken to you. I truly appreciate you taking the time to talk with me."

"It was my pleasure," Bessie told him. "You know where to find me if you have more questions."

"Mostly, at this point, I'd like to know who killed Walter Gray. I'm only slightly worried that I might have been the intended target."

Bessie frowned. "I hadn't considered that," she said softly.

The man nodded and rose to his feet. "I really must go," he said, "but I may be back. Thank you again for your time."

Doona opened the door and then stood and watched as the man walked to his car. As it pulled away, Bessie noted that it had a sticker from a hire car firm on the back bumper.

"That was interesting," Doona said as she sat back down across from Bessie at the table.

"It was, wasn't it?" Bessie replied. It was getting late and she wanted to tell Doona to leave, but she wasn't sure she was ready to be alone in her cottage yet. As she opened her mouth to broach the subject, once again someone began knocking on the door.

CHAPTER 11

*D*oona frowned. "It's too late for visitors," she said.

"Clearly not," Bessie replied, as whoever it was knocked again.

"Maybe I should ring John," Doona said hesitantly, "or Hugh."

"For goodness sake, just open the door," Bessie snapped. While she was nervous about who might be on her doorstep, she really hated it when Doona fussed over her.

Doona shook her head and then walked over to the door. "You need a window in this door," she said.

"Yes, well, it's a bit late in the day for that now," Bessie replied. "Are you going to open the door, or am I?"

Bessie knew Doona didn't want to open the door, but she did so anyway.

"Andy? What brings you here this late at night?" Bessie asked as she recognised her visitor.

"The kitchen lights were still on, otherwise I wouldn't have knocked," he explained. "It's just, well, after we got home, Mum and I were talking, and we agreed that we weren't happy about you being here on your own. Not while the person who broke into the cottage hasn't been found, anyway. Mum wondered if you'd like to come and stay with us, but I didn't think you'd like that idea. I reckon I stayed here a lot when I was a teenager, so maybe you wouldn't mind if I stayed over again for a few nights."

"That's a very kind offer, but I'm perfectly fine on my own," Bessie said firmly. She wasn't sure she actually believed it, but she wasn't prepared to admit that to herself, let alone to anyone else.

"I was going to stay tonight," Doona told them both. "I just need to pop home and get my things. I was so focussed on getting the cottage clean that I forgot to bring them when I came earlier."

"You go home and don't worry about me," Bessie said, "and Andy, you can go home as well. I'm sure my intruder is long gone."

"Yeah, halfway down the beach," Doona muttered. "I'll go home and stay home if you let Andy stay."

Before Bessie could reply, Andy held up a hand. "Don't argue," he said sternly. "I'm not leaving. I brought a bag with everything I'll need for three or four days, and Mum has promised to come by and collect my laundry and bring me clean clothes if I want to stay longer."

"I appreciate the offer, but it really isn't necessary," Bessie said.

Andy crossed the room and sat down next to Bessie. He took one of her hands and held it tightly. "You were one of the most important people in my childhood," he said. "I'm not sure I would have made it through without your support. I'm sure you're perfectly safe in your cottage, but I don't think I'll be able to sleep at home for worrying about you. Please, just let me stay a few nights. As soon as the police arrest someone for the break-in, I'll go quietly."

Bessie sighed. "I'm sure you have better things to do."

"Oh, I brought all my things to do with me," he laughed. "I'm working on a few new recipes. I brought all of my ingredients. I was hoping you might help me taste-test some of my ideas."

"What sort of recipes?" Doona asked.

"Puddings, mostly, as that's my favourite thing to make," Andy told her. "I've been working on an American-style brownie for a few days now and I think I've just about got it where I want it, but I want to try adding chocolate chips or maybe topping them with caramel sauce. I want them to be just a tiny bit more decadent."

"If Bessie won't let you stay, you can come and stay at my house," Doona offered.

Bessie and Andy both laughed. "You'll have to come and visit tomorrow," Andy told her. "I plan on baking brownies all day tomorrow."

"If I let you stay," Bessie said.

"You can't throw him out," Doona told her. "He's going to make me brownies."

Bessie chuckled again. She knew she was being manipulated into letting the man stay, but it was hard to argue with fresh brownies, especially extra-decadent ones. "Okay, you can stay," she told the young man, "but you can't fuss over me."

"I have no intention of fussing over you," Andy retorted. "Fussing isn't my style."

Bessie looked at Doona. There was no way her friend could say the same. Doona fussed nearly all the time, or at least it felt that way to Bessie.

"I should get home, then," Doona said, ignoring the look. "I've the day off tomorrow. Would you like to do something?"

"I thought you were taking Thomas and Amy into Ramsey," Bessie reminded her.

"Oh, that's right. I am. Would you like to go to Ramsey?"

"Actually, I suppose I could," Bessie grinned.

"I'll collect you around half nine. I'm collecting the children at ten. We'll make a morning of it, if you'd like, and maybe have lunch there before we head back."

"That sounds good," Bessie replied.

"Bring the children in when you get back," Andy suggested. "I'm sure they'll be brutally honest if I have them taste the brownies. If I have the cottage to myself for a few hours, I should be able to bake several different batches."

"The children and I will all come in when I bring Bessie home," Doona said. "I can be brutally honest if I need to be in order to be allowed to try the brownies."

With everything agreed, Bessie let Doona out of the cottage. She watched as her friend drove away and then spent a minute staring out the door down the beach. It was almost impossible for her to believe that someone had broken into her cottage, even though she'd seen the mess they'd left behind with her own eyes.

The beach was empty and nearly all of the holiday cottages were dark. Bessie fancied that she could see a few lights on in Thie yn Traie, high above the beach, but the mansion was so far away that she was probably seeing street lights rather than anything there.

"I'll just bring in my things," Andy said behind Bessie.

She moved out of the way and the watched, stunned, as he unloaded several large bags from his car boot. "I thought you were only staying for a few days," she said weakly as he struggled back inside with the bags.

"I am, or I hope I am," he grinned. "This is my bag for me," he said, holding up a small backpack. "Everything else is work." He unzipped the largest bag and let Bessie look inside. It was packed full of cooking utensils, baking pans, and weighing scales.

"I have all of those things," Bessie said. "I'll admit mine probably aren't as nice as yours, but they all work."

Andy shook his head. "When I'm working on a recipe, I always use the same pans and scales and whatnot. Precision is important until I get the recipe exactly where I want it. Once it's just right, then I can relax a bit about everything."

"But surely the most important variable is the oven that you use," Bessie suggested. "My oven won't bake anything like the oven in your mother's house."

"But I can adjust for that easily," Andy assured her. "I'll start with a test batch or two of the recipe I already have. Once I've worked out the differences in the ovens, I'll be good to go."

A second bag was full of flour, sugar, and other ingredients. With Bessie's cupboards already full to bursting, Andy had little choice but to leave the bag largely packed. He put the perishable items into the rather full fridge and left the rest of the items in the bag.

"Are you sure you don't mind being here on your own tomorrow?" Bessie asked as he finished.

"I'd rather be alone, if I'm honest," Andy said. "I love Mum, but when she's underfoot, I can't get anything done. I'm afraid if you were here, I'd feel self-conscious about my baking. I learned everything I know about it from you, after all."

"I may have taught you the basics, but I'm sure you've learned a great deal since then." She yawned before she could continue. "Maybe it's time for bed," she said eventually.

"I'm ready when you are. When I'm home I tend to go to bed early. Mum likes early nights, especially when she's working, which she's doing one or twice a week at the moment."

"I don't know who the girl was who was behind the till the last time I was in the shop. She seemed nice enough, I suppose, but she didn't seem to like the job very much."

"It's a tough job, I reckon. Mum never complained, at least not to me, but I know she didn't much like it. She only does it now as a favour to the owner, even though I don't think she owes him any favours after the way he treated her."

"She probably likes getting out of the house," Bessie suggested, "and spending time with the regular customers."

"She does. It's a bit frustrating, because she doesn't have to work, but she simply can't relax and enjoy herself at home all day, every day."

"I've never had a problem doing that," Bessie laughed. She gave the man a hug. "Thank you for coming to stay with me," she told him. "I don't need you, but I am glad that you're here."

Andy followed Bessie up the stairs, carrying his backpack. "Do you still get up at six every morning?" he asked from the guest room doorway.

"I do. I'll try to be quiet."

"No need. I probably won't be far behind you."

Bessie got ready for bed as quickly as she could in the small bathroom. When she came out, she tapped on Andy's door. "Good night," she called.

"Good night, Aunt Bessie," he replied.

Bessie wasn't sure if it was Andy's presence in the house or just exhaustion after her stressful days of late, but she was asleep as soon as her head touched the pillow. When she woke up, she felt slightly disoriented, as if she'd overslept, but her clock showed that it was only one minute past six. She showered and dressed and then had a slice of toast with honey, all while trying to be as quiet as possible. When she let herself out of the cottage, she breathed a sigh of relief. Out on the beach she didn't have to worry about how much noise she made.

With that thought on her mind, she headed for the water's edge and then kicked off her shoes and splashed into the sea. The water felt ice-cold and surprised her feet. It wasn't long before she headed back up the beach to slip her shoes back on. She walked as far as Thie yn Traie and then continued for a short while longer. As the skies began to cloud over, she turned and headed for home.

"My goodness, I didn't even think you'd be up yet," Bessie exclaimed as she opened her cottage door and found Andy working at the cooker.

"I really am an early riser now," he replied, "and since I was up, I thought I would make breakfast."

Bessie had opened her mouth to tell him that she'd already had toast, when she spotted the pancakes he was expertly flipping. Maybe I can find room for a few pancakes in spite of my earlier snack, she thought as she shut the cottage door behind her.

Andy had a pile of pancakes with strips of bacon on a plate at the table for her before she'd crossed the room. "I brought maple syrup," he told her. "It's the best for on pancakes."

Bessie wasn't about to argue. She sometimes bought maple syrup herself, although she hadn't done so lately. While Andy cooked his own breakfast, Bessie poured the syrup onto her pancakes.

"Go ahead and start eating," Andy told her. "Pancakes are best when they are hot."

"These are delicious," Bessie said after her second bite. "They've come up much fluffier than mine ever do."

"I have a trick, but I'm not going to tell you what it is," Andy teased.

"I don't need to know. If I could make pancakes this good, I'd have them for breakfast every morning, and that would be bad for my health and my waistline."

"But it would make you happy," Andy suggested.

"I think I'll settle for being pancake-happy only once in a while," Bessie told him.

"Well, while I'm here, I'll probably make them every morning. I don't have time to make breakfast when I'm at culinary school. I eat a lot of cold cereal while I'm walking back and forth to class. Being able to make pancakes is a real treat for me."

"It's a treat for me as well, and I'll enjoy them while you're here, as long as you don't stay for more than a few days."

"Let me know when you want to me to stop," Andy replied.

Bessie insisted on doing the washing-up since Andy had cooked.

"I'm going to be dirtying dishes all day," he argued. "I can wash the breakfast dishes while I'm washing everything else later."

"This way you can start with a clean kitchen," Bessie told him. "That will be nicer for you."

Doona arrived at exactly half nine. Bessie was sitting on the rock behind the cottage when her friend drove up. She waved as Doona climbed out of her car.

"I hope this doesn't mean that Andy is getting on your nerves already," Doona said as a greeting.

"Not at all," Bessie assured her, "but he wanted to get started on his baking and I was in his way."

When Doona looked surprised, Bessie continued quickly.

"He didn't tell me that I was in the way, but I could tell that he wanted to be alone."

"I just can't wait to see what he comes up with," Doona said. "I dreamed about brownies all night last night."

Bessie laughed and then got down off the rock. "I just need to grab my bag, and I'll be ready to go."

"No rush. We aren't due to collect the children for nearly half an hour. They probably won't be ready when we get there, either."

Bessie nodded and then crossed back to the cottage. She let herself in the back door and headed up the stairs. After running a comb through her hair and adding a touch of lipstick to her lips, she went back down and stuck her head into the kitchen. The wonderful smell of warm chocolate filled her nose.

"Someone should bottle that smell and sell it to restaurants. I'm sure they'd sell many more puddings if that smell was always in the air."

Andy laughed. "You could be right," he said. "Maybe I'll try that for my restaurant."

"I'm going with Doona now. I should be back some time after one. I need to make dinner for my friends who are coming over tonight, so I will need to get into the kitchen at some point."

"Right," Andy nodded. "What are you planning to make for them?"

"I'm not sure. I might throw a chicken in the oven or make spaghetti Bolognese. We'll see how much energy I have when I get back from shopping all morning."

"I hope you have fun," Andy told her. "I'll be hard at work on the perfect brownies."

Bessie met Doona back on the beach. Doona had taken Bessie's spot on the rock.

"Is everything okay?" Bessie asked her friend when she joined her.

"My solicitor from across rang last night," Doona replied, still staring at the sea. "He's unearthed another life insurance policy on Charles that's payable to me. I should be getting a cheque for a fairly large six-figure sum in the next few weeks."

"My goodness," Bessie gasped, "but that's wonderful news, isn't it?"

Doona sighed. "Of course it's wonderful, but it's also strange and odd and, well, I don't know what to do with that much money. It's a life-changing amount, you know? I'm sure Doncan will have all sorts of excellent advice, but he's booked up until next week, so for now I'm just imagining selling up everything and moving to the south of France or some island in the Caribbean, or something equally crazy."

"Doncan always has excellent advice," Bessie agreed. The man had been her advocate for many years, following on from his father. His son, the third generation of advocates, was also turning out to be very good at the job, even if Bessie couldn't quite believe that he was even old enough to drive a car.

"I think I'm just feeling a bit overwhelmed," Doona told her. "The solicitor in the UK has been warning me all along that there might not be any more money, and that the legal fees will probably take nearly everything by the time it's all sorted with Charles's former partner, and then he dropped this on me yesterday with no warning."

When Doona's second husband had died, she'd been shocked to learn that she was still his heir even though they'd been separated for some time. She'd received a large lump sum right after his death, but the rest of the estate had been tangled up in legal proceedings ever since. Charles's business partner had been arrested for illegal business practices within days of Charles's death, and the police, the solicitors, and the courts were all still working to determine a fair settlement of the man's estate.

"Try not to think about it until after you've spoken to Doncan," Bessie suggested.

"I've been trying that, but it's hard. I can think of a million things I'd like to do with the money, all of them stupidly indulgent. Would you like to go to Disney World with me for a month or two?"

"Disney World? In Florida? I'm sorry, but I don't think that's my sort of holiday."

"It may not be mine, but I'm tempted to find out. Maybe I should take Thomas and Amy with me. They'd probably love it."

"They probably would, but you'd have to talk to John about that."

"Yeah, and I'd probably have to take John with us, and that would be, well, awkward," Doona sighed. "Never mind. Maybe I'll go on a cruise around the world or buy a totally unsuitable car or something. Let's go into Ramsey and see what I can buy."

"Are you sure you should be shopping right now?"

"I promise not to go crazy in Ramsey," Doona assured her. "I might buy a few more books than normal, or even buy myself the hardcover version of a new release rather than wait for the paperback to come out, but I won't be any more extravagant than that today."

"Let's go, then," Bessie said with a smile.

Thomas and Amy were standing in front of their father's house when Doona pulled up. They quickly jumped into the back of the car.

"You didn't have to wait outside," Doona told them.

"We were ready to go, and it's a nice day to be outside," Amy replied. "I was worried about rain, since we're planning to go to the park, but it's lovely."

"It is nice," Bessie agreed. "I hope it stays that way."

Doona dropped the children off at the large park in the centre of Ramsey. "You know how to get in touch with me if you need me," she reminded them. "We'll meet you at the café here at midday for lunch. Do you have money for crazy golf or the boats?"

"Yes, Dad gave us both money," Thomas assured her. "Thanks for bringing us."

Doona watched them from the car park until they were both inside the park gates. "I know they'll be fine, but I'm going to worry until we see them again at the café," she told Bessie as she put the car back into gear.

"Do you want to stay here instead of going shopping?"

"I don't want the children to think I don't trust them," Doona replied. "John gave them permission to spend the morning at the park on their own. He's their father, so the decision is his, really."

"He's also a police inspector. If he thinks it's safe, he's probably correct."

"Yes, I know. It's very odd, feeling responsible for them, really. It complicates things."

"Things with you and John?"

"Yeah, that," Doona sighed, "but I really don't want to talk about it."

Bessie bit her lip and tried to work out the best reply. "You know where I am if you ever do want to talk about it," she said eventually.

Doona nodded. "Let's go shopping," she said in an artificially bright voice.

The pair spent far too long at the town's large bookshop, browsing the shelves for favourite authors and new ones. Bessie ended up buying three books and Doona found five.

"See, that's my idea of extravagant," she told Bessie as they put their bags in the car's boot. "Five new books, and one of them is hardcover. I wonder what the solicitor would say if I told him I didn't want the money."

"I'm sure he'd be happy to take it off your hands," Bessie said dryly.

Doona laughed. "Yes, you're probably right about that," she said. "Never mind. I shouldn't even be talking about it. I really want to put it out of my mind until I can talk to Doncan. If I bring it up again, just tell me to be quiet."

The pair walked up and down the main shopping street, looking in shop windows and popping into a few shops that looked interesting. Having not found anything else to spend any money on, they headed back to Doona's car a little early.

"We may as well drive over to the park," Bessie said. "It's a bit of a walk to the café and it's the perfect day to go around the long way."

The café was situated along the small boating lake in the centre of the park. Bessie and Doona walked slowly from the car park around the lake, arriving at the café only a few minutes before twelve. Thomas and Amy were sitting on a bench near the door.

"I hope we aren't late," Doona exclaimed.

"We were early," Amy replied, "but I was hoping that I could have more time with my friends after lunch. A bunch of them are having a round of crazy golf at one. It should only take an hour."

"Do you have to be home at any particular time?" Doona asked Bessie.

"No, not at all. I don't mind spending an hour at the park after lunch," Bessie replied.

"Maybe I'll have a round myself," Thomas said. "Although I'm not sure I want to play alone. Doona, I challenge you to an epic crazy golf battle."

"Epic battle? I'm not sure I'm quite up for that, but I'll give it a try," Doona laughed.

"Bessie, you can join in as well," Thomas added.

"Thank you, but I think I'll miss it out and simply take another stroll around the lake," Bessie replied. "I've never been especially good at crazy golf."

The foursome enjoyed their lunch at the café. When they were finished, Doona smiled at the children. "Ice cream?"

"Oh, yes, please," Thomas said quickly. Amy's "Yes, please," followed a moment later.

"I won't," Bessie said, "because I know what will be waiting for me at home."

Doona stared at her for a minute and then grinned. "Dozens of brownies, that's right. Maybe I won't have ice cream either, then."

"Brownies?" Amy asked.

"I have a friend staying with me at the moment," Bessie explained. "He's training to be a chef and while he's staying at my cottage he's working on a recipe for brownies. He told me that he'll be baking several batches today to try different things."

"Yummy," Amy replied.

"You're both welcome to try some of the samples when we get back to my cottage," Bessie told them.

"Maybe we should skip ice cream too," Amy said. She looked at her brother. "Nah," they both said as they shook their heads in unison.

When the ice cream was eaten, Doona and the children headed for the crazy golf course. Bessie sat down on the nearest bench and let out a long sigh. She loved spending time with her friends, and John's children were incredibly well mannered, but after spending the morning with Andy, she was grateful for some time on her own. After a few minutes, though, she began to get restless. She was never one for simply sitting around.

Getting to her feet, she began a slow stroll around the lake. She waved to Doona and Thomas as she passed them. Amy was in the middle of a crowd of teenaged girls and didn't notice Bessie as she walked past. At the boat rental end of the lake, Bessie found another bench and sat down for a short while. She watched families and groups of teens renting paddle boats and taking them out for a trip around the lake. It looked like fun, but also like hard work. More than one father came back from the excursion dripping with sweat on the warm day.

There was another bench on the perimeter of the lake opposite the café. Bessie walked that far and then sat down and stretched out her legs. Very few people actually walked around the entire lake and for a moment she felt as if she had the entire park to herself. She could just see the crazy golf course, but the players were not much more than specks in the distance. Doona had promised to ring Bessie when they finished playing, so Bessie didn't have to worry how the games were going.

She was trying to decide if she wanted to walk further or simply wait there until Doona rang when she heard footsteps approaching her. When she looked around, she was surprised to see Constance Hamilton walking towards her.

"Ah, I should have known someone would already be on my favourite bench," the woman said as she reached Bessie. "I don't suppose you're planning to leave soon?"

Bessie was shocked by the woman's words, and perversely, they made her want to stay right where she was. "I'm enjoying the view," she said in the politest tone she could manage under the circumstances. "You're welcome to join me, though."

"I suppose that will have to do," Constance replied. "I don't want to go any further into the park. I'm trying to stay away from people."

"I'm sorry to hear that."

"Yeah, everyone is sorry, but no one really cares," Constance sighed. "I'd get off this damn rock if I could, but they won't let me leave."

Bessie didn't doubt that the police wanted to keep Constance on the island. She might have an unbreakable alibi for the murder, but after she'd lied to them about her relationship with the dead man, it was hardly surprising they didn't trust her.

"Yep, I'm stuck here," Constance continued, "even though all I want to do is go home."

"That's a shame," Bessie murmured, not sure what else to say. She wasn't certain if the woman recognised her from any of the previous times they'd met, but she wasn't about to remind Constance of them. Bessie was quite happy to play dumb if the occasion called for it. If Constance did remember Bessie from the church hall the night Walter had been murdered, she'd know that Bessie was fully aware of why she was stuck on the island.

"What about you? Do you live here by choice?" Constance demanded.

"Yes, I do, actually," Bessie replied. "I've lived on the island for all of my adult life."

"Really? And you haven't died of boredom yet? I mean, you may only be twenty-five and just look older because you've nothing to do all day but wait to die, but I'd guess you're closer to ninety than twenty."

Bessie gave the woman an icy stare. "My age is none of your business," she said after a moment, "and I don't find the island boring in the slightest. It has an incredibly rich history, fascinating museums, all the necessary shops, excellent restaurants..." She trailed off when Constance held up a hand.

"Okay, I get it. You love it here. But then you've probably never lived anywhere else."

"Actually, I grew up in Ohio in the United States," Bessie told her.

"You grew up in the US and you're happy here? I'd love to go and live in the US. My last partner and I were talking about doing that, you know. He was going to find us a way to move there before, well, before."

"Before?" Bessie echoed.

"Before his wife murdered him," Constance replied.

CHAPTER 12

"Is wife murdered him?" Bessie gasped.

Constance looked around and then leaned closer to Bessie. "The police haven't quite worked it out yet, but yeah, his wife killed him. I'm sure of it."

"That's a very serious allegation."

Constance shrugged. "I can't prove it, if that's what you mean. She was very clever about it. She's here with her family and some friends as well. I'm sure they'll all give her an alibi so the police will never be able to charge her."

"Surely her friends wouldn't cover up a murder," Bessie suggested.

"That brother of hers would, for sure. I used to be very good friends with Brandon. He's a nasty piece of work, that guy."

Bessie nodded. She certainly agreed with Constance's opinion of the man. "Maybe he killed Walter, then."

"Maybe. It was one of them: his wife, her brother, their father, one of them. And now they're all covering up for one another, and I'm stuck here while the police waste their time looking into Walter's past indiscretions."

"Indiscretions?"

"Walter was, well, he didn't always follow the rules. I'm sure he made a few enemies over the years, too, but don't we all? No one was angry enough to kill him, except his wife and her family, though."

"Why were they angry with him?"

"He left Dawn, didn't he? And he ran away with me, even though Brandon thought we had some sort of a relationship. They couldn't stand the thought of me and Walter living happily together."

"But he wasn't who he claimed to be," Bessie pointed out. "How long was he planning to stay on the island?"

"We were happy here. Walter was going to start introducing me to people and letting people know that I was more than just the housekeeper. He was hoping to quietly get a divorce so that we could get married and simply stay here forever."

Bessie wasn't sure she believed the woman, and even if that's what Walter had been telling her, she didn't think those were actually the man's plans. Was it possible that Constance had learned the truth and been angry enough to kill Walter? Maybe she'd deliberately established her alibi while an accomplice was off murdering the man.

"You haven't had a chance to meet many people on the island, then?" Bessie asked.

"No, not really, and now I'm not interested in doing so. Without Walter, I don't really want to be here. I'd have left already if the police would have allowed it."

"You had some friends visiting from across the night that Walter died?"

"Yeah, I only told a few people where we were going when we left the UK, but one of them was already planning a week's holiday over here. She managed to persuade a handful of others to join her, some I knew, and some I didn't. Obviously, none of them knew that Walter was living here under a different name. That's one of the reasons why he didn't come to Douglas with me that night. We couldn't afford to see any of his Laxey parishioners, could we?"

"That would have been awkward," Bessie agreed. "Your friends knew that Walter was here, though?"

"None of them knew Walter, just that I'd moved here with a man. Anyway, I told them that we'd had a huge fight and he'd moved back across. I told them that I'd found a job as a housekeeper for the vicar in Laxey. They weren't really interested in what I was doing, anyway. People would always rather talk about themselves."

Including you, Bessie thought but didn't say. "Of course, Walter's wife didn't know he was here, either, did she?" she wondered.

"She did," Constance replied. "I, well, I may have said something to Brandon about our plans, you see. We were, well, very good friends for a time, and when Walter and I decided to go away, I, well, I mentioned to Brandon that we were leaving. Brandon and I stayed in touch. He was actually going to meet me in Douglas that night, but there was some sort of problem with their accommodations and he never managed to get away."

"Or that's what he's telling you," Bessie remarked thoughtfully.

"Oh, I believe him. He's never been able to lie to me," she said smugly. "He told me all about having to fill time while they waited for their cottage to be ready and then getting drunk with his mates. The only thing he's evasive about is where his sister was while all of this was going on."

"What about his father?"

"Lucas? He's okay. I'm sure he was angry that Walter left Dawn, but as long as Dawn wasn't planning to go back to him, I don't think Lucas would have cared. He hated Walter, but all he was concerned with was keeping Dawn away from him."

"Do you know either of Brandon's friends?" Bessie decided to simply pepper the woman with questions. So far Constance hadn't objected, even as Bessie had grown increasingly direct.

"Horace and Mike? They're both dumb as rocks, really. Horace and I were friendly for a while, but it never went anywhere. Mike bought me dinner a few times, but I was never actually interested in him. I'm sure they're both chasing after Dawn now that she's a widow. Horace has been pining for her for years, actually."

"Can you imagine either of them as the murderer?"

Constance stared at her for a minute and then laughed. "What a question," she exclaimed. "No, I can't imagine either of them as the killer. Neither of them hated Walter. While Horace would love to get together with Dawn, there's no way he'd actually kill anyone to accomplish that. He and Mike simply aren't the type."

"But Dawn and Brandon are?"

"Dawn is a vicious, nasty woman who was scorned, and her brother is cruel and brutish. I can see either of them killing Walter if they accidently came across him, and anyway, they knew he was here."

"Brandon did, anyway."

"Oh, he shares everything with his sister, or he would have told his father and Lucas would have told Dawn. Either way, I'm sure Dawn knew and planned the whole thing. She's..."

Constance stopped talking when Bessie's mobile began to ring. Bessie frowned as she answered the call.

"We're ready when you are," Doona said brightly.

"I'll meet you at the café in a short while," Bessie replied tightly.

"Is everything okay?"

"It's fine." Bessie ended the call and dropped the phone back in her bag. "You were saying?" she said to Constance.

"Probably too much," the woman replied. "I should be going, really."

Before Bessie could react, Constance got to her feet and walked rapidly away. Bessie sighed deeply and then stood up and headed back towards the café. She'd learned a great deal more than she'd expected to learn, but she was still frustrated that Doona had interrupted the conversation.

"Is everything okay?" Doona asked again as Bessie joined her and the children on the bench in front of the café.

"I was talking with Constance Hamilton," Bessie replied. "She had some interesting things to say."

"And I interrupted," Doona sighed. "I'm sorry."

"You didn't know. She got up and left right after you rang me, so she probably wasn't going to say anything more, anyway."

Doona frowned. "I am sorry, though."

"It's fine. Let's get home and see if there are any brownies ready."

"Yay!" Amy shouted.

Thomas grinned. "I get Doona's share, because I beat her at crazy golf."

"That doesn't seem quite fair," Bessie said.

"That was the bet we made, though," Doona told her. She winked at Bessie. "Maybe you can distract him long enough that I'll be able to at least sneak a few crumbs or something."

As they drove back to Laxey, Bessie got a hole-by-hole rundown the entire golf game between Thomas and Doona. By the time Doona had parked at Bessie's cottage, Bessie felt as if her head were spinning.

"How was your game?" she asked Amy as they all climbed out of the car.

"We didn't bother to keep score," Amy replied with a shrug. "We were just having fun."

Bessie grinned. She was sure that all three of the trio had had fun, but it seemed as if Doona had enjoyed herself the most. As she pushed open her cottage's door, she breathed in warm chocolate and something else. The kids were already exclaiming happily about the smells as they all walked inside.

Andy was standing at the cooker, stirring something on top of it. "You're back just in time," he told them. "There are three trays of brownies coming out in the next two minutes and I want everyone to try them all and tell me what you think."

"That doesn't look like brownies," Bessie said, pointing at the pot on the cooker.

"It isn't. This is my secret recipe spaghetti sauce," Andy replied. "I created it while I was at school. It's fairly quick and easy, but the longer it simmers the better it tastes. You weren't sure what you wanted to do for dinner tonight, so I thought I'd mix this up while I was waiting for the batches to bake. If you don't want it for tonight, it will freeze nicely."

Bessie crossed to his side and looked into the pot. The sauce was a deep, rich red flexed with fresh herbs. It smelled gorgeous.

"Here, try it," Andy urged. He pulled a spoon out of the drawer and scooped up a bit of sauce for Bessie.

"I want the recipe," Bessie said after a taste, "or you can just come and make it for me every week. It's incredible. It tastes really fresh, with just a hint of garlic and herbs."

"I'm glad you like it," Andy grinned. "There should be enough here for you to freeze some, even if you have it tonight for dinner. And I will share the recipe with you, but you must promise not to pass it on. It's going to be a staple in my restaurant when I open it, and I don't want everyone on the island duplicating it at home."

"In that case, don't give me the recipe," Bessie replied. "I'll just enjoy it when I can get it. The question is, do I share it with my friends tonight, or do I keep it all for myself?"

"I hope you decide to share," Doona said, "because it truly does smell delicious."

A buzzer saved Bessie from having to make an immediate decision. Andy began to pull trays full of brownies out of the oven. The scents of warm chocolate and vanilla replaced the smells of tomato and garlic in Bessie's nose.

"Everyone sit down," Andy instructed them. "The trays need to cool for a minute or two before I can try to cut the brownies."

"When you make brownies from a packet, they tell you to cool them completely before you cut them," Amy said.

"Yeah, and who does that?" Andy laughed. "I love my brownies hot, or at least warm, and I don't mind if they come out in a crumbled mess instead of a neat square."

"Me, too," Bessie and Doona both said at the same time.

A few minutes later Andy set plates in front of everyone. Bessie was relieved to see that Andy had given them fairly small portions of each type.

"The one on the left of the plate is a classic chocolate brownie with chocolate chips," he told them. "It took a long time to work out the ratio of chips to batter, but I think it's about right now. The idea is to give you one or two chips in each bite, but no more. I don't want the chips to overpower the brownie, but I do want you to get a soft, melting chip in every bite."

"This is the best brownie I've ever had," Thomas said after his first bite.

"It's wonderful," Amy told Andy.

"It's very good," Bessie said. "The texture is excellent. Brownies often dry out, but these haven't at all. And I did get one or two chips in every bite."

"I think I got three in a one of my bites," Doona said, flushing, "but I was taking rather large bites."

"Let's move on, then," Andy said. "The brownie in the centre is the same chocolate brownie, but without the chips and with a generous drizzle of caramel sauce baked inside."

"I liked the first one better," Amy said as she scraped up the last of the second brownie.

"Me, too," Thomas said.

"I preferred the caramel one," Bessie told Andy.

Everyone looked at Doona. "I just loved them both," she said with a shrug. "I couldn't possibly choose between them."

"The last brownie is a blonde brownie," Andy told them. "It's a vanilla batter with chocolate chips in it."

"It's almost like a chocolate chip cookie," Bessie said after her first bite, "a very tasty chocolate chip cookie."

"I love it," Amy said, "but I still liked the first one best."

"I like it, but the first was my favourite," Thomas added.

Bessie looked at Doona, who shook her head. "It's wonderful and I love it, but I loved them all," she said.

Andy laughed. "Let's hope I only ever get customers like you at the restaurant when I open it," he said.

"You'll definitely get me," Doona replied.

Bessie got up to let Doona and the children out so that Doona could take Thomas and Amy home. Andy packed up a large box of brownies for them to take with them.

"Some of them won't be as good as the ones you tried," he said as he piled the treats high. "They were all test batches, so some have more or fewer chocolate chips or too much caramel sauce. I hope you don't mind."

"We don't mind," Amy said emphatically as she took the box from Andy.

Bessie shut the door behind the trio and then sighed. "I'm not going to want any dinner after all those brownies," she said. "It was worth it, though."

"What time are your friends coming over?" Andy asked.

"Around six."

"You have a few hours to get hungry again, then," Andy pointed out. "If you don't mind, I'm going to pop home while they're here. I'm going to put a lot of this stuff through Mum's dishwasher, for one thing."

"I can help with the washing-up," Bessie offered.

"I'd rather let the dishwasher do it," Andy replied. "It gets everything spotlessly clean. Anyway, the dishwasher needs to be run occasionally to keep everything working properly, and Mum never uses it. I thought it would be a big help for her, but she won't even touch it."

Bessie helped Andy pack all of his bowls, pans, and utensils into a large box. "I'll just wait for your friends to get here and then I'll go," he told her.

"You can go now," Bessie replied. "I'll be perfectly fine. It's the middle of the day. No one is going to bother me."

Andy shook his head. "I'll wait. I don't want you here alone unnecessarily."

Bessie opened her mouth to argue further, but someone knocked on her door.

"Hugh? You're very early," she said, smiling at the young man on her doorstep.

"I had an odd shift at work today, so I finished early. I thought maybe I could just come here and wait for the others rather than going home. Grace is spending the day with her mother, shopping for baby things, so the flat would be empty if I went home."

"You know you're always more than welcome here," Bessie said, stepping back to let the man into the cottage.

"Doona did tell me that you had brownies too," Hugh admitted sheepishly.

Bessie and Andy both laughed, and then Andy cut Hugh a piece of each of the three types.

"Not too much before dinner," Bessie chided as Andy worked.

When he'd finished serving Hugh, he smiled at Bessie. "As long as you aren't going to be alone, I'll pop home now. I should be back before your friends leave for the night."

"I'll wait for you," Hugh said around a mouthful of brownie.

"Excellent. You can tell me what you thought of the brownies when I get back," Andy said to Hugh.

"I will," Hugh promised.

"You and your friends are welcome to eat them all," he told Bessie. "After baking and tasting all day, I don't think I'll want brownies again for months, if not years."

Bessie laughed. "You'll change your mind," she said, "but maybe not for a week or two."

After she let Andy out, Bessie sat down next to Hugh. "Is everything okay?" she asked the man.

"Everything is wonderful," Hugh replied. "Grace is doing great with the baby. I can't even imagine how it feels, but she's taking it all in her stride and just carrying on is if she weren't actually growing a whole tiny person inside of her."

"I'm glad to hear that."

"And we should be able to start moving into the house soon too. It's taken a while, but I think everything is finally ready. We had the carpets taken out and replaced and had everything painted as well. Grace's parents insisted on paying for it all as a housewarming gift. They aren't all that happy about our buying a house that someone was murdered in."

"But you're getting it for a wonderful price," Bessie reminded him. "It's a much larger house than you could afford otherwise and in an amazing location."

Hugh nodded. "I never imagined that we'd be able to afford a property on the beach, right down from your cottage. And as we've been living in flats, we don't even mind that the neighbours are quite close by."

"I'm really pleased that everything is working out for you and Grace," Bessie said, "and I'm terribly excited about the baby."

"We are, too, most of the time. Everyone once in a while, I feel terrified instead, but I'm told that's perfectly normal."

"I'm sure it is. But now I should start thinking about dinner, I suppose."

"Those brownies were wonderful," Hugh said, pushing his empty plate away. "I liked them all."

"Andy will want to know exactly what you liked and didn't like," Bessie told him. "He's trying out new recipes for the restaurant he wants to open one day."

"Are we having spaghetti for dinner? I could smell the sauce as soon as I walked in. It smells really good."

"Andy made it, so it's wonderful. Yes, we'll have spaghetti. I know I have everything I need for a salad and I think I can make some garlic bread as well."

"What can I do to help?" Hugh asked.

Bessie gave him a few little jobs as she pottered around the kitchen, getting everything ready for her friends. The water for the pasta had just come to a boil when someone knocked on the front door. Hugh let John and Doona in while Bessie added dried pasta to the water. When they were all sitting together, enjoying their meal, Bessie told them about her conversation with Constance.

"So she thinks that Dawn killed Walter," Bessie concluded.

"I think it's interesting that she claims she told Brandon that she and Walter were here," John said. "That's not what she told me in her interview, and Brandon denied having any knowledge of where Walter was when I spoke to him, as well."

"He was hardly going to tell you that he knew that Walter was here, though," Bessie retorted. "He'd have to know that that would make him a suspect."

"He's a suspect anyway," John replied. "It's more a question of whether the murder was premeditated or spontaneous. I'm going to have to speak to both him and Dawn again."

"Let's talk about the suspects, then," Hugh suggested. "Is Dawn at the top of the list?"

"She's on the list, but maybe not at the top," John replied.

"She didn't seem angry to me," Bessie said. "She was crying over Walter when I first met her. I simply can't see her killing him."

"Killers do cry over their victims," John said softly, "but in this case, I'm inclined to agree with you. I'm more interested in whether she knew he was here or not and whether she planned to see him while she was on the island."

"She can deny it, and you'll struggle to prove otherwise," Doona pointed out. "Constance hasn't exactly been an honest and trustworthy witness thus far, either. If I had to believe one or the other, I think I'd believe Dawn."

"We know Dawn had the means and opportunity, even if her family is providing a loose alibi for her," Hugh said.

"I still think it was Brandon," Bessie said firmly. "I didn't like him when I met him and I still believe he was behind the break-in here."

"We haven't found any usable fingerprints from the cottage," John told her, "but we'll talk about the break-in after we finish with the murder."

Bessie nodded and then got to her feet. She and Hugh cleared away the dinner dishes before Bessie brought the three trays of brownies to the table. "Everyone can choose a favourite or try them all," she said as she put them down.

"They all look wonderful," John said.

"Doona, Hugh, and I have all tried all of them," she admitted. "Maybe you should start with a small piece of each and then go from there."

Once everyone had pudding in front of them, John brought the conversation back to the murder. "Brandon is certainly a possibility," he said, "as is Lucas."

"I don't really feel as if I've met him," Bessie said. "He doesn't talk much, but he watches everything."

"That was my impression as well," John told her. "I'm convinced that he knows something, but I'm sure he won't share it until he feels the time is right."

"If ever," Hugh muttered.

"What about the two friends?" Doona asked.

"They both had means and opportunity, if we discount the alibis provided by the others in their party, which I'm inclined to do," John replied. "I'm not aware of any solid motive for either of them, though."

"Horace is in love with Dawn," Doona said. "That's enough motive for some people."

"I'm not sure Horace feels that strongly about her," John replied. "I can't see Dawn getting involved with him in any case. I suspect he knows she isn't interested, and I can't imagine he thought that he might win her heart by killing her husband."

"What about Constance?" Bessie asked. "I know she has an alibi, but could she have hired someone else to do it, or something like that? What have you found out about her friends from across?"

"At this point I've nothing to connect them to the murder," John replied. "I've spoken to them all and they all tell the same story. One of the women planned the trip initially and invited the others to join her. The original plans were made before Walter and Constance moved to the island. They came as foot passengers on the ferry and none of them had access to a car, aside from Constance."

"Maybe she killed him and the camera footage was faked somehow," Doona suggested.

"It's been gone over very carefully," John told her. "There's a gap of about eleven minutes where Constance can't be seen, but that isn't enough time to get to Laxey and back, let alone kill anyone along the way. There are other gaps without her, but they are even shorter than that."

"Isn't it odd that she managed to be on camera all the time?" Bessie asked. "Are you sure it's the same woman who came back after the gap?"

"I'm not, but our video expert is," John replied. "It never looks as if she's trying to stay on camera or is even aware that the camera is there. When we questioned her, she was surprised to hear that we had her on videotape."

"Pleasantly surprised, no doubt," Bessie said, "otherwise she'd be the main suspect."

"Her friends are in and out of the video a bit more frequently than she is, but none were gone long enough to have gone to Laxey and back," John added. "If she did hire someone, it wasn't one of her friends."

"Maybe she arranged it with Brandon," Hugh suggested. "She told him where to find Walter and then got herself out of the way while he did the dirty work."

"That sounds possible," Bessie said. "She said they'd been very close. I'm not clear on why she rang him to tell him where she was, actually. Maybe she and Walter were having problems and she wanted to get back with Brandon."

"All possibilities," John sighed, "but there are others as well."

"Are there?" Bessie asked.

"Tomorrow's paper is going to have an interview with a man called Herbert Dunkin," John told her. "He was cheated out of several thousands of pounds by Walter Gray about ten years ago."

"He's on the island?" Doona wondered.

"He is. He and his wife moved here to get away from everything that had happened to them in the UK. They live in Peel," John replied.

"If he wanted to get away from it all, why did he give an interview to the local paper?" Hugh asked.

"Dan Ross tracked him down and threatened to write his own version of events unless Mr. Dunkin cooperated," John said. "Oh, not in so many words, but that's basically what he did," he added before Bessie could react.

"The poor man," Bessie said.

"Is he still angry about what happened?" Doona asked.

"As I understand it, he said something in the interview along the lines of, 'If that man weren't dead, I'd kill him myself,' or something similar," John said.

"I don't suppose he has an alibi?" Bessie wondered.

"He was with his wife at home in Peel. They've alibied each other, which means very little. His wife is also quite bitter, actually, but she has mobility issues that make it very unlikely that she was involved," John told them.

"What you need to know is whether or not they knew Walter was here," Bessie said.

"They say they didn't, but they would, of course," John agreed. "From what I've been told about the pair, they rarely leave Peel, but that doesn't prove anything. Walter might have been in Peel for some reason, or they could have crossed paths in Douglas, or anywhere, really. It's a very small island when you get down to it."

"Is he the only other suspect?" Bessie asked.

"I have a constable working his way through the lists of people we know were victimized by Walter," John told her. "I'm not sure how Dan Ross got onto Mr. Dunkin so quickly, but I suppose I should be grateful that he saved us having to track the man down."

"Of course, Walter may have had a number of victims that the police know nothing about, and any of them could be living on the island," Bessie said.

"And we can't investigate every single person on the island to see if we can find a connection between them and Walter," Hugh said.

"So where does that leave us?" Doona asked.

"I still think Brandon was the killer," Bessie said. "His family and friends will cover for him, of course."

"I think we should take a closer look at Constance," Hugh said. "She lied to the police from the start. Anyway, I find unbreakable alibis very suspicious."

Doona nodded. "That bothers me as well. It's almost like she knew she'd need an alibi, which means she must have been involved in some way."

"Then she talked Brandon into killing him," Bessie said. "I can see that happening, actually. It may even be more likely than him killing Walter simply because Walter treated his sister badly."

"They do seem very close, Brandon and Dawn," Doona mused. "Having said that, maybe his father suggested it to Brandon. Lucas seems to have a lot of influence on both of his children."

"So maybe Lucas told Brandon to kill Walter," Bessie sighed. "At the end of the day, I still think Brandon was holding the knife."

"Maybe Mr. Dunkin found out that Walter was here and hired Brandon to kill him," Doona suggested.

"We've found nothing to connect Mr. Dunkin with Brandon or anyone else in the family," John told her.

"Maybe he hired someone, then," Doona replied.

"From what we've been able to determine, money is quite tight for the Dunkins. They still haven't recovered financially from what Walter did to them," John said.

"So he killed Walter himself," Doona suggested.

"Maybe," John replied.

"No one is suggesting Horace or Mike as possibilities," Bessie pointed out. "I'm crossing them off my list."

"They're still on mine," John told her, "but near the bottom. Let's just say there seem to be others who are more likely suspects."

"If Brandon did do it, they're probably covering up for him," Hugh pointed out.

"What about the break-in?" Bessie changed the subject.

"I said we'd talk about it later, but there really isn't anything to discuss," John told her. "We're still processing evidence, but we haven't found any fingerprints that can help. Whoever it was may have worn gloves or they may just have been lucky."

"I hope their luck is going to run out soon," Bessie muttered.

"We're doing everything we can," John assured her. "I have extra men working on the case on the grounds that it may be connected to Walter's murder in some way."

"I hope it is. I'd hate to think that someone broke in here at random," Bessie sighed, looking around her snug kitchen.

"We're pretty sure it wasn't random," John replied.

A knock on the door a few minutes later interrupted a second round of brownie-eating and nothing useful in terms of the conversation. Hugh let Andy in and then he and John shared their thoughts on the different brownies. Bessie was yawning by the time they finished.

"We should all go and let you get some sleep," Doona exclaimed. "You've had a rough couple of days."

Bessie didn't argue. While she was saying goodbye to her friends, Andy tidied the kitchen. They were both in bed only a few minutes later and Bessie was asleep as soon as she closed her eyes.

CHAPTER 13

Knowing that Andy would be making breakfast, Bessie didn't bother eating anything before her walk. She wouldn't feel as guilty about pancakes with maple syrup that way. A small child, maybe two or three years old, was running around the beach and shouting as Bessie let herself out of her cottage. A woman in her thirties, presumably the child's mother, was sitting on a blanket watching the child run. Bessie gave her a sympathetic smile as she walked past.

"I hope you couldn't hear him from your house," the woman said.

"No, not at all," Bessie replied. She was pretty sure the folks in the holiday cottages weren't as lucky, but she didn't mention that to the exhausted-looking woman.

"His father gave him too much sugar yesterday and now he won't sleep," the woman continued. "I keep telling him that we can't treat little Montgomery any differently while we are on holiday, but he doesn't listen to me."

"Maybe he should be the one sitting out here, then," Bessie suggested.

The woman grinned. "He's cleaning up the cottage. Monty was

sick everywhere from tummy ache. I'd much rather be out here, thank you."

Bessie nearly laughed out loud as she continued on her way. It was impossible for her to imagine what life would have been like a parent, but once again she felt as if she hadn't missed out on much.

She walked to Thie yn Traie, and then continued on. It was only the thought of Andy's pancakes that made her turn around before she got to the new houses. As she walked past Thie yn Traie again, she heard someone calling her name.

"Good morning, Elizabeth," Bessie called back to the young girl who was making her way down the stairs behind the mansion on the cliff top.

"Good morning," Elizabeth shouted back. She jumped down the last couple of steps and gave Bessie a quick hug.

"You're up early," Bessie said.

"I have lots to do," Elizabeth replied excitedly. "I'm planning lots of parties for all kinds of people, a wedding, and a holiday to Florida for one of my mother's friends."

"I'm glad to hear things are going so well," Bessie said. "Will you still have time to plan Grace's baby shower?"

"That's why I wanted to catch you. I've been working on the plans and I'm getting really excited. Mum has lots of great ideas as well. She's hoping the two of you can get together soon to discuss everything."

"I'm always happy to spend time with your mother. I'll ring her later, shall I?"

"That would be great, I'm sure she'd appreciate it. The thing is, I was just wondering, well, have you found out anything more about the murder or the break-in at your cottage?"

Bessie shook her head. "The police are still investigating both cases. I talked to John last night, but he wasn't able to tell me anything more than that."

Elizabeth sighed. "Mum is more worried about the break-in than the murder. She's worried that someone might try and break into Thie yn Traie while I'm here on my own."

"I don't think she has anything to worry about. Don't you have security, anyway?"

"We do, but you know what my mother is like."

"I'll see if I can set her mind at rest when I talk to her later today," Bessie said.

"That would be terrific, thank you."

"Was there anything else?" Bessie asked, sensing that the girl had something on her mind.

"No, not really," Elizabeth said. "It's just, well, I mean, someone said that Andy Caine is staying at your cottage at the moment."

"He is," Bessie agreed. " He's worried about me and doesn't want me staying on my own, at least not until the person or persons behind the break-in are found."

"That's very kind of him," Elizabeth said. She looked down at the sand and then gave Bessie a shy smile. "Do you know if he has a girlfriend?"

Bessie did her best to hide her surprise. "I believe he and the girl he was seeing at school are no longer together," Bessie replied. "You're welcome to come back to the cottage for breakfast, if you want to ask him yourself."

"Oh, goodness, no," Elizabeth said, looking flustered. "I mean, we do need to talk about the baby shower, but I wouldn't want to impose on your breakfast."

"It's no imposition," Bessie assured the girl. "I'm sure Andy can make extra pancakes without any difficulty."

"Pancakes? I didn't actually have any breakfast. I wouldn't mind some pancakes."

Bessie grinned. "Come on, then," she said. "Let's go see if Andy has breakfast ready yet or not."

When Bessie opened the cottage door, she was greeted by the scent of warm chocolate yet again. "I thought we were having pancakes for breakfast," she said to Andy, who was once again standing at the cooker.

"I had a lot of leftover chocolate chips after yesterday, so I thought I would throw some into the pancake batter for a treat," he explained.

"I hope you don't mind that I brought home a friend," Bessie said.

Elizabeth had been standing behind Bessie; now she gave Andy a small wave. He flushed and quickly turned back to his cooking. "Of course not," he said. "I've more than enough for three."

Bessie invited Elizabeth to sit down and then poured the girl a cup of coffee from the pot that Andy had made. She made herself a cup of tea and then sat down next to Elizabeth as Andy handed them each a plate piled high with chocolate chip pancakes.

"There's maple syrup," he told Elizabeth.

"Yum," she replied before blushing and looking down at the table.

Bessie found the entire situation amusing. She never would have expected to see worldly and sophisticated Elizabeth Quayle blushing over pancakes in her cottage. Andy seemed quietly confident as he filled his own plate. He sat down opposite Elizabeth.

"I should thank you again for sending so much business my way," he said to Elizabeth after everyone had taken a few bites. "I'm almost too busy now, really."

"Should I stop referring clients to you?" Elizabeth asked. "You've been ever so good about meeting everyone's needs, even on short notice. I'm not sure who else I could find who would be as flexible and produce such excellent results."

Andy flushed. "Thank you," he said. "I'm on the island for another month. I suppose I could handle a few more orders before I go back. And I can make a list for you of some of the island's best bakers. I'm certainly not the only one here who can get you what you need."

Elizabeth nodded. "And that's a good thing, since you're leaving soon."

"I'll only be gone for six months to finish the course," he told her. "Then I should be home for good. I certainly don't plan on leaving again, at least not for a good while. I may do some short courses elsewhere to learn new techniques or styles, but nothing like the eighteen months of culinary college."

"You're going to open your own restaurant once you're back, aren't you?" Bessie asked.

"That's the plan," Andy told her. "Mum thinks I'm crazy, because restaurants are very hard work, and I don't really need the money. I can't imagine what else I'd do with my time if I don't start a restaurant, though."

"You could do catering," Elizabeth suggested. "I could probably keep you busy doing birthday parties and weddings most weekends. I was worried about starting a party planning service. I didn't know if there would be any actual demand for my services, but I'm already almost too busy as well. I never imagined so many people wanted help planning their events."

"Maybe you could do catering and also open a bakery or something like that," Bessie said. "That might be less work than an actual restaurant, and I'm sure you'd enjoy doing all of that baking."

"I truly would," Andy nodded. "I've promised myself that I won't make any decisions until I finish school. One of our classes next semester is all about starting a business, actually. I'm fortunate that I don't have to worry about writing a business plan or finding investors and all of that, but we're meant to be spending some time talking through all of the different options and their relative likelihood of success."

"I'm sure you'll be successful, whatever you decide to do," Bessie said.

"And Doncan is already on board to make sure I don't spend too much on the business and end up broke," he laughed.

The trio ate their pancakes and chatted about the weather and nothing much until Elizabeth glanced up at the clock. "My goodness, I must dash," she said. "I didn't realise it was that late."

Bessie walked her to the door. "I'll ring your mother later," she told the girl.

"Excellent." Elizabeth looked at Andy. "I may have to ring you later to talk about a wedding cake. Should I ring Bessie's or use your mobile?"

"Oh, use the mobile," Andy told her. "I would never answer Bessie's phone."

As Bessie shut the door behind the girl, she remembered that Elizabeth had wanted to talk about Grace's shower. It was too late now, but the more she thought about it, the more convinced Bessie was that the shower had only been an excuse to spend some time at Bessie's cottage. Bessie suspected that Andy was the real draw, whatever Elizabeth said.

When Bessie rang Mary Quayle a short while later, Mary was quick to invite Bessie to lunch. "Let's go to Lonan and see how Dan and Carol are getting on," she suggested.

Bessie rarely said no to lunch at the little café in Lonan where the day's special was always a sampler platter of amazing creations. Andy was busy working on bread dough, with no plans to go out.

"I want to try different amounts of yeast and varying rising times," he told Bessie. "Since I'm more or less stuck inside, this is the perfect time to do it, because I can monitor everything closely."

"You aren't stuck inside," Bessie said, aghast.

"I didn't mean it quite that way," Andy laughed. "Since I'm choosing to stay inside all day, how's that?"

Bessie still didn't like it, but she didn't argue any further. Instead, she went upstairs and got herself ready for lunch with her friend. Mary was always impeccably and expensively dressed, so Bessie pulled on a black dress and low heels. She even added a touch of makeup to her face before combing her hair. She was watching for her friend when the black limousine pulled into the parking area. A uniformed chauffeur was at her door a moment later.

"Miss Cubbon? Mrs. Quayle is waiting in the car for you," he said when Bessie opened the door.

Bessie exchanged glances with Andy before locking the door behind herself and following the man to the car. He held open the passenger door and Bessie slid inside. Mary was already sitting comfortably with a glass of something in her hand.

"I wasn't expecting the fancy car," Bessie said in a whisper.

"He can't hear you," Mary told her, "not unless we want him to hear us, of course."

"How, um, interesting," Bessie said, feeling completely out of her element.

Mary glanced at the driver, who was now driving slowly away

from Treoghe Bwaane. "Our regular driver had to have some surgery and won't be back for at least six months, if ever. We've had dozens of applicants for the position, so we're trying out a few of the best. George is using one man to get all around the island today on business, and I'm having this man drive us to lunch. Maybe, after lunch, you'd like to go home via some long and scenic route?"

"I don't see why not," Bessie said.

"Would you like a drink?" Mary asked, waving the glass in her hand. "It's far too early for me to drink. This is just juice, but you're welcome to anything. Part of the driver's job is to keep the drinks cabinet back here fully stocked. Tomorrow I shall check to see if he's remembered to refill everything when he puts the car away tonight."

Bessie took a bottle of water from the drinks cabinet and poured some of it into a glass. She'd only taken a single sip when they arrived at their destination.

"We shall have to drive more after lunch," Mary said as the driver opened their door, "and drink more."

The little café was busy, but that was always the case. Dan Jenkins, one of the owners, was seating guests himself.

"I had a quiet moment in the kitchen, so I came out to help," he told them as he showed them to the only empty table in the room. "Now I shall go back and check on everything that's busy baking."

He was gone before Bessie could ask him about the day's specials or his wife. A pretty young waitress was at the table moments later. "Mrs. Quayle, how lovely to see you again," she said brightly. "Can I get you drinks?"

Mary and her husband, George, were investors in the small café, so Mary always received extra-special treatment from the staff. They ordered drinks, but before the girl could walk away, Bessie stopped her.

"What has Dan prepared today?" she asked the waitress.

"Today he has been baking," the girl replied. "Our entrée sampler has small squares of shepherd's pie, cottage pie, and lasagne, as well as a small piece of pork tenderloin baked with stuffing inside."

"That all sounds amazing," Bessie sighed. "I'm afraid to ask about pudding."

"Again, the theme is baking," the girl said. "You get a chocolate chip cookie, a small piece of chocolate cake, a tiny individual apple pie, and a small portion of bread and butter pudding."

"I know I'll never be able to manage it all," Mary said, "but I can't possibly not order everything."

The girl smiled. "I've only worked here for a month and I've already put on a stone," she said. "It's been completely worth it."

While the girl went to get their drinks, Bessie looked around the room. "It's full of men in suits again," she said to Mary. "They must have all driven up from Douglas for lunch."

"I understand it's the place to bring colleagues whom you wish to impress," Mary told her.

"I'm so happy for Dan and Carol," Bessie replied. "I was worried when they first opened that the location would be a problem for them."

"We were as well, but the building was affordable. Luckily for us and for them, it's turned out just fine."

"That's because Dan is a genius," Bessie suggested.

"He's certainly very talented. I expect he gets a lot of offers from Douglas-area restaurants."

"He does," the waitress said as she put their drinks down, "but when I answer the calls he always tells me to tell them he's not interested. Having his own place was always his dream and he's not going to give that up for anything."

"Good for him," Bessie said.

"The food should be out in just a few minutes," the girl told them.

Bessie and Mary talked about the plans for Grace's shower while they ate the incredibly delicious food that came out of the kitchen a few minutes later. Mary had extravagant ideas and she was more than willing to fund them, but Bessie managed to persuade her to temper them slightly.

"We don't want to overwhelm Grace and Hugh," Bessie reminded her. "Grace still feels as if we did too much for their honeymoon."

"I wanted to do a great deal more," Mary said. "In this case, though, they'll won't feel as guilty because it isn't for them, it's for the baby."

"I'm so happy for them," Bessie said. "That baby may not have everything money can buy, but it is going to be incredibly loved."

"That's very true, and I do believe that's a good deal more important than money," Mary replied.

"Elizabeth seems to be doing well with her business."

"Yes, it's lovely to see her doing something she enjoys. I don't know that she's actually making any money at it, but I suppose that doesn't really matter."

Bessie hid a smile. She didn't have many friends who wouldn't care if their adult children were making money or not.

"Ready for pudding?" the waitress asked as she cleared their plates away.

"As long as we can take our time eating it," Mary said. "I'm awfully full, really."

"You know you're welcome to stay all day," the girl replied. "Dan would never ask a customer to leave, and especially not you."

The puddings were everything that Bessie had hoped they'd be and then some.

"I've eaten thousands of chocolate chip cookies in my life, and I've baked at least that many myself," Bessie said after her first bite. "But this is the best chocolate chip cookie I've ever tasted."

They were lingering over their sweets and coffee when the café door swung open and Dawn Gray walked in. Bessie gasped as the woman looked around the room.

"Can I help you?" one of the waitresses asked.

"I was supposed to meet some people here for lunch," Dawn replied, "but they aren't here yet."

"We can find you a table while you wait, if you'd like," the girl suggested.

"Yes, I suppose so. I'll need a table for six," Dawn told her.

Bessie was relieved when the girl led Dawn to the opposite side of the room. The café was tiny, but Dawn sat facing the door. She didn't appear to have noticed Bessie, and now she'd have to turn around to see her.

A moment later the door opened again and Constance Hamilton strolled in. Bessie held her breath, waiting for Dawn to notice the new arrival and start shouting. Instead, Dawn waved. Constance crossed the room and sat down opposite her. A few minutes later Brandon and his two friends came in. They quickly joined the women at the table.

Bessie was surprised to see Brandon sit down next to Constance. He slid his arm around her as soon as he was seated.

"Is everything okay?" Mary asked in a low voice.

"Everything is fine," Bessie replied. "That's the widow of the man who was murdered in the churchyard." Bessie nodded towards the table in question.

"Which one?"

"The brunette," Bessie told her. "The blonde was his live-in housekeeper."

Mary raised an eyebrow. "I'm surprised they're having lunch together."

"Yes, me, too," Bessie told her.

"Who's the man wrapped around the housekeeper?" Mary asked.

"The widow's brother," Bessie whispered.

"My goodness," Mary exclaimed.

The café door swung open again and Lucas joined the party. As he approached the table, Brandon removed his arm and sat up straight in his chair.

"You want to be careful you don't get people talking," Lucas told his son. "We have enough to worry about already."

Brandon said something back, but Bessie was too far away to hear it. Lucas's voice had carried well across the café in the silence that had followed his entrance, but now, as the general noise level increased, Bessie could no longer hear anything that was being said on the opposite side of the room.

"And the man who just joined them?" Mary asked.

"The widow's father," Bessie explained. "Also the father of her brother."

Mary nodded. "Do you think one of them killed the pretend vicar?"

Bessie hesitated and then nodded slowly. "I think it was the brother, but I haven't any real reason for feeling that way except that I don't like him."

"That's good enough for me," Mary laughed.

"I think he's the one who broke into my cottage, as well, but again, that's based on my feelings rather than on any evidence."

"The police have to worry about evidence, we don't," Mary said. "I'm quite prepared to believe the worst about the man on your word alone."

Bessie grinned. "He may be a perfectly nice man," she suggested.

"He doesn't look perfectly nice," Mary retorted. "He was hanging all over the blonde, who doesn't look particularly nice either."

"She and the widow used to be good friends, but they had a falling-out over the dead man," Bessie explained. "I'm not sure what they're doing having lunch together."

"Maybe they thought they could meet here and no one would see them together," Mary suggested.

"I hope they don't spot me, then," Bessie said.

"We can go out through the back," Mary offered, "or I can have Dan create a distraction."

Bessie smiled at her friend. It was difficult to imagine what sort of distraction anyone could make in such a small space, but Bessie didn't want to cause any trouble. "If we could slip out the back, that might be best," she said.

Mary nodded and then beckoned to their waitress. "We need to sneak out without being noticed by the people at table six," she told the girl.

"I'll go and take their order while you go," the waitress suggested. "I'll take my time describing everything."

Mary got up and then stood deliberately between Dawn's table and Bessie. Bessie watched as the waitress walked over and stood so that while they were looking at her, everyone had their backs to Bessie. After a moment, Bessie picked up her handbag and then walked quickly to the door marked "Kitchen – Staff Only." She and Mary were through the door and out of the building in less than a minute.

"That was exciting," Mary said as she and Bessie walked back to Mary's car. "I felt as if I were in a James Bond film or something."

"I was too busy worrying that I'd trip over something and ruin everything," Bessie sighed, "but I think we got away without being seen."

"It doesn't much matter if they saw me," Mary laughed. "They've no idea who I am."

Mary had the driver take them along the coast road for some distance before having him turn back towards Laxey.

"He seems competent enough," Mary said as she poured Bessie more water. "I rarely use a driver, anyway. He'll mostly be working for George. George should be dealing with the trial sessions, not me."

Treoghe Bwaane smelled like yeast as Bessie walked back inside. "My goodness, I ate far too much at lunch and that smell still makes me hungry," she exclaimed.

"I love the smell of bread baking," Andy told her. "Almost as much as I love the smell of warm chocolate. I hope you aren't going to be too full to try a few different breads at dinner. I thought I'd make a chicken and leek pie, if that sounds good."

"It will sound wonderful in a few hours," Bessie told him. "Right now, though, I'm almost too full to think about food."

"I'll have four, no, five types of bread for you to try for me as well," he said. "Garlic and parmesan bread rolls, a French baguette, an American-style sourdough loaf, a whole wheat loaf that should be healthy and delicious, and a chocolate bread that's almost a pudding rather than a bread."

Bessie groaned. "You can stay here as long as you like," she said. "Now I have to find a way to work up an appetite. I want to try all of those, and we went to the café in Lonan for lunch."

Andy nodded. "Dan does great things over there. It's an interesting concept, really, his sampler plates. I wasn't sure when I first heard about it, but I understand it's proving very popular."

"The café was full when we were there," Bessie confirmed.

"Of course, Dan's incredibly talented, as well. A lesser chef would struggle to continue to create combinations that work well together day in and day out. It's far more work than I'm prepared to undertake, I think."

Bessie nodded. "He seems to love it, though."

"I think his wife does a lot of the menu planning, too, which probably helps. I'm sure it's easier when they can bounce ideas off one another."

"No doubt. They seem to have a good partnership. She's not actually at the café much these days, though, as they are hoping to start a family."

"I hope I find someone I can work with like that one day," Andy sighed.

Bessie wanted to ask him what he thought about Elizabeth, but she didn't want to interfere, at least not yet. Maybe once Andy was finished with school and back on the island for good she might say something. She wasn't convinced that Elizabeth was interested enough to wait for six months while Andy finished college, anyway.

A buzzer sounded and Andy pulled open the oven. A rich yeasty smell filled the air. "Which one is that?" Bessie asked.

"Sourdough. An American friend at college gave me the recipe. You have to make a starter and feed it regularly. You use the starter to make the bread rise. It's very different from anything else I've done, but I really like it. The flavour gets increasingly sour as you keep using the starter."

"It smells wonderful, anyway. I must work up a huge appetite, mustn't I?"

Andy set the loaf of bread to one side to cool. "I'm going to start on the chicken and leek pie now. I'll plan dinner for six, if you think that will give you enough time to get hungry."

Bessie looked at the clock. Surely she'd be hungry again in three hours? "Six is fine. I may just have small portions of everything, but I'll definitely be ready to eat by then."

She headed up to her office and spent some time looking for a book, but nothing seemed to hold her interest. What she really needed was a long walk on the beach. That would fill some of the time and also help her work up an appetite for the wonderful meal that Andy was preparing. It wasn't actually raining, although it was overcast. Bessie checked her appearance in her bedroom mirror and then shrugged. It was bound to be windy; there was no point in combing her hair, really.

"I'm going to take a long walk," she told Andy, "unless I can help you in some way."

"Oh, no. I have everything under control here," Andy assured her. "You go and get some fresh air."

"You haven't been out of the house today, have you?" Bessie asked, suddenly concerned.

"No, but Mum is working at the shop at the moment. She's going to come here when she's done. I'll run home and get some clean clothes and whatever else I need while she's here."

"I don't need a minder every minute of the day," Bessie complained. "You can go home and get what you need, or even simply go home and stay there, if you like. I'll be just fine on my own."

Andy nodded. "I know, but I feel better knowing that you're safe and that the cottage isn't empty. Once whoever broke in is safely behind bars, I'll go home. Mum wants to talk to you about something, anyway. I hope you don't mind that she's visiting."

"Is everything okay?"

"I think so," Andy shrugged. "She doesn't want to talk to me about whatever it is, but she didn't seem upset, just, I don't know, mildly disconcerted."

Bessie chuckled. "May all of your troubles be only mildly disconcerting," she replied.

Andy grinned. "Yeah, well, maybe that isn't the best way to describe it, but anyway, she was hoping to have a chat with you about something."

"I'll look forward to it," Bessie told him. "For now, I'll get my walk in."

She pulled on a pair of comfortable shoes and grabbed a light rain jacket, just in case. "I'll be back before six," she told Andy. "But maybe not much before, unless it rains. I feel as if I haven't had a proper walk in a long time, so I'll probably walk to the new houses and even beyond."

"I hope the weather holds up for you," Andy replied. "Enjoy your walk."

Bessie nodded and then let herself out of Treoghe Bwaane. Even though the weather wasn't all that nice, the beach behind he holiday cottages was busy. After a moment's hesitation, Bessie turned and walked in the other direction, away from the holiday cottages.

She didn't get very far, though, as the tide was coming in and there wasn't much beach to walk along before the cliffs rose up over the sand. Not wanting to get stuck as the water came in, Bessie turned back around and sighed. She'd simply have to put up with the holiday-makers on the beach. Once she was past them, she should have the beach to herself, anyway.

CHAPTER 14

*B*essie wasn't sure if it was her mood or something in the air, but as she walked it seemed as if everyone was doing his or her best to get in her way. She didn't mind so much when small children ran across her path, but when grown adults simply stopped right in front of her, their eyes seemingly on the sea, Bessie felt a bit put out. When a large man with a huge anchor tattooed on his arm suddenly stood up and nearly knocked Bessie over, she almost told him what she thought. His muttered "sorry" didn't do much to improve Bessie's opinion of him.

As she'd hoped, though, once she'd passed the last holiday cottage, which was empty, the crowds almost disappeared. A few families had ventured further down the beach, spreading themselves out across the large empty patch under Thie yn Traie, but they were easy enough to walk around. And beyond them, Bessie had a large stretch of sand all to herself.

It didn't seem to take her more than a few minutes to walk from Thie yn Traie to the new houses that had been built on the beach. The stretch of sand behind the houses was surprisingly empty, but maybe the people who owned the homes didn't feel as if they needed to be outside at every opportunity as much as those in the holiday cottages did. Bessie walked past the houses, glancing into the window of the home that Hugh and Grace were buying. It was empty, but Bessie was able to admire the new carpeting that they'd chosen for the large sitting room. If she'd not known about it, she never would have guessed that a man had been murdered in the lovely house.

A bit further down the beach, she was surprised to see a sign advertising another new row of houses. At the moment, there was nothing to see but empty beach, but the sign showed a row of terraced houses lit by brilliant sunlight. Bessie couldn't help but grin at the artist's depiction of the homes. She couldn't imagine it would ever be as sunny on the island as it was in the picture.

Curiosity got the better of her and she walked up the beach to read the sign. The new houses were going to have two or three bedrooms each, she learned. If Hugh and Grace hadn't already found a place to purchase, one of these properties might have been good for them. Bessie glanced at her watch. She probably should turn around and head for Treoghe Bwaane. She didn't want to be late for dinner, and getting back through the crowd might take some time.

She walked back down to the water's edge and wandered slowly back towards home. Jack, one of the new house owners, was outside the houses, exercising his dog, Spot.

"It looks as if it might rain," he said to Bessie as she walked past.

"It does, doesn't it? I've been lucky so far, though," she replied.

"I was worried about getting Spot out for his walk before it started, but we made it," he laughed. "Spot loves the water, anyway. He wouldn't have minded a walk in the rain, even if I would have."

"How are you finding your new home?"

"We love it down here. It feels a million miles away from Douglas, even if I do have to drive in every day for work. It really rather feels as if we're on holiday all the time, which is splendid."

"A friend of mine has just purchased the empty home," Bessie told him.

"The one where that man was killed? That's very brave of your friend."

"He's a police constable, and it was a sensible choice for him and his wife. It's a lovely house."

"I understand it was sold for considerably less than the others," Jack said. "That's hardly surprising under the circumstances. I hope your friend and his wife will like living in Laxey."

"They already live in Laxey. Hugh works for the local constabulary and Grace is a teacher. They have a baby on the way, as well."

"How exciting for them. We're hoping to start a family in the next year or so, once we've repaid my mother-in-law. She lent us the money for the deposit on the house, but we've paid most of it back."

"It's nice to think of these houses full of families with small children," Bessie said.

"Yes, I think it will be great to have our own little neighbourhood down here."

Bessie patted Spot on the head and then continued on her way. As she approached the beach behind Thie yn Traie, she felt a few drops of rain. Several families jumped up almost immediately and began to drag their things inside. As the rain stopped almost as soon as it had started, Bessie didn't increase her pace. She was making her way between a red-faced woman who was shouting at three preteens to collect their things and get in out of the rain, and a man who appeared to be fast asleep on his blanket, when someone called her name.

"You're nearly always on the beach, aren't you?" Dawn asked as Bessie stopped and turned to look at her.

"I walk on the beach every day," Bessie replied. "I always walk in the morning. When I have time, I like to walk more later in the day."

Dawn nodded. "It must be wonderful to live right by the water," she sighed. "Walter and I always talked about getting a house on the water, but he couldn't seem to stay out of prison long enough to make it happen."

Bessie wasn't sure how to respond to that statement, so she simply smiled at the woman. After an awkward moment, Dawn spoke again.

"We're going home tomorrow," she told Bessie. "My father has gone to talk to the inspector to let him know."

"I'm not sure he's going to allow that," Bessie said slowly.

"He can't stop us," Dawn replied. "We have jobs to get back to, and appointments and things. Walter's death doesn't have anything to do with us, anyway."

"Constance told me that she'd told Brandon that they were here," Bessie said in what she hoped was a casual tone.

"Constance talks too much," Dawn snapped.

"Who has she been talking to now?" Brandon asked as he joined his sister in the cottage doorway.

"You remember Bessie from the cottage down the beach," Dawn replied.

"Of course I do," the man said, looking at Bessie and smiling. It was a nasty smile that nearly made Bessie shiver.

"Did Constance tell you where she and Walter were?" Bessie asked, feeling brave on the crowded beach.

"I don't really talk to Constance," the man replied. "She was Dawn's friend, not mine, after all."

Bessie opened her mouth to ask about their lunch together that afternoon, but she shut it again as Brandon walked out of the cottage and onto the patio. Dawn followed, and before Bessie could speak they were joined by Horace and Mike.

"Is it raining yet?" Mike asked. He had a can of lager in his hand, and he popped it open and took a long drink as he waited for someone to reply.

"You're standing outside, surely you can answer that question yourself," Dawn snapped. "I thought we were going to wait to start drinking until Dad got back."

"He's not my father," Mike laughed.

Horace looked at Dawn and then at Mike. After a moment he shrugged and opened his own can with a resounding snap. "It's our last night, right? We should enjoy it," he said.

"Why can't you enjoy it without alcohol?" Dawn asked.

Horace took a drink before he replied. "I can enjoy it anyway, it's just better with booze."

"Everything is better with booze," Brandon said loudly. He stepped back into the cottage for a minute and then emerged with his own can.

Dawn frowned. "You should wait for Dad, anyway," she suggested.

"If I drink a few before he gets here, he'll never know how many I've had," Brandon argued.

"Dad can count the empties," Dawn replied.

"I'll just tell him Mike drank them all," Brandon retorted with a wave of his hand. "You're just grumpy because we don't have any more wine, and you think you're too sophisticated to drink lager."

"That's not it at all," Dawn told her brother. "What if the police come back with Dad to ask us more questions? I'd rather deal with that when I'm sober, thank you."

"Nah, the police are best dealt with after a few drinks," Brandon laughed. "Besides, why would they come back with Dad? They must be done with their investigation by now. What do you know about that?" he challenged Bessie.

"Nothing," she replied flatly. "I believe the investigation is ongoing."

"You can't expect an inspector on a tiny island like this to actually catch anyone," Brandon told his sister. "This is probably his first-ever murder investigation."

Bessie almost laughed out loud. While she'd have loved to set Brandon straight, maybe it was better that he was underestimating John and the local constabulary.

"I just hope they let us leave," Dawn said. "I need to get back for work."

"We'll go, no matter what," Brandon said. He glanced at Bessie. "You can tell your friends at the police that I said that, as well. They've no cause for keeping us here."

"Take it easy, mate," Horace said. "Have another beer. We need to get it all gone before we leave, right?"

"There's no point in taking any back with us," Brandon replied. "We have plenty at home."

"Exactly, so drink up and relax," Mike said. "Cheers." He waved his can in the air and then emptied it. "Bring me another," he added as Brandon went back inside.

"I really wish you'd all stop until Dad gets back," Dawn said, sounding anxious.

"I'll stop, if it matters that much to you," Horace said. He drank whatever was left in his can and then threw the empty can through the cottage door. It clattered loudly as it bounced across the tile floor. "Come and sit with me and relax," he told Dawn.

There were a few chairs on the patio, and Horace crossed to one and sat down. He pulled a second one closer to him and gestured towards it. "There you are," he told Dawn. "Sit down and we'll talk. I've been wanting to talk to you since we arrived, but I haven't had the opportunity."

"That's because Lucas is always around," Mike said loudly. "He stays real close to his little girl to protect her from men like you."

Horace laughed. "I don't think it's me he's trying to protect her from."

"He isn't trying to protect me from anyone," Dawn said angrily. "He's just been trying to keep an eye on me because he knows how upset I am about Walter, that's all."

"More fool you," Brandon said as he walked back out of the cottage. He handed Mike a can and then opened the one he'd kept for himself. "You knew Walter was trouble when you married him. He treated you badly, but you kept going back to him, time after time. Even after he ran off with your best friend, you still cried when he died. I don't understand it."

"You've never been in love," Dawn snapped.

"Love should be a two-way street," Brandon argued. "Walter never cared about you. He just wanted a place to stay between prison sentences."

"That's a horrible thing to say," Dawn replied. Bessie could see tears in the woman's eyes. "He did love me and we might even have made things work again, if Constance hadn't interfered."

"You can't keep blaming Constance for everything," Brandon told her. "Walter was the one who left. It doesn't matter that Constance went with him."

"It does matter. It matters a lot," Dawn countered. "He would have come back to me if she hadn't persuaded him to run away."

"So she did you a favour," Brandon sneered. "You should send her a thank-you card."

"When hell freezes over," Dawn said.

"What is going on out here?" a loud voice interrupted.

"We were just talking," Brandon said as his father appeared in the cottage doorway.

"And drinking?" Lucas countered.

Brandon looked at the can in his hand as if he weren't quite sure how it had appeared there. "Just the one," he said. "We have a lot to finish before we leave tomorrow."

"We aren't leaving tomorrow," Lucas told him, "not unless something changes in the next few hours. The inspector is going to be here in another hour or so to talk to all of us again."

"Why?" Brandon barked. "He's questioned us over and over again. Does he think one of us is suddenly going to confess to something?"

"He said he'd learned a number of new things and that he wanted a chance to discuss them with each of us in turn," Lucas explained.

"What sort of new things?" Dawn asked.

"He wouldn't answer any questions," Lucas told her, "and he didn't ask me anything, either. I assume he didn't want me coming back here and telling you all what he was asking about."

"Constance has been talking to him," Dawn suggested. "I can't even begin to imagine what she's told him."

"Hopefully they realise that she can't be trusted," Lucas replied. "As the police will be here soon, I suggest you all stop drinking for now, though."

"I wasn't drinking," Dawn said. "We don't have any more wine."

"So let's go and get some," Lucas replied. "We can run up to the shop at the top of the hill and get what you want. It won't take more than a few minutes."

"You'd better be back before the inspector gets here," Brandon said tightly.

"We will be," Lucas assured him.

Bessie watched as Dawn followed Lucas into the cottage. A minute later she heard the front door open and close. Turning, she started back on her way home.

"Hey, wait," Brandon shouted.

Bessie glanced over her shoulder, hoping he was talking to someone else. He was staring straight at her. She stopped and waited to see what he would do next.

"Why were you talking to Constance?" he asked.

"She sat down next to me in a park and started a conversation," Bessie said, working to keep her voice steady as the man approached her.

"And she just happened to mention that she'd told me that she and Walter were here? I don't believe it," he challenged.

"You'll have to take that up with her, then," Bessie said, taking a step backwards as he got too close.

"I might just do that," he muttered.

"How about a drink?" Mike shouted. When Bessie caught his eye over Brandon's shoulder, she thought he looked worried.

"I can't have another drink right now," Brandon yelled back, his eyes never leaving Bessie. "You heard what Dad said. The police are on their way."

"I meant something fizzy or maybe coffee," Mike said. He walked over and stood next to Brandon. "Coffee might be good."

"I don't want coffee," Brandon replied. "I'm just having a little chat with our neighbour here."

"Except I need to get home and get my dinner," Bessie said. "I hope that everything goes well with the police and that they let you go home soon."

"They will," Brandon said in a low voice. "But don't rush off. You were just telling me about your conversation with Constance. What else did she tell you during your little heart-to-heart?"

"It was hardly that," Bessie replied. "We only spoke for a minute or two."

"I know Constance better than that. If she had a captive audience, she'd have talked for hours. What else did she tell you?"

Bessie shook her head. "As I said, it was a short conversation, but she happened to mention that she'd told you where she and Walter were, that's all."

"That's all? That's pretty significant in light of subsequent events, wouldn't you say?"

"That's for the police to consider, not me."

"Have you told the police what Constance told you?" Brandon demanded.

"I have, yes," Bessie said quickly. "I've also told them that I saw all of you having lunch with Constance this afternoon." That last part wasn't true. She'd completely forgotten to ring John when she'd arrived at home.

Brandon took a step closer to her. "You do get around, don't you?" he hissed, "and you stick your nose everywhere it doesn't belong, as well."

"Having lunch with an old friend is hardly a crime," Mike said brightly. "I mean, we were all good friends with Constance before she moved over here. We were all happy to see her again, to get caught up."

Bessie nodded. She'd have agreed to just about anything at that point. She just wanted to get home. The crowded beach didn't feel particularly safe with Brandon standing only inches away from her.

"Maybe that's what the police inspector meant when he said he had new information," Brandon speculated. "Maybe he wants to ask all of us about our lunch with Constance. I suggest we all tell him that it's none of his business."

He looked around and then stared at Horace. "Maybe you could tell the police you had lunch here today. Maybe we could all tell the police that. Then it would be our word against the little old lady's. They'd probably believe us. She's probably half-senile, anyway."

Bessie nearly bit her tongue in half as she struggled with the urge to reply. There was no doubt in her mind whom John would believe if Brandon and his friends denied having been in Lonan for lunch today. After a long, deep breath she smiled at the man. "They do have security cameras in the café in Lonan," she said lightly.

Mike took a step closer to Brandon, almost getting between him and Bessie. "Let's talk about this inside," he suggested, staring hard at his friend.

"I'd rather talk out here with the old lady," Brandon replied. "You seem to think you know something. Go on, then, what do you think you know?"

"I don't know why you're so upset about my mentioning that you had lunch with Constance," Bessie told him. "If you didn't want anyone to see you with her, you should have met privately, not in a busy restaurant."

"I don't have anything to hide," Brandon said. "It's just that Constance and I are trying to keep our friendship quiet until certain things get sorted."

"I really must go," Bessie said, looking at her watch. It was nearly six. Andy would start to worry before too much longer.

"I'm not done talking to you," Brandon objected.

"Let her go," Mike suggested. "You don't want her complaining to the police about you."

"And there's no doubt she would," Horace added from where he was still standing on the patio.

"Yeah, she would," Brandon agreed. "She's the type that runs to the police all the time, complaining about her neighbours or getting upset when kids break into her cottage."

Bessie very nearly asked the man what he knew about the break-in at her cottage, but she stopped herself. He was already angry. She didn't want to upset him any further. Instead, she turned and began to walk away, slowly at first, but gradually increasing her pace as she went.

"That's it," Brandon shouted after her. "Run away home. Go up to your pathetic pink bedroom and your collection of cuddly toys and hide."

Bessie's blood ran cold at his words. There was only one way he could possibly know about her bedroom. She started to walk even faster, telling herself not to turn around or react to his words.

He must have realised what he'd said, though, because he began shouting again. "Wait. Hold on. Wait a minute," he yelled.

Bessie could see the front door to her cottage, but she could hear the man gaining on her, as well. She glanced around the beach and then made an impulsive decision.

"I need your help," she said in a low voice as she sat down on the blanket in front of her.

The very large man with the anchor tattoo gave her a confused look. "Pardon?"

"There's a man chasing after me, and I'm afraid he's going to hurt me," she explained. The words were barely out of her mouth when Brandon reached them.

"Come on, granny. Stop bothering the nice man," Brandon told her. "I'm very sorry. She wanders off and then she gets disoriented. She forgets who I am, as well, which complicates things."

Bessie met the other man's eyes and shook her head very slightly. He looked from her to Brandon and back again.

"Come on, now," Brandon said. He put his hand on Bessie's arm and began to try to pull her to her feet.

The tattooed man sighed and then stood up slowly. Although Brandon was well over six feet tall, the other man seemed to tower over him. "I don't believe the lady wants to go with you," he said in a conversational tone.

"She needs to come with me. It's time for her medication," Brandon said. He pulled again on Bessie's arm.

"I think you should take your hands off her," the other man said. He took one step closer to Brandon and then another. "If there's a problem, I can ring the constabulary and have someone come and sort it for you."

Brandon let go of Bessie's arm and took a step backwards. "It's all good," he said. "I just want to take Granny home, that's all. She needs her meds."

"I'll just talk to her for a minute or two and then help her get home if that's where she wants to go," the man said. "You go home and let me worry about her for a few minutes."

Bessie could tell that Brandon wanted to object, but the larger man clearly intimidated him. After a few seconds, he turned and stormed back down the beach. Bessie sighed with relief.

"Thank you," she told the stranger. "I'm going to get home before he comes back with his friends."

"I'm not worried about them," the man said as he helped Bessie to her feet. "I was in the Royal Navy. Anyway, I've seen him and his friends around. None of them would be any good in a fight."

Bessie gave him a shaky smile and started to walk away. He fell into step with her. "I'm Dave Horton, by the way," he said.

"I'm Elizabeth Cubbon, but everyone calls me Bessie," she replied.

"You're Aunt Bessie," the man said, sounding delighted. "My closest friend in the Navy talked about you all the time. You probably don't remember Oliver Boyd, but he had very fond memories of you."

"I do remember Oliver," Bessie said. "I wouldn't have thought he was tall enough to join the Navy, actually."

Dave laughed. "That's Oliver. He told me he always got bullied as a kid because he was so much smaller than the other boys. I think he bribed a doctor to lie about his height in order to get in, but he loved the Navy. The first day of training, he came up to me and asked me to be his friend. He reckoned that no one would pick on him if his closest friend was the biggest guy in the fleet."

Bessie chuckled. "That sounds like the Oliver I remember. He isn't here with you?"

"He, um, that is, he passed away a few years ago. Lung cancer, I'm sorry to say. We all started smoking in training, and he was never able to break the habit. He'd always talked so much about the island that I had to come and see it." He paused and looked at Bessie for a moment. "The thing is, this is the first time I've been able to get over here. I promised Oliver that I'd scatter his ashes on Laxey Beach when I could, but I haven't been able to do it."

Bessie patted his arm. "It's very kind of you to have agreed to do it for him. You're a good friend."

"I will be, if I can find the nerve."

"If you need help, I'm available. I'd welcome a chance to remember Oliver, actually."

"That would be great, I mean, in a sad way, but still."

Bessie nodded. "I just have to ring the police right now, though. It may have to wait a short while."

Andy was pacing around the kitchen as Bessie and Dave walked in. "I was starting to worry," he told her. "I was just about to ring 999."

"No need. I'm fine. I just need to ring John and then we can have dinner," she replied. "Oh, and this is Dave. He saved me from a very angry Brandon Mason."

She picked up the phone and dialled a number she knew well.

"Laxey neighbourhood..."

"Doona? It's Bessie," Bessie interrupted. "I'm sorry to interrupt, but I need to speak to John rather urgently."

"He just walked out on his way down to talk to Brandon and Dawn again," Doona told her. "Do you want me to try to catch him?"

"Yes, please," Bessie replied.

She winced when her friend apparently dropped the phone. While she waited, she could hear conversations in the background, but she couldn't make out exactly what was being said. After a few minutes, Doona was back.

"I missed him, but I rang him. He pulled over to take the call, and since he's only a short distance from your cottage, he's going to stop there before he goes to talk to the others."

"That's wonderful. Thank you," Bessie said. She put the phone down and then gave Andy a rueful smile. "I'm sorry, but dinner is going to have to wait a few minutes. John is on his way here."

Andy laughed. "I'll just keep the pie warm in the oven, then," he said. "Is John joining us for dinner?"

"I doubt it. I suspect once he hears what I have to say, he'll be even more eager to talk to Brandon."

"What about Dave?" Andy asked.

Bessie looked over at the other man and shrugged. "You're more than welcome," she told him. "We're having chicken and leek pie, and knowing Andy, there's enough there to feed an army."

"I was Navy," the man laughed. "We eat more than they do."

John knocked on the door only a few minutes later. Bessie quickly told him everything that had happened on the beach.

"You know you should never confront suspects in a murder investigation," he told her as he rang into the station for backup.

"I didn't mean to confront him," Bessie replied. "I was talking with Dawn. I didn't even know he was behind her."

"And now he knows that you know he was behind the break-in here," John said. "I'd be very surprised if he hasn't already run."

"Just because he broke in here doesn't mean he's the murderer," Bessie said, "but I've been saying all along that I thought he did it."

"Yes, you have, and you may well be right. You've given me some things to discuss with him, anyway," John said.

A police car with flashing lights rolled past Bessie's cottage. When a second one went past a minute later, John got to his feet. "There's my backup. I probably won't be able to tell you anything until tomorrow at the earliest."

Bessie nodded. "Good luck."

John gave her a hug and then headed out, walking across the beach towards the holiday cottages. Bessie stood in the doorway and watched him go. She would have loved to have been there when he confronted Brandon, but instead she pushed the door shut and had dinner with Andy and Dave.

They were working their way through the various breads when someone began banging on the cottage door. Bessie got to her feet, but was waved back into her chair by Dave.

"I'll get that," he said.

Andy walked behind him to the door. When Dave swung the door open, Brandon was standing there, his face bright red with anger.

"This is all your fault," he shouted at Bessie. "You're nothing but a meddling old lady."

Bessie stared at him, not sure how to respond.

"I believe the police are looking for you," Dave said casually.

"They aren't going to find me," Brandon replied. "You can hide me in your cottage to make up for what you've done," he told Bessie.

"I'm not letting you in here," Bessie exclaimed.

"I'm coming in," the man shouted, glancing back down the beach.

As he took a step forward, Dave took a step back. A moment later Dave's fist crashed into Brandon's jaw. The man looked stunned for a moment and then slowly sank to his knees and then slid to the floor.

"Maybe you should ring your inspector friend," Dave suggested.

Bessie was too stunned to react for a moment, but eventually she managed to find John's mobile number and ring him. He was there in less than a minute, with several uniformed constables.

"What happened?" he asked as he looked down at the unconscious man.

"He tried to push his way inside, and ran into my fist," Dave said.

John looked at the man and then nodded. "Thank you for looking after Bessie," he told him.

"I was happy to do it," he replied.

Dave helped John get the slowly recovering Brandon into the back of a police car before he rejoined Bessie and Andy in the kitchen.

"Oliver said you were really special," he remarked as he sat back down at his place, "but he never mentioned this much excitement."

"This last year has been rather different," Bessie told him. "Things are usually much quieter."

CHAPTER 15

*J*ohn rang later that evening, after Bessie had helped Dave scatter Oliver's remains on the beach Oliver had loved.

"I'm going to have to come back and visit Oliver once in a while," Dave told Bessie when they were done.

"I hope you'll visit me as well," Bessie replied.

"I'll look forward to it," the man had said.

"I just wanted to let you know that Brandon has confessed to breaking into your cottage," John told her. "Just in case you want to send Andy home."

Bessie looked at the slice of toast she'd just made from Andy's sourdough loaf. She wasn't really in any hurry to send Andy home. "Thank you for letting me know. Has he confessed to the murder as well?"

"Not yet, but I suspect he will. Constance is doing her best to get him put away for a long time. She's insisting that she told him they were here and that she told him all about her plans for the evening that Walter was killed. I suspect he may end up trying to implicate her in some way, but it's early days yet."

Andy went home the following morning, after one more round of pancakes with bacon. Bessie was sorry to see him go, but she was also looking forward to having her cottage to herself again.

"Feel free to drop in and cook for me anytime," she told the man after he'd loaded up all of his things into his car, "and thank you for looking after me. I really appreciated it, even if I did grumble about it."

Andy laughed. "You wouldn't be the Aunt Bessie we all love if you didn't grumble when we try to fuss over you," he told her. "Anyway, I'm planning to visit regularly for the next month while I'm here. I have lots more recipes I want you to try."

Bessie grinned. "I'm always happy to try anything you make," she assured him.

The cottage felt strangely empty for a few hours, but by late afternoon she was feeling at home again. She took a short walk on the beach before dinner.

"I'm sorry," a voice said from behind Bessie as she walked.

She spun around and met Dawn's eyes. "Pardon?"

"I'm sorry," Dawn repeated. "I'm sorry that my brother killed my husband. I'm sorry that he broke into your home and destroyed your things. And I'm sorry that he chased you down the beach and then later tried to barge into your cottage. I, well, I wondered about him and Walter, I truly did, but I didn't want to believe it was possible."

"I'm sure this is very difficult for you," Bessie said softly.

"It is, yes. My father isn't taking the news very well. He worked hard to raise us right and, well, he feels as if he failed."

"You and Brandon are adults now. You're making your own choices and your own mistakes."

"Yes, I know. Marrying Walter, that was my big mistake. I can't help but blame myself for all of this, really."

"You didn't tell Brandon to kill the man," Bessie said sharply. "Even if you had, it was up to him to actually do it. You can't possibly take any of the blame."

"I never should have befriended Constance, either," Dawn continued as if she hadn't heard what Bessie had said. "She was the one who told Brandon to kill Walter, although she'll never admit to it and he'll never tell."

"Why would she do that?" Bessie asked.

"I suspect she was bored with life here and wanted to get away. Just leaving Walter would have been too easy, though. She thrives on drama."

"Murder seems a step too far."

"Maybe she didn't tell Brandon to kill him. Maybe she just suggested that he get rid of him or something. Who knows what she had in mind? All Brandon would have had to do was tell the bishop who Walter really was and everything would have blown up in Walter's face. Why Brandon didn't think of that, I'll never know."

"I'm sorry," Bessie told her.

"Now I've lost my husband, who was lost to me anyway, and my brother. I'm not sure my father is going to get through this either. He doesn't look like it, but he's had a lot of health issues in the past year. All of this might just kill him."

Bessie didn't want to keep repeating how sorry she was, but she couldn't think of anything else to say.

Dawn sighed. "Anyway, I just wanted you to know that I'm sorry about what Brandon did. The murder was awful and horrible, but breaking into your cottage was just him being childish. He used to do stuff like that when he was younger, breaking into homes and making a mess, but we all thought he'd outgrown it. Apparently, once he got really drunk, he decided it was a good idea. He was mad at you because you were talking to me about Walter, you see."

Bessie didn't see, but she didn't argue. "When are you leaving, then?" she asked.

"We're allowed to go whenever," Dawn shrugged, "but Dad doesn't want to leave Brandon here, and I don't want to leave Dad. Horace and Mike have both gone home, so at least we don't have to deal with them anymore. Dad and I are moving down to the last cottage in the row later today. Apparently, they can't find anyone to stay there because someone died in the cottage, but Dad and I don't care. All of the other cottages are fully booked, of course. We were lucky they managed to move a few people around to let us stay this long."

"I suppose I'll see you around, then," Bessie said.

"I hope you'll understand if I seem to be avoiding you," Dawn told her. "Dad's visiting Brandon right now, but if he's here, I don't want him to see us talking. He seems to blame you for Brandon's arrest."

Bessie opened her mouth to object, but Dawn held up a hand.

"I know you were part of it," she said. "Brandon told me that he messed up and let slip that he'd broken in here and that you ran home and rang the police. I'm actually grateful to you for doing so. He killed Walter. I want him in prison for a very long time."

On that note, Dawn turned and went back into her cottage, and Bessie continued on her way back down the beach.

GLOSSARY OF TERMS

House Names – Manx to English

- **Thie yn Traie** - Beach House
- **Treoghe Bwaane** - Widow's Cottage

English to American Terms

- **advocate** - Manx title for a lawyer (solicitor)
- **aye** - yes
- **bin** - garbage can
- **biscuits** - cookies
- **bonnet (car)** - hood
- **book** - make a reservation
- **boot (car)** - trunk
- **car park** - parking lot
- **chemist** - pharmacist
- **chips** - French fries
- **cooker** - oven

- **cot (for a baby)** - crib
- **crisps** - potato chips
- **cuppa** - cup of tea (informally)
- **dear** - expensive
- **fairy cakes** - cupcakes
- **fizzy drink** - soda (pop)
- **hire car** - rental car
- **holiday** - vacation
- **icing sugar** - powdered sugar
- **jumper** - sweater
- **lie in** - sleep late
- **midday** - noon
- **notes** - paper money
- **primary school** - elementary school
- **pudding** - dessert
- **starters** - appetizers
- **supply teacher** - substitute teacher
- **telly** - television
- **torch** - flashlight
- **trolley** - shopping cart
- **uni** - university (informal)
- **windscreen** - windshield

OTHER NOTES

CID is the Criminal Investigation Department of the Isle of Man Constabulary (Police Force).

When talking about time, the English say, for example, "half seven" to mean "seven-thirty."

With regard to Bessie's age: UK (and IOM) residents get a free bus pass at the age of 60. Bessie is somewhere between that age and the age at which she will get a birthday card from the Queen. British citizens used to receive telegrams from the ruling monarch on the occasion of their one-hundredth birthday. Cards replaced the telegrams in 1982, but the special greeting is still widely referred to as a telegram.

When island residents talk about someone being from "across," they mean that the person is from somewhere in the United Kingdom (across the water).

"Touch wood" is used where in the US we might say "knock on wood."

The term "pull" is similar to "pick up" when it comes to dating.

The emergency number in the UK is 999, not 911.

One stone of weight is equal to fourteen pounds.

ACKNOWLEDGMENTS

Thanks to my hard-working editor, Denise, who spends far too much of her time correcting my mistakes!

I'm grateful to my beta readers who give up their valuable time to offer their thoughts on these books.

Thanks to Kevin for the wonderful photos that I use for my covers.

And thanks to all of you for continuing to spend time with Bessie and her friends.

AUNT BESSIE REMEMBERS

RELEASE DATE: JULY 19, 2018

Aunt Bessie remembers nothing about the party that Elizabeth Quayle insists she invited Bessie to attend.

Elizabeth Cubbon, known as Bessie to nearly everyone, is confident that she would have remembered being invited to take part in a murder mystery evening. After everything she's been through over the past eighteen months, it doesn't sound the least bit enjoyable to her.

Aunt Bessie remembers thinking the whole thing was a bad idea.

And when someone at the party ends up dead, it looks as if she was right.

Aunt Bessie remembers as much as she can as she tries to help Inspector John Rockwell work out exactly what happened at Thie yn Traie. But can she remember enough to put a murderer behind bars before he or she kills again?

ALSO BY DIANA XARISSA

Encounters and Enemies

Friends and Frauds

Guests and Guilt

The Markham Sisters Cozy Mystery Novellas

The Appleton Case

The Bennett Case

The Chalmers Case

The Donaldson Case

The Ellsworth Case

The Fenton Case

The Green Case

The Hampton Case

The Irwin Case

The Jackson Case

The Kingston Case

The Lawley Case

The Moody Case

The Isle of Man Romance Series

Island Escape

Island Inheritance

Island Heritage

Island Christmas

ABOUT THE AUTHOR

Diana grew up in Northwestern Pennsylvania and moved to Washington, DC after college. There she met a wonderful Englishman who was visiting the city. After a whirlwind romance, they got married and Diana moved to the Chesterfield area of Derbyshire to begin a new life with her husband. A short while later, they relocated to the Isle of Man.

After over ten years on the island, it was time for a change. With their two children in tow, Diana and her husband moved to suburbs of Buffalo, New York. Diana now spends her days writing about the island she loves.

She also writes mystery/thrillers set in the not-too-distant future as Diana X. Dunn and middle grade and YA books as D.X. Dunn.

Diana is always happy to hear from readers. You can write to her at:

Diana Xarissa Dunn
PO Box 72
Clarence, NY 14031.

Or find Diana at:
www.dianaxarissa.com
diana@dianaxarissa.com

Made in the USA
Lexington, KY
29 September 2018